THE ESCAPE OF
ROSE ALLEYN

Vivien Freeman grew up in North London and graduated in Art History from the University of East Anglia before settling in Ware, Hertfordshire. A published poet as well as a novelist, she taught Creative Writing for many years and has an MA in Scriptwriting from Salford University. She is a professional script reader.

She now lives in rural Wales in the Vale of Glamorgan with her husband, the poet, John Freeman. Between them they have four children and three grandchildren. She likes visiting family and friends as well as frequenting art galleries and historic houses. She also enjoys gardening, walking, reading and listening to classical music.

To Jan and Philip

THE ESCAPE OF
ROSE ALLEYN

with very best wishes

Vivien Freeman

VIVIEN FREEMAN

ACCENT

First published in 2017 by
PublishNation

This edition published in paperback in 2020
by HEADLINE ACCENT
An imprint of HEADLINE PUBLISHING GROUP

1

Cataloguing in Publication Data is available from the British Library

ISBN 978 1 7861 5802 4

Typeset in 10.5/13pt Bembo Std by Jouve (UK), Milton Keynes

Printed and bound in Great Britain by Clays Ltd, Elcograf S.p.A.

MIX
Paper from
responsible sources
FSC® C104740

Headline's policy is to use papers that are natural, renewable and recyclable
products and made from wood grown in well-managed forests and other
controlled sources. The logging and manufacturing processes are expected
to conform to the environmental regulations of the country of origin.

HEADLINE PUBLISHING GROUP
An Hachette UK Company
Carmelite House
50 Victoria Embankment
London EC4Y 0DZ

www.headline.co.uk
www.hachette.co.uk

To the memory of my parents, Betty and Stan,
and of my dear friend, Ruth

Chapter One

I come downstairs in my stockinged feet, avoiding the creaking places. The ashes glow faintly red, taking the chill from the room. I throw in a handful of offcuts from Father's workshop, which snap as flames catch them. When I hear her moving, I will heft the coal hod and tip in its noisy contents, but for now I am a shadow amongst shadows. Let her sleep. Let her rest.

I move the black saucepan of porridge to warm and set the kettle to boil. I filled it from the pail last night, just over half way so that its weight will be less of a trial when she next comes to use it after I have left her. All this I do by habit, needing no more than firelight. Passing the window, I gather back one curtain enough to see that the dark morning is made bright by a round moon showing a sharp frost which glimmers on the path and hedges.

I light the lamp. Soon, I will hear her slow, gentle tread above me, and when I do, I shall make a pot of tea and place on the fire two fronds of juniper I cut and brought in to dry. The room will greet her with fragrance.

The bed springs creak. Too heavily for her. Father, awake early. A shiver of unease runs through me. She must be feeling poorly to miss being down to share my final breakfast at home. Father's voice murmurs. I put my own selfish disappointment to one side and feed the branches to the fire that their scent may drift upstairs and lighten her pain.

I hear the sing-song three syllables of her name again, and there is something in that questioning repetition which, despite the blazing flames, turns me to ice. A silence, then swift footsteps. I turn round, and for one extraordinary moment, I do not recognise the wild-eyed figure in a nightshirt, stumbling on the stairs.

'Run as fast as you can, Rose,' Father cries. 'Fetch Dr Jepp – if only for the baby's sake.'

I am already at the door, feet in my boots, fingers shaking and slipping on their hooks. I run out into the moon's glare, heart bursting up into my mouth in great sobs.

I reach our lane, which leads to the road into our little town of Markly. The doctor's house is on the edge, thank goodness, beyond the field next to ours. I run onwards, slipping on stones slick with frost. I burn with exertion, throw back my shawl. *Please let him be awake and dressed. Please let all be well.*

I am on the road now, its resistance jarring every step, but I have acquired an extra bout of strength as I round the bend. There is Dr Jepp. He stands in the street, leaning on his bicycle, lifting the hasp of his side gate. His whole posture bespeaks exhaustion. In the midst of my anguish, it comes to me that he has probably spent the night attending to another's emergency. He hears my pounding footsteps, stiffens, looks up and before I even gasp his name, he is turning the bicycle my way, swinging aboard.

'It's Mother,' I begin, but he arrows past me, all weariness put aside. His face is set as if angry. As I start to run back, trying not to give way to a stitch, I find myself recalling a conversation, unintentionally overheard, which took place when my mother first became ill after falling pregnant this latest time.

The doctor was called, and went upstairs to see her. I had been picking peas, and sat down on the bench in front of the cottage, about to shell them. Suddenly, there were footsteps, voices in the room behind me, clearly audible through the open door and window.

'I advised you, after the last miscarriage, that she should not conceive again.'

The sternness of the doctor's tone held me entranced with fear. My mother had lost that baby late in term. In her previous confinement, the newborn died within days. These events had been preceded by a troubled decade, in the time of the old doctor. Little Annie and poor, simple Jim had not survived beyond the age of five. There had been a stillbirth and, as I now know them to have been, five miscarriages. These had not been brought to medical attention.

'But what's a man to do?' My father sounded plaintive, less than his usual manly self.

I blushed with shame for him. Are men really so primitive that they can control their urges no better than animals?

'I gave you guidance – on more than one occasion,' said the doctor, curtly.

'I've tried, God knows,' said Father, '. . . and my wife . . . but she . . . she couldn't cope . . .'

'I understand.' The doctor spoke more gently, 'I am thinking of *her* well-being now, though.'

They began to move towards the door, and I fled around the corner. The exchange hardened my resolve never to marry.

By the time I reach home, Dr Jepp is upstairs. Father leans on the mantelpiece, staring into the red heart of the fire. He does not acknowledge me.

I hear the doctor splashing water in the bowl. Steeling myself, I go up, taking a clean towel from the linen chest on the landing. As I enter the room, he walks towards me, blocking my view. He takes the towel, but simply clutches it. 'I'm sorry, Rose. She'd already gone.'

The tears flow quietly out of me. I feel faint, drained.

'There is nothing either of us could have done, for your mother or the baby,' he says, patting my upper arm. Underneath his well-meant words, I hear true grief.

'Thank you, Dr Jepp,' I say, trying to compose myself, 'for all you *have* done.' He sighs and shakes his head. 'May I stay with her a moment?' I ask.

'Of course.' He picks up his bag and leaves the room.

Now I look across. The doctor has kindly smoothed her sheets. She looks serene. She could be sleeping, but free from pain at last. I say goodbye, leaning over to kiss her forehead. Her skin is cool. All is stiffening. She is my mother, yet no longer my mother. I take the candle from the room and blow it out.

Downstairs, Dr Jepp is sitting at one end of the table, writing Mother's death certificate. There are three sounds in the room: his fountain pen, the ticking clock and the kettle lid, falling, falling. I make tea. It seems the only thing to do.

'The patient succumbed to her weakened heart.' The doctor says this to my father, now slumped at the table's other end. 'From my own observations and from what you have told me, I estimate that cardiac arrest took place at about six a.m. this morning. Foetal demise would have followed within minutes. Rose can verify that this is what I have written.' He hands my father the certificate, puts his pen away and prepares to leave.

A little later, we force ourselves to eat, though the porridge sticks in my throat. Father speaks: 'You'll have to go to the Hall, Rose.'

Sawdons Hall. I had completely forgotten my new employment.

'You must make sure that you inform your brothers and sisters.'

These are Phyllis, Dorothy and Hilda and the boys, Ralph and Jack, already working there. It was through Phyllis that I was accepted at the higher position of tweeny because I had good references from the solicitor's family in our town. Unfortunately, they moved away. The new people brought their own maid with them.

'And you'll have to tell them at Sawdons that you can't take up the post. I shall need you here to run the house for me.'

Although I have not been relishing my new job, the thought of staying within these four walls fills me with a different apprehension.

'You'd better go,' he says. 'Besides, I have plenty to get on with in your absence.'

He will be thinking of the green oak in his workshop, from the great tree brought down in the autumnal storms. We little knew then how personal its significance would be.

'And when you come back, you must help me write to Joe and Hubert.' These are my brothers who work in a town, bigger than ours, not far from here. 'By then, I shall have spoken to the vicar and seen Will.' Will Sturgess is Father's partner, also the undertaker for our town and its neighbourhood.

This leaves only my two eldest brothers, Bob and Ted, who left for America ten years ago. They live and work in New York City. I imagine, briefly, their shock when they receive my letter.

I clear the dishes. By the time I come back from the scullery, Father has gone. I set the chairs straight and turn out the lamp. A faint light curls around the edges of the curtains. I throw open the door. The sky in the east is suffused with a delicate pinkish gold along the horizon. By the minute, darkness above is giving way to blue. I stand motionless, until I can breathe without sobs threatening to burst out of me. All around, from the shadows of the garden, come the soft chirrups of the birds' winter waking. It is going to be a beautiful day, the kind Mother would have loved.

I go back indoors and open the curtains wide, as she would have done. It comes to me, as I take this step, that there are, no doubt, countless rules of etiquette for mourning and people who enjoy not only the leisure to put them into practice but the opportunity to wag a finger if they have been neglected. I am thankful that, here, we are simple country folk, untroubled by such conventions.

I am wearing what I would have worn if I had been setting out for my first day's employment: my best clothes, consisting of a navy skirt and white blouse. I put on my matching barathea jacket, hat and gloves.

As I walk down our path, the moon pales as if transparent and the sun comes up over the horizon, gilding the bare branches of trees and hedges. There is no need to take the long way round by road. The footpath across the fields is dry. We have had two summers of drought and it has yet to turn to mud. I feel my mother's presence, not walking beside me but a little above. This seems as it should be. I derive some comfort from the notion that she is watching over me.

After I have walked about three miles, I come to the stone wall encircling the deer park. I start down the drive and, after another mile, the Hall comes into view surrounded by its formal gardens. It is an impressive building, rising three storeys at its centre with lower wings on either side.

I enter the stable yard and find Jack, cleaning harness in the sunshine. He straightens up, the smile draining from his face. I realise that there are tears running down my cheeks. Jack is my closest brother. We share a birthday a year apart, he being seventeen. Today, as I hug his shaking body, I could be the elder.

Everyone is very kind. Cook, Mrs Brandon, makes us both a cup of tea and presses upon us a plate of fresh-baked muffins, surplus to the breakfast table upstairs. The housekeeper, Mrs Gilliatt, puts her sitting room at our disposal. Jack and I wait there whilst the rest of the family are located and released, temporarily, from their duties. They will have grasped, from this extraordinary measure, that something grave has happened.

We stand in an unhappy circle in the neat, cold room, whose fire is laid but not yet lit. 'I'll come back as soon as I have news of the arrangements,' I say, after finishing my account. 'Let's say a prayer for Mother's soul.' Ralph and Jack are visibly relieved to be able to focus their attention on the stumbling words which are all I can manage as a blessing. It serves to conclude our meeting and allow them back to find some solace in routine. We clasp each other, and they leave the room followed by Dot, who says that she is needed in the kitchen.

I move to follow. I begin to tell Phyllis and Hilda that I must explain to Mrs Gilliatt about no longer being available to take up my position. Hilda bars my way, urging me back into the room.

'Please let me be the one who comes home to tend the house for Father.'

'What's happened?' I look from her frightened face to that of Phyllis, which is set hard.

'They are short of an upstairs maid,' Hilda says.

'We all know why.' Phyllis's mouth is a thin line.

'Master Greville has noticed me already.' Hilda speaks of the elder son of the house. 'He takes delight in chasing me. I live in fear.'

Hilda is the prettiest of us, with her auburn curls and blue eyes just like Mother's.

6

'Where is he now?' I ask, ready to take her home with me this instant.

'He left for Ireland with his father yesterday to look at horses. He wants a new hunter.'

'And when do they return?'

'In ten days' time.'

Mrs Gilliatt agrees without demur to the proposal that it should be Hilda who remains at home after the funeral, I taking her place here at the Hall. 'And if the situation should change in the meantime,' she says to Hilda, nodding towards upstairs, 'you may leave straightaway.'

We thank her, and the three of us say goodbye. Even in my sad state of mind, I cannot help the wry reflection that my own safety is not considered to be at risk. This comes as no surprise. My father never ceases to remind me that the style of my looks and my direct manner make me unattractive to men. Phyllis is cut from the same mould as me, and poor Dot's birthmark is, no doubt, her saving grace, keeping her below stairs. 'His gaze does not dwell on Dot or me,' Phyllis had remarked with satisfaction.

As I skirt the building, I hear young, animated voices, running footsteps, laughter. Across my line of vision run a young fair boy of about eight followed by two fair girls, a good deal older by their height and dress. These two are enjoying the fresh air and winter sunshine with the probable excuse that they are looking after their younger brother, since all three are engaged in a game of tag around the knot garden. Had this been a normal day, their gaiety would have lifted my own spirits, but today it underlines my grief and somehow sharpens a sense of anxiety about my future, which has been stealing up on me. Suddenly, I feel overcome. As I turn the corner, my eyes well up.

'Good morning. Lovely day.'

I nearly bump into a tall young man. I take a deep breath and try to regain my equilibrium. 'Yes, indeed,' I just manage.

'Or perhaps it's not so lovely.' He speaks in a considerate tone.

Surprised, I look straight at him. He must be about my brother

Hubert's age, in his early twenties. Fine-featured and well-spoken, he could be one of the gentry. Yet his face, framed by black hair, is open and friendly, his dark eyes showing concern for my troubles, which I have clearly failed to conceal.

'Come and sit down in the sunshine,' he says, indicating a stone bench recessed in one of the yew hedges. 'I'm Leonard Pritchard, by the way.'

Now I have placed him: the tutor. Phyllis has mentioned him and said that he was a pleasant fellow.

'I'm Rose Alleyn,' I answer him. 'My brothers and sisters work here.'

'Ah, yes,' he claps a hand to his forehead. 'Of course.' He offers his condolences. How word has travelled.

'You are very kind, but I mustn't detain you from your charges.' I am regretful, for it's warm here in the sun, and he seems well-intentioned.

'Oh, blow them!'

I sit straight down again.

'You fear we will both be compromised if we're seen.'

This had been my thought exactly.

'No window overlooks us here.'

It is true. The wall nearest this corner of the garden offers a blank face to the outside world. I can see that at one time it supported windows, but they have been bricked up.

'Besides, we're in the twentieth century now,' he says, smiling, sensing my lingering unease. 'You and I may speak to whom we please, how we please, Rose. "The old order changeth –"'

'"Yielding place to new",' I respond.

'"And God fulfils himself in many ways,"' he goes on, and I conclude,

'"Lest one good custom should corrupt the world."' By now we are both laughing.

'If you believe in God, that is,' he says, almost to himself, still chuckling. Seeing he has startled me, he tactfully changes the subject. 'You are a devotee of Tennyson?'

'I prefer Keats and Shelley.'

'Of course.'

As he talks about the poets and asks me for my views, he looks as if someone had given him a tonic. I think: what a good teacher he must be. Not once does he imply surprise or patronise me, but in case he is wondering, I tell him about Mother's bookshelf of the classics and the fact that I have read every book in the subscription library, or so it feels, not that most of its stock is really to my taste.

'No, I can imagine.' He sounds thoughtful.

'But I shall have no time for reading once I come to work here.' The words are out as of their own volition and, because he is sympathetic company and seems to want to know, I tell him the implications of what has happened today, though I merely say that Hilda will take my place at home because she is Father's favourite, which is true enough.

'So, you exchange one kind of servitude for another?'

'I have to earn a living. It's what I can do,' I say, but although I'm slightly irked, Leonard Pritchard's analysis is the crystallisation of a thought which has been surfacing ever since Hilda made her plea to me.

'You have no idea,' Leonard says, 'how much I have enjoyed talking to a like mind. We must meet before I leave.'

This last sentence cancels all the pleasure I derived from being called a 'like mind'. 'When is that?'

'Next week, Master Hector will go to boarding school to have all his lovely sensitivity beaten out of him. He should have gone last autumn, but he was too sickly. The girls are never in the schoolroom, these days. They can't wait to be sent to Switzerland for finishing.'

'And what of you?' A tiny flame in the looming shadow of my employment is snuffed out.

'I,' he cannot help a wide grin spreading across his face, 'am opening a bookshop in Widdock.'

I must look surprised. I explain that this is the town where my two brothers, Joe and Hubert live.

9

'I like it, though I don't know it well,' he says.

I have to admit that I have never left Markly.

He looks thoughtful. 'I would never have expected to have left my own home town. But then I went to South America.'

'Goodness! What were you doing there?'

'Teaching in Buenos Aires. Then, I came back and took this job to be near my father, who died last year.'

I offer sympathy, for which he thanks me.

'With my inheritance and the money I'd saved, I had enough to start a business. Widdock is expanding. It's to gain a teacher-training college. It needs a good bookseller.'

'When do you expect your bookshop to open?' It seems another world.

'Before the end of the month, I hope. My stock is ordered. The next task is finding staff and furnishing my –'

'Mr Pritchard?' Small running footsteps resound on gravel.

'Coming, Hector.' He rises, as the small fair boy appears, rubbing his eyes.

'They say I'm a sissy because I don't want to get my feet wet.'

'You are not a sissy at all, you're very sensible. Come with me.' He takes young Hector's hand. 'Let's see whether Cook has made the pies for luncheon yet. There might be a makeweight jam tart or two going begging.' He turns to me. 'You expect to return within the next few days, Rose?'

'As soon as the arrangements are confirmed. I'll come at this time of day.' Again, the words speak in spite of me.

'I'll look out for you. We must talk again.'

We say goodbye till then.

I am downstairs in the bunk bed, which makes me think of the time when I was very small and we were all at home. The fire is low. I shall fall asleep in its soft light. Mother has been laid out and rests in the temporary shell which Will Sturgess brought this afternoon. Father sleeps in my room, exhausted.

As soon as I returned, I went to see him at his workshop, where he'd gone after carrying out the necessary duties. Already, he had planed the oak. If it is possible for a coffin to be a thing of beauty, Mother's will be, for he is putting every iota of his craftsmanship and all his love into its lines.

I have been busy, too. The funeral will take place in five days' time. I found, at the back of Mother's writing desk, the notepaper and envelopes last used when little Annie died. I wrote to Joe and Hubert with the details and then, seeing that I still had time, comfortably, to catch the last post, I broke the news of Mother's death to Bob and Ted in America. At least my handwriting on the black-bordered envelope will brace them for the worst.

Father and I ate early, the leftover broth which I made yesterday, in another life. His head was nodding over his dish. As soon as he had finished, he retired to bed. Five minutes later, all was quiet above me in my old room. I went up with my own candle's light to make sure that his was out. He was sound asleep.

I came down, found plain notepaper and, before I could lose faith in myself, started writing. For I have had an idea. It is a very audacious one, which has been growing inside me this long, tumultuous day. I still cannot believe that I, Rose Alleyn, am about to execute it, but I have debated with myself every consequence and can see no good reason to prevaricate. I can feel my mother willing me to proceed, repeating Leonard Pritchard's words: *We're in the twentieth century now.* The more I consider my idea, the sweeter it becomes.

Chapter Two

I climb out of the bunk bed, which has been like a friendly little boat carrying me through the night. I recall how Phyllis, Jack and I used to play pirates and explorers in it until Mother pointed out that we should have to remake it thoroughly before we could comfortably sleep in it again. I chivvy the fire and put the black saucepan on the hob. There is tepid water in the kettle. I pour it into my bowl, which I thought to bring down from my room last night, and quickly wash and dress.

Outside, the air is softer, sweeter than yesterday morning. There is no frost and no visible moon. I sense, in the darkness, that it may already have rained. Standing quite still, taking the measure of the day for a few moments, I gauge that it would not be sensible to wear one's best coat and hat for a prolonged outing. I sense, too, that it is later than my normal getting up time so, when I turn round, I am not altogether surprised to see the lamp alight.

Father, fully dressed, is building up the fire with dry twigs and half-burnt coals. He nods but does not look at me until he has encouraged new flame to catch and hold the kindling. He straightens up. 'You won't be able to lie in, once you start at Sawdons.' He could almost be amused.

I have elected not to tell him of my plan. I don't underestimate his almost certain resistance should anything come of this endeavour which, even I have to admit, is headstrong. If – and I must look this likelihood squarely in the face – it all comes to nothing, Father need never know. So, I let his barb pass, a not unusual state of affairs between us.

He does not wait for me to serve him, but fetches his bowl and spoon from the dresser, and helps himself to porridge. I notice a vigour about his movements and it comes to me that, not only is he channelling his grief into crafting Mother's coffin to the best of his ability and with all his heart, but he has been given a renewed purpose, albeit a distressing one, in applying the skills of his trade.

Even in my short lifetime the population of our town, not large to start with, has dwindled. My four older brothers are not the only young men – and women, too – who have left Markly. The people who remain do not require new furniture very often. These days, cartwheels, farm implements and gates, along with household utensils and repairs, form the majority of Father's trade. He gladly leaves the production of coffins to Will Sturgess but not, of course, this time.

'Don't make tea for me,' he says, as I move towards the boiling kettle. 'I must get on while it's light, which won't be for long today, by the look of it.'

He's right. I have not yet pulled the kitchen curtains. Beyond them, the darkness still presses. I take the kettle off the heat. 'Then I shall leave shortly, too.'

Father puts on his cap and jacket, and tucks in his muffler. 'I don't suppose you'll see all your brothers and sisters again,' he says.

'No, I'll speak to whoever I can find, and ask them to pass on the message,' I say. 'They're hardly likely to forget.'

'That's true enough.' He pauses a moment, hand on the latch, head bowed. There are tears in his eyes when he looks up, but he manages the shadow of a smile. 'If you see Hilda, tell her I'm glad she's coming home to keep house for me.'

I say I will, and we bid each other goodbye. He means no harm. He does not intend to slight me. And who can blame him for preferring Hilda's instinctive grace about the home? Apart from Dot, who beats all of us girls at making appetising meals from nothing and who excels at every culinary skill, Hilda is peerless. Neither Phyllis nor I have her light touch with pastry or sponge. It is Hilda who inherited Mother's gift for brightening a home. A table laid by

13

Mother or Hilda would always look inviting, even if the food to be served was plain and scant.

I quickly clear up, chiding myself for sleeping on that extra hour. Our two old hens will again have to scratch around till I get back, poor things. I hurry upstairs.

Mother's pier-glass stands with its back against the wall next to the window, so that the light falls correctly on the person in front of it, not on the surface of the mirror. The stand which holds the looking-glass was lovingly crafted by Father as a wedding gift to his bride. She told me he had said that he understood how important it was to women, for their peace of mind, to preserve a neat appearance, although she would never look anything other than beautiful to him.

As I face the glass, Mother's presence in this room is so powerful, I expect to see her figure behind me squeezing my shoulders and telling me that I look perfectly presentable in this worn worsted coat once Phyllis's, before that Hilda's, and owned originally by Dot. From the corner of my eye, I can see, reflected, the casket on the bed. If I were to lift the lid, surely, it would be empty, for Mother is everywhere but in that oblong box.

With that thought the heavy weight, which has been lying on my heart ever since I woke and instantly remembered everything, subtly shifts and redistributes itself so that I do not feel quite so constricted, as if I would suffocate with sorrow. I hesitate to say that the pain eases, but I do take the change in me to be a sign, sent to console me and give me strength, which I shall need today.

I set my old hat at an angle, take one last appraising look at myself and go downstairs. The all-important letter is hidden at the back of Mother's writing desk. I almost imagine it not to be there, but it is, of course. I press the envelope deep into a capacious pocket, making sure I do not crush it.

The morning sky has no blue in it. Reluctantly, I accept the encumbrance of an umbrella and strike out with it grasped in one hand, the other in my pocket, compulsively touching the corner of the letter.

As Sawdons comes into sight, I have to take command of my nerves and remember that my primary purpose is to relay to at least one member of the family the day and time of Mother's funeral.

I have been walking fast. I can see the leading edge of rain as it swiftly advances. It is visible against a far line of trees. It is crossing the parkland on the other side of the Hall. Soon, it will be sweeping over the building, the gardens and then over me.

Now, I am almost running, but I pause to put up the umbrella. The wind, which has been gusting for most of my journey, snatches at the unfurling folds of cloth. I fumble with the mechanism. A sudden squall of stinging rain hits me in the face. I grab my hat before it lifts from my head and button it inside my coat, against my chest. As I slide the catch and the spokes begin to open, a crosswind surges underneath them and blasts the whole frame inside out. I turn into the wind and somehow nurse all the limbs back into shape, but I've gained a drenching in the process. I march forward. It takes two hands to hold the umbrella in place and, now, my mind is playing tricks with me. Since I can no longer hold onto the letter, I imagine it somehow working its way out of my pocket and, caught up by a capricious eddy of wind, whirling away into oblivion. Similarly, I dare not jog-trot any faster, so powerful is the malign fancy that I shall get to the Hall and find my pocket empty. I see no one as I skirt the building, which is hardly surprising. They have all found jobs indoors.

At last I am standing, dripping, in the dark corridor by the back door, shaking out my umbrella. The next thing I do is slip my hand into my pocket. My relief at touching the corner of the envelope makes me feel, for a moment, light-headed. It is followed, however, by renewed anxiety. How on earth am I going to deliver the letter? If I were to follow this uninviting corridor it would, no doubt, lead to the back stairs which, in turn, would take me to the grand rooms where the members of the family who own this large house, more like a village, pass their days. I am not even tempted to try this out. It is unthinkable.

I feel the smallest of nudges, a kindly nudge. Although I flush with guilt, I am not riven. The intention, I am sure, is to guide me back to my primary task. I pass a series of closed doors behind which must be the laundry room, the pantry, the housekeeper's sitting room, where my family gathered yesterday — was it only yesterday? — to learn from me of Mother's passing. Behind the furthest door, I hear voices and the clatter of pans. This must be the kitchen. If I find none of the others, Dot will surely be there. I knock and enter.

My heart jumps and I'm temporarily at a loss, for seated at the nearest end of a big table in the centre of the room, with his back to me, is Leonard Pritchard. Master Hector is sitting on a stool beside him. They are both tucking into toasted teacakes, I have time to notice whilst, at the other end of the table Dot looks up from glazing the top of an enormous veal and ham pie, using a little brush dipped in a teacup of beaten egg. 'Rose.' I am blessed with her sweet smile.

Before I can speak, Master Hector has twisted round, and says, 'We were watching you.'

'Good morning, Rose. Not that it is.' His tutor has turned, too. 'Yes,' he continues, 'we happened to be looking out of the schoolroom window and saw you wrestling with your umbrella.'

'Not a day for fresh air,' I begin, but Dot has wiped her hands and is bustling to me.

'Don't just stand there. Come over to the fire and dry off.'

I have no sooner propped my umbrella against the wall next to the huge range and spread my hands to warm in its glow, when another pair of hands closes them around a toasting fork on which a teacake is speared. I turn to thank the kind person. It's Mrs Brandon, Cook herself, and she smiles and sweeps on to taste the soup which a maid is stirring across from me.

'Give me that and take off your coat,' Dot says, 'the hem's soaking.'

As I do so, I tell Dot, 'Mother's funeral is to be on Tuesday at midday.'

She nods, 'I thought it would be Market Day.'

Travelling will be easier for Joe and Hubert, who could come in with one of the regular stallholders.

'I'll make sure the others know,' she says, bringing my teacake to the table and buttering it liberally from the pat in front of the two visitors from upstairs.

I follow, spread my coat out on the long bench which I have pulled out slightly, and sit down. Dot pushes my plate towards me, then lifts her masterpiece of a pie and carries it over to the ovens. The teacake is delicious, moist with butter. I taste all my favourite flavours, clove, nutmeg and soft, rich sultanas. It makes me think of Christmas, and I am caught with a sharp grief. I will my eyes to stay dry, as I am being addressed.

'I had hoped we could continue our open air discussion, Rose.' Leonard – I must get used to this freedom from formality – is smiling, as if encouraging me to be strong.

'Indeed.' I reach for my handkerchief to dab my mouth. It is in the other pocket from the letter, but it comes to me that this might be my only opportunity to deliver it discreetly. 'Actually, arising from all we spoke of yesterday, I have something to give you, if you don't mind, that is.' I can hear how breathy my voice sounds, the words knocking into each other.

'Not at all,' says Leonard, calmly.

All the time that I spent on the walk here, worrying that the letter would somehow liberate itself and blow away, and now it seems to have got caught in the narrowest recess of the pocket.

'Is it a present?' Young Hector asks.

'Er . . . no.' I try to smile, to compensate for this inadequate answer, and now I have freed it. I pull out the envelope whose stark whiteness seems to draw attention to itself.

Just at this moment, two things happen simultaneously: the door opens and in walks Phyllis bearing a redundant tea tray, pale eyes lighting up at the sight of me; Master Hector says, loudly: 'Oh, it's a letter. Look, it has your name: Mr Leonard Pritchard. That's you.'

Phyllis's gaze freezes like blue ice on the envelope. My cheeks must be scarlet.

In one swift movement, Leonard grasps the letter and tucks it briskly away in his inside pocket. He cannot be aware of Phyllis

17

advancing behind him with a puzzled frown, but he says, quite loudly as if to the room in general, 'I shall be happy to look over the Bible readings you've suggested, Rose.' The hint of amusement in his eyes is replaced with an earnest intensity. 'I'll let you have my response tomorrow, I promise.' He holds my gaze a moment. It is almost as if he has guessed the letter's contents.

'Thank you,' I manage to say, my wits having deserted me.

Phyllis is level with me now. She turns to include us all. 'Hello, Rose. Good morning, Leonard, Master Hector.' Her face is a study of contained curiosity.

'Good morning, Phyllis,' Leonard says. 'I expect you're wondering how your sister and I became acquainted.'

Another person might look flustered at having such thoughts exposed. Phyllis's slight frown has gone to be replaced by what, on the face of it, looks like an enquiring smile – one undergirded with steel.

'We bumped into each other, literally, in the knot garden, yesterday, and somehow started chatting about poetry. I'm afraid I delayed Rose's return home.'

Now all the tension has melted, and Phyllis's smile is simply her wry one. 'You'd better make the most of your discussion,' she says to me, 'hadn't she?' – turning to Leonard. 'It's not encouraged down here – that sort of thing.'

They exchange a keen glance, and it comes to me that they are friends. They have a complete history to which I am not party. I have the feeling that everything is moving too fast.

'You know my views,' says Leonard, quietly.

'I do.' Again, a look of complicity passes between them. Phyllis straightens. 'Anyway, I can't stand here hob-nobbing.' She turns to me and drops her voice. 'I expect you've got some news.'

'Tuesday, at noon,' I tell her.

She nods and takes her tray through to the scullery. I know, from the awkward way she keeps her head down, that she is trying not to cry.

'We have to get back to the schoolroom,' says Leonard. 'Lessons

18

till one o'clock, then Master Hector is free of me until Monday morning.'

'I am very bored on Saturday afternoons and all of Sunday,' says his young charge.

Leonard lightly touches the front of his jacket where my letter resides in his inside pocket. 'You'll have a reply by tomorrow night, Rose.'

The lad is sharp, and senses some business between his tutor and me, so I hope to distract him. 'What are your interests, Master Hector?'

'History,' he answers, quickly. 'Did you know that after The Great Plague there was a Great Fire in London?'

'I believe I did.'

'And do you know the date of the Fire?'

He looks so eager. I hope I step the right way. 'Will you tell me, please?'

'1666,' he cries, delighted. 'It's easy, but young ladies are no good at facts and figures.'

He gives me a sympathetic smile, which I try to return without showing the weariness engendered by this all-too-familiar remark.

'You haven't learnt that opinion from me,' Leonard says, evenly.

'No, Father told me,' says Hector, with pride, 'so it must be true.'

I send a reassuring almost-smile to Leonard to let him know I am unscathed. I ask Hector, 'Where did the Fire start?'

But he is tired of this game. 'Pudding Lane,' he answers, without interest. Then, the idea provokes another. 'Cook?'

'Yes, Master Hector?' Mrs Brandon pauses to give him her full attention, a great jar of eggs in isinglass held against her broad, white-aproned chest.

'What's for pudding, this luncheon?'

'For you, syrup sponge and custard.'

She includes Leonard in her satisfied smile. He closes his eyes. 'Mmn . . . delicious.'

'Thank you, Cook,' says Hector.

She nods and moves on as Phyllis returns, evidently within

earshot. 'You will stay, Rose . . . ? You can't walk home. I've seen outside and it's tipping down.' Since the three walls which do not house the range and ovens are lined with shelves and cupboards, the windows in this room are high, admitting no view, only light and not much of that on a day like this. 'We'll be having our dinner soon. You can join us.'

'I'd feel embarrassed, Phyllis,' I say, for the thought is daunting.

'Nonsense, you're almost one of us – will be next week.'

Something hits me deep down: *No, I do not want to be here*, an instinctive reaction which shocks me with its vehemence and conviction. I can't begin to examine it before I am assailed by the most desperate guilt. I have never kept a thing from Phyllis. Her eager anticipation of my forthcoming employment at the Hall reminds me forcibly that I have embarked upon a double life, if only for the time being.

I must look stricken. Perhaps Leonard senses something of my unhappiness and strives to break its spell, which he does by standing up, 'I will say goodbye, for the moment, Rose.'

'Goodbye, Leonard.' I hope my eyes reflect my thanks.

'Well, it's up to you.' Phyllis touches me lightly on the shoulder. 'I must go back upstairs.'

I catch at her hand, but she has already whisked out of the door, after Leonard and Hector.

I suddenly feel very conspicuous, even though I am ignored. The fact that everyone else has a job to do for either the enormous luncheon which will take place in an hour upstairs or the plain meal which will be eaten beforehand here somehow makes me feel worse. I run my hand across my coat. It is dry enough to wear without too much discomfort. I stand and shake it out, but before I even find a sleeve, Dot comes in.

'I'm sorry I had to leave you, Rose. Cook required me in the pantry.'

I tell her Phyllis was down and that I spoke to Leonard and Master Hector. Her sweet smile, 'They'll have entertained you.' Knives and forks are being set out. There is a strong smell of greens, but also a savour of some tempting meat dish. 'You will stay for dinner, won't you? We're having Irish stew. I made the dumplings.'

Dot's suet dumplings are a serious rival to Hilda's in their lightness. I can almost taste one as it crumbles in the mouth, fat without being fatty, moist enough to absorb gravy without going to mush, a hint of marjoram tempering all that richness. Just the thing on a wet winter day, when everything else in the world is bleak. I am feeling very unsettled and, just at the moment Dot presses me, I can do nothing but give in to the solace of dumplings.

I am seated next to Jack, and am glad of his and Ralph's benign and protective presence, as I do not care for the appraising looks directed at me by the two footmen, who must be about the same age as my brothers. These young men would not speak to me, of course, especially with Phyllis on my other side. I do not need to see her face to know she is my champion. Hilda is on her other side. She is transformed from the grey, anxious shadow of herself I encountered yesterday. 'Father is looking forward to you coming home,' I say. 'Tell him, I can't wait,' she whispers.

After grace, said by the butler, I wonder whether it is my being here and having to convey sad information to the family or simply the imperative to eat quickly in order to return upstairs to serve luncheon, which subdues conversation to the functional minimum. Jack observes that when he crossed the yard, the rain had stopped and it looked as if the sun might be trying to break through. Phyllis says she just has time to walk with me a few paces on the gravel. The little scullery maid, who looks much younger than the twelve years she must be to have finished school, begins to collect the dirty dishes. I notice that her fingers are red and raw, swollen with chilblains.

'We look forward to your joining us next week, Rose,' says the housekeeper, Mrs Gilliatt.

Luckily, she does not wait for more than a smile from me, before she leads her retinue upstairs. Other faces smile back at me. I feel dreadful and yet, for all I know, this life will be my fate, so I am pleased to have been accepted. I put on my coat and my poor hat, whose appearance has not improved from being flattened against my chest during the windswept journey here. I remember my umbrella and say a brief goodbye to those remaining in the kitchen, but all is action and no one takes much notice, for which I am glad.

A weak sun is shining now and the whole garden glistens. Mist rises from the stunted winter plants. A horse neighs in the stables, and I think of Jack and his calming way with all creatures, even the boldest stallion. The only other sound is our two pairs of footsteps on the gravel path through the knot garden.

'You'll fit in well,' says Phyllis.

My insides freeze.

'Don't look so worried, Rose. I won't let them eat you.'

We hug goodbye, but briefly. Displays of affection would not be tolerated and, in any case, Phyllis has to go. I watch her straight-backed stride which is almost a run. She turns at the door and I wave. Then she disappears inside the dark corridor and the door shuts on her.

When Phyllis and I were little, long before school age, we had a make-believe family. In summer, when we played outside, Father and Mother would be a larger and smaller stone, their children named pebbles. In winter, playing under the table in the warmth of the range, our family would be assorted buttons. In just the way that, occasionally, one of the others, such as Jack or Hilda, would join us and play a part, we sometimes brought in other characters to augment our little family's adventures.

I must have been about eight when our church acquired a curate for a year. At probably no more than thirty, he still seemed old to us, with a florid face and portly profile, as if he had enjoyed too many roast dinners. Young children though we were, we could not fail to notice his pomposity. On top of this, he had a manner of speaking in which his small, round mouth barely moved, contorting the words which issued. One Sunday, walking home after Matins, Phyllis and I were giggling about him. Suddenly, feeling wicked, I turned to her and said: 'May the Dervane late shane upern you.' In her shout of laughter, shushed by Father, a new character was added to the stone and button family. Whole episodes were created so that Uncle Bottomley, as we called him, could appear and dispense his wisdom. This was usually through me, because Phyllis loved to hear me do his voice. We would hold back his entrance the more to enjoy the anticipation of his eventual performance.

Years have passed, and though we no longer play our childhood game, of course, if we should be together on one of Phyllis's rare half-days or holidays and a situation calls for it, perhaps a local elder holding forth, we only have to catch each other's eye to know that Uncle Bottomley lives on in our imagination and our stifled giggles.

All this and much more comes to mind as I walk back across the Park, avoiding the places where the rain has turned the path to mud. We were best friends. I fear, in all the internal debate about my big idea, I have managed to underestimate the extent to which Phyllis, assuming my imminent residence at Sawdons, has been counting on a resumption of that friendship. This makes me feel bad, not only selfish but foolish, as if I thought I could follow my whims with no repercussions.

Then I recall my sense of desolation, when Phyllis left to take up a position at the Hall. I was ten. That final year at school, walking there and back on my own, I was miserable and lonely. Poor Jim's winter cough turned to pneumonia, which took him quickly and little Annie was beginning to ail, but we did not know it at the time, nor the reason why, and simply thought her tendency to tire easily was because she had a delicate constitution. Mother's health was, of course, not good, and these two little deaths, each at under five years old, made her very low. I began to take on as many of the household tasks as I could manage before and after school and when I started as a maid at the solicitor's house. I would sit and read to her from one of her own books kept upon her shelf, Jane Austen, or a poem from her anthology of English poets. She had always been easy to talk to, even though she was our mother. Gradually, without my knowing it, she took Phyllis's place and became my closest friend.

All of which does not mean that I feel any the less for Phyllis now. On the contrary, our time together today, albeit brief, has rekindled a good deal of our old feeling for each other. Have I set in train something I might regret? As I have told myself before, the likelihood of gaining the position is not high. Leonard, for all his welcoming ways, has to be business-like about this venture. He will probably be looking for someone considerably older, with experience in the world of retail and, although he might not admit it to himself, a man. I imagine the ideal candidate for the job: a sober-sided gentleman with spectacles who can speak Latin, knows his Shakespearean quotations and is well-equipped to advise on the merits of one encyclopaedia in preference to another. He will be a gentleman of authority, someone whom the public will respect. Yes, he's the man for the position. I'm almost glad. I come out of these reflections to realise home is in sight. This has turned into a lovely afternoon, the winter sun dipping now, the sky suffused with apricot. Beyond the silhouette of winter trees and hedges, a further expanse of faded blue has a hint of green about it. I feel as if it is a gift. I cannot be downhearted.

I wake unrested, aware of having experienced active dreams full of presences. I remember that this is the Second Sunday after the Epiphany. It would be unthinkable, on every count, to attend church before the funeral on Tuesday. At least we will be spared the added pang of seeing the church cold and bare, all its decorations having been taken down by Twelfth Night. Besides, we need the intervening days to summon our courage for the emotional ordeal.

In our raw state, we would not want to meet anyone. I feel strongly, however, that after the turbulent night which I have suffered – and, judging by Father's face, so has he – we cannot remain cooped up in these four walls all day. Expecting him to reject the idea of a walk down our field path to the river and back for a breath of air, I am surprised when he agrees.

We set out when I have cleared up after breakfast, soon reaching the river. It is not yet in its winter spate but looks black under the bare branches of the willows and alders, which line its banks. Instead of turning for home, Father walks on along the towpath. In a while, we pass the end of Dr Jepp's garden, with its little gate under the arching boughs of two tall horse chestnut trees which, in springtime, are a glory of white candles. Several smaller gardens follow and, now, we are coming to the yards of the shops and workshops in the town. Here is the back of the blacksmith's forge, with Father's workshop next door.

He pauses, gazing at the barn-like building. 'I think I'll just . . .' He tails off.

'Of course,' I say, but he probably doesn't hear me, as he walks up the yard. 'I'll leave you . . .' I begin, but he is already entering and closing the door behind him. If this were not the Day of Rest, he would be bent over Mother's coffin, ensuring every detail is correct. As it is, standing in the unusual stillness of his place of work, at one with what he has created, this will be his act of Sunday worship and communing.

I head home to add jacket potatoes to my casseroled shin of beef, one of the last cuts available when I ran down to the butcher's yesterday. I open the door. On the mat is an envelope. We have had notes and letters from those such as the doctor, thoughtfully composed and written in Mrs Jepp's elegant copperplate and from one or two, such as the midwife who, though barely able to write, are yet moved to express their condolences in a form more permanent than speech. I shall treasure them all for their wonderful appreciation of our mother and concern for us. I pick the envelope up. It is addressed to me in a distinctive, Italic script. My heart lurches.

Chapter Three

Dear Rose,

I have given your application careful consideration, and hope you will be pleased to know that I have decided to offer you the position of assistant in my bookshop, Pritchard's.

I am unable to go on reading, for my hand is shaking too violently. My heart is pounding. I feel faint. Seated, I try to calm my breathing before I lift the letter again, gripping it with both hands, my arms resting on the table to keep them steady.

The hours will be 10 a.m.–6 p.m., Monday–Saturday.

Your starting pay will be 10 shillings per week.

I have reserved board and lodging for you, from Saturday 20th January, with Mrs Florence Fuller, who runs a women's hostel called Apple Tree House. You will, therefore, be in place to start work on Monday 22nd January.

If you do not have the funds to support yourself, I am willing to advance you two weeks' wages.

I shall be at Sawdons from today till the morning of Wednesday 17th. Letters addressed to me there will find me. I should be grateful to know by that date whether you accept the post.

I hope to hear from you in the affirmative, and look forward to working with you.

Yours sincerely,
Leonard Pritchard

I close my eyes and imagine myself leaving a tall building, inside which is my room. I am on a street, busy with cabs and carriages. I fall into step with other young women – or perhaps we have come from the hostel together – a group of us laughing and chatting, each splitting off towards her own place of employment. Could this really be me?

... I am brought to my senses by the sound of Father's footsteps. I push the letter under the bedclothes of my bunk.

I have made a fearful mistake. My heart beats as loud as a soldier's drum. I should have waited, let Father have his rest, then told him everything. But I was too agitated, aware that tomorrow would be taken up with preparation and Tuesday would, rightly, be devoted to Mother's funeral. And so the days would slip away.

As soon as Father had finished his baked apple and pushed the empty dish from him, therefore, I told him of the letter offering me a better position than I would have held at the Hall.

'Better?' This one questioning word conveyed not only complete incomprehension that I should be setting the merits of one form of employment against another when a steady job, already offered and accepted, was not something to be dismissed, but that I should have the temerity even to undertake such an appraisal.

Unnerved by his dumbstruck stare, and before he could collect his thoughts into forbidding utterance, I rattled reassurances: how I had met Leonard and been impressed, how Phyllis clearly trusted him as a friend. I faltered to a halt.

Now, Father sits, elbows on the table, fingers ploughed through his thick hair, his forehead resting on his palms. His eyes are shut. 'Oh, Rose, this is all too much,' he says, as if each word weighs on his soul.

'I'm sorry, Father,' I whisper into my lap, where my hands lie clenched.

'I should have known,' he says, almost to himself, 'trouble where you least expect it.'

My heart feels as if it has been squeezed. A tear springs from each eye. 'Father, I would never –'

His chair grates back. I jump.

'This fellow, Pritchard, he's at Sawdons now?'

My mind freezes.

'He put the letter under the door this morning, on his way back there – yes?' Father barks.

'Yes . . . yes,' I stutter, shocked by Father's peremptory tone, yet at the same time trying to guess where this is leading.

'Right. Well, I'm going to see him. You can gasp, Rose. Some fathers would give you a reason for gasping.'

'But –'

'No "buts",' he slams into his outdoor clothes. 'You, in the meantime, can go in place of me to see your aunt, uncle and grandmother. My sister will, no doubt, have heard of our loss, but she'll expect a personal invitation to the funeral. Tell her I'm sorry not to have come myself, but I've had to go to the Hall to sort things out. And that's the plain truth of it.'

I stand in the ringing silence after he has left.

I clear the dishes in a trance of anxiety. Father is a man rarely given to anger but, on a few notable occasions when circumstances have had him cornered, he has lost control. I can only hope that the tumult of emotions, which it pains me to own he will be feeling, will have blown themselves out by the time he has walked the four miles to Sawdons.

I take the towpath for the second time today. This is the sort of quiet, winter afternoon I usually like, grey but with a kind of luminosity. I find, as I walk, that the meeting between Father and Leonard is being edged out of my imagination by what might be to come at the mill house.

I come up through Uncle Adam's vegetable patch, his neat rows of January Kings, past the hen-coop whose occupants mutter and jib, and across a small strip of cobbles to the back door, behind which is the kitchen-cum-living room. There is a parlour beside the front door, but I have never been inside it. I raise my hand to tap on the adjacent window but before I can make contact, the heavy door is dragged back by my aunt.

I know instantly, from her tight little smile of satisfaction, that I have nothing to tell her which she does not already know.

'I guessed my brother would send you, Rose.' Her words confirm my supposition.

'Father is very busy.' Mine sound limp, defensive. It was always a cause of anxiety in Mother that Father neglected to call more often upon his family.

'On a Sunday?' Aunt Mary draws herself up.

'He had to go to Sawdons. He says he's sorry.' I hold my breath, hoping she will not question me further, hoping I shall not have to confront a choice whether to lie about the reason.

She seems to accept this meagre explanation, thank goodness, and holds the door open. 'You'd better come in, Rose. You've got time to take tea with your grandmother before the evening draws in.'

I follow her into the room, which is larger than ours but feels airless, crammed with heavy furniture. Apart from the one casement, whose panes are small and dense, the only source of light is the red glare of the open range. Next to it sits my grandmother, in black bombazine, a large white apron and lace mob cap styled in the fashion of the olden days with which I'm sure she feels more at ease. In her lap, she has a number of colourful pieces of square rag. At first glance, it looks as if she is sorting them for the purpose of making a rug. It soon becomes evident, however, that there is no method to her plucking and shuffling. I sit on the low stool next to her. 'Grandmother, it's me, Rose.'

She looks up, at the proximity of my voice. Some fleeting change may have registered in her pale eyes but, if it did, it has vanished. She mumbles something anxious in tone, and returns to her toiling.

While the tea is brewing, Aunt Mary sits down in the big armchair on the other side of the hearth. 'God rest your mother's soul, Rose. This is a hard cross for you to bear.'

'Thank you for your sympathy, Aunt,' I say, responding to the softening of her expression.

I remember being shocked when Father told me once that his sister, when young, had been considered pretty and 'quite a catch'.

Where Father's hair still keeps the colour of honey with few grey strands, Aunt Mary's has turned completely white. Where Father's eyes seem composed of many hues, all warm, as if dappled by sunlight, hers are a lighter, more uniform shade of oatmeal. Above all, it is the set of mouth which I find hard to imagine as being anything other than reproving.

'Prayers were said for her in chapel, this morning, your uncle tells me.'

Is this a reproach, or am I being over-sensitive?

'Not that we can go to the funeral. Tuesday is a busy day for your uncle, and I can't leave Mother. This afternoon she's docile, other days she wanders from the house. We think she's looking for her old home. If I turn my back for any length of time, she strays down to the river. Still,' she rises to pour the tea, 'we're not vouchsafed this life in order to ask for recompense.'

Despite the resignation implied by these words, she looks worried and unhappy. It comes to me that my aunt is probably rather lonely. All activity takes place at the mill itself, not here. If, after all, I had been the one to stay at home and care for Father, I can see I should have felt it my duty to visit regularly. The thought has barely time to touch my heart with a creeping dread when Aunt Mary says, as if intuiting some part of it: 'Now you'll be looking after your father, you can come and see us any time, Rose.'

I carefully explain that Hilda will be doing this instead of me. Aunt Mary's face lights up at this news, which solution she considers 'quite right'. So delighted is she, at the prospect of Hilda's return home, that she does not think to pursue my future. I wonder how on earth things are going at the Hall.

'Here you are, Mother.'

Aunt Mary scoops up the rag squares and puts a plate with a slice of Christmas cake on it in Grandmother's lap. There is still a sizable chunk of cake left on its silver board, which makes me think of ours with a rush of emotion – consumed with relish over two days, parcelled up for Joe and Hubert and anyone else to take away, gone by the New Year.

'Oh, good,' Grandmother says, quite distinctly, then picks up the cake in both hands and crams it into her mouth, making short work of it.

I accept a small slice with my cup of tea. It is of a drier texture than Mother's. No alcohol, of course, this being a Methodist household. Again, my father's words return to me of how, initially, Adam's parents had opposed the match with Mary, thinking he would be marrying into a family of drunkards. Father told this story, partly as a joke: Mary was teetotal and their fears were soon allayed, but also to show the contrasting attitude of Mother's parents to their prospective son-in-law. They saw the good in Father and accepted him.

Whilst I am eating and drinking, my aunt wipes Grandmother's hands carefully with a damp cloth, then pours her tea into the saucer, tests it then tilts it into her mother's mouth, spilling nothing nor hurrying her. I am not surprised when my offer of assistance is politely brushed aside.

In the meantime, the sound of heavy footsteps above us, then on the stairs, heralds the arrival of Uncle Adam, rubbing his eyes from his afternoon sleep. He offers his condolences and helps himself to tea and cake. 'I will try and get away on Tuesday,' he says.

'Everyone understands your situation,' I assure him.

As soon as he has finished, he takes the cup and saucer from Aunt Mary and sits down to finish feeding Grandmother, so that Aunt Mary can have her tea. This is clearly a routine, which the old lady accepts with equanimity.

There has always been so much to occupy my time and thoughts in our family. It is as if I am seeing for the first time why things are the way they are between us and this little family. It is, I believe, what the Greeks would have called dramatic irony. Every year as our family grew and grew, my aunt and uncle were not blessed with children. No wonder Mother always seemed uncomfortable here and, when she became too infirm, ceased to visit. No wonder Father found it easier to forget.

'So, Rose,' says Aunt Mary, between sips, 'when do you start at Sawdons?'

My mind seizes up. 'I'm not sure –'

A sudden clatter of hooves on cobbles. We all, except Grandmother, look up. A black blur of horse across the window, and I can't believe my eyes. 'Good Lord,' says Aunt Mary, then claps her hand to her mouth looking at Uncle Adam, but he stands transfixed grasping Grandmother's empty cup and plate. It is Father riding Will Sturgess's mare, Sable, whom he may borrow because she spends a large part of the year in our field. When not grazing or pulling the hearse, she is often harnessed to Father's cart.

He slides down, landing with a little bounce, and hitches her to a ring in the wall. Uncle Adam hurriedly places the crockery on the table and, squaring his shoulders, goes to the door, followed by Aunt Mary. I notice, as I join them, that her face has resumed its customary set. I had relaxed while Grandmother was the centre of attention, now there is a knot of tension inside me.

Uncle Adam is at the door, offering condolences. Aunt Mary echoes him, then says: 'We weren't expecting you. Rose said you had business at Sawdons.'

'I did, but I hoped Rose would still be here so I could take her home. Are you ready to go?'

I try not to make my 'yes' sound too eager. I turn to say goodbye to Grandmother, but she is right behind me and pushes past with surprising strength.

'Mother,' my father says. 'How are you?'

'Oh dear, now we'll have to get her back inside,' says Aunt Mary.

'Robert,' says Grandmother, with clarity.

Father smiles, 'Yes, that's right.'

Aunt Mary looks exasperated, Uncle Adam wary.

Then Grandmother walks to Father and takes his arm, looking up at him sideways, girlishly. Heat rushes to my cheeks. I feel both embarrassed and ashamed of being embarrassed. Everyone looks at each other. Then, as one, we all realise Grandmother's sad and understandable mistake.

'Home?' Grandmother asks, uncertain now.

'Yes, we're going home,' says Father, escorting her back inside the house. As she passes me, she has a sweet smile on her face.

I hear Father making her comfortable in her chair and saying, 'we're home now', several times. When he comes out, he looks shaken. He speaks in a low voice. 'I've given her my clean handkerchief with the embroidered R. It was Father's, of course. I think she recognised it. Anyway, it's keeping her contented.'

Aunt Mary looks anything but contented. She gives her speech about not attending Mother's funeral, which Uncle Adam qualifies with ifs and buts. Father nods. While they have been speaking, he has untied Sable and led her over to a large, worn stone evidently used as a mounting block. Almost in one movement, he slots his left foot into the stirrup and jigs his right leg up and over her back. He settles in the saddle above us. Just before he speaks, I have a flash of terrible intuition. 'Right, come on, Rose.' He has the reins firmly gathered in his right hand which rests on Sable's neck. He opens his left and dangles it towards me. 'Put your left foot in the stirrup and pull on my arm. I'll swing you up.' He has slipped his own foot obligingly from the iron.

I am petrified. Sable has been a formidable presence in our field every summer of my life. I have been on her back before, but that recollection is particularly unhelpful now. Aunt Mary speaks before I can. 'You don't mean her to sit *astride*?' This last word is a shocked hiss.

'I do. For the time it takes to get back to the stable, what does it matter? Besides, I've met no one else the whole afternoon and we'll be on the towpath.'

I think of the river on one side, brambles on the other. 'I'll walk,' I say, quickly.

'You won't keep up once Madam guesses she's going home.'

Aunt Mary says, 'Let me fetch a shawl so that Rose can put it –'

'I can't fart-arse about anymore. I'll be shielding her modesty, won't I?'

Aunt Mary has been tutting the whole way through while Father spoke. I am rather shocked, too. Father never uses foul language – at least, not in front of us. I feel a dropping sense of disappointment. They've driven each other back to fit the idea one has of the other. I have to admit a certain admiration for Father's succinct eloquence. I have the urge to giggle. This prompts me to act. I advance on the mass of Sable's brown-black, glossy flank, reach my leg up, up till my foot finds secure purchase in the stirrup iron whilst grabbing Father's arm, and then it is as if the world has tilted as I swing, he pulls and I land hard on her rump behind him, winded, my skirts round my calves.

'Tch! Tch!' Aunt Mary begins again, as if she cannot stop herself.

'It was kind of you to visit – both of you.' Uncle Adam tries to curb her disapproval and conclude the afternoon in harmony. 'We shall be thinking of you all over the coming days.'

I can feel the mare's impatience to be moving which must be obvious to my relatives. We all say goodbye, and she's off, taking us down to the river in no time. As soon as her head points for home, she breaks into a little trot. I assure Father I am all right, even though I am clinging to his middle and feel far from all right.

'She always manages to rub me up the wrong way, my sister,' he says.

I don't answer. This is not tact on my part nor loss of the right words, but because my breath is being buffeted out of me on every down-beat of Sable's hooves. Father doesn't seem to notice my lack of response, however, because he is now telling me about his ride over to Sawdons which, apparently, the mare enjoyed.

'You think of her daily life, Rose. She never gets the chance to go through her paces, so where the ground wasn't too firm, I let her canter and then, on that bit of fallow just before the Hall, I put her to the gallop.'

It occurs to me that the mare was not the only one who enjoyed the exercise. I try to enjoy this bouncing ride, and give thanks for the moon, nearly full, silvering the river and lighting our way.

'I saw Phyllis.'

I catch my already-limited breath, feel light-headed, grip Father tighter.

'Well, she saw me,' Father is saying. 'She'd been called upstairs and glimpsed me coming through the Park – nearly dropped her tea tray, she said.'

'Did you speak to her?' I manage to jerk out, a knot inside me tightening.

'She met me in the yard. Told me off. She said it was all right you visiting because you're about to start work there, but friends and relatives are forbidden. I could have lost her job for her. I said it was an emergency. I had to speak to Leonard Pritchard.'

I feel faint, hot and cold. 'So, you told her –' I begin.

'I didn't tell her anything,' Father cuts in. 'As soon as I said the name, Leonard Pritchard, she calmed down. She seemed to think I'd come to consult him about passages from the Bible, suitable for reading at the funeral. That's what she told Jack.'

'Jack?'

'He came out when he heard our voices. They're all having to work this afternoon to make up for Tuesday. Anyway, he took Madam, here, and gave her some hay, and Phyllis went to fetch Mr Pritchard from his room.'

At this point, we both have to duck to avoid an overhanging branch as Sable veers into the undertaker's yard and, hooves ringing in the Sunday night quiet, jogs to her stable door, where she stops with a great huff as if to emphasise that we are to expect no more of her.

'You'll have to get off first, while I'm still holding her,' Father says, offering me his left arm. 'Hang onto me and just slide down.'

He looks determinedly forward whilst I make an undignified descent, glad that no one else is here to witness it. It feels a very long way down before one foot, then the other, touches the ground. The sensation, as I bear my own weight, is as if I were sinking, sinking. I feel immensely tired and weak. Tomorrow, I shall ache.

Father unsaddles Sable by the light of the moon, then leads her to her stall. I begin to follow, wobbly and feeble, but wait at the door. The stable is dark and sweet smelling. I hear Father hang the tack on its hook and Sable pulling at her manger. Father comes out, and we head towards the glimmer of gaslight in the High Street.

'I liked him, young Pritchard,' Father says, as we turn for home. 'He looked me in the eye and he called me Sir. I like that. Firm handshake, too. Honest. Trustworthy.'

Leonard's steady gaze holds my mind's eye. 'Yes, that's what I think,' I say.

'He told me what your duties would be and gave me a good description of the hostel. It all sounded above-board, I must say.'

I dare not hope, but I have to ask. 'Please, Father, may I know your decision?'

'I said I would sleep on it' – my heart misses a beat – 'but I couldn't see why you shouldn't accept the job.'

Relief and fatigue sweep over me. 'Thank you, Father, thank you.' I am close to tears. He supports my arm.

'Mr Pritchard said you can hand him your written acceptance on Tuesday afternoon when I take the family back to Sawdons. He'll be looking out for us. I thought that was decent of him in the circumstances. You can tell them at the Hall that you won't be taking up the position there. You'll be coming home with me and, apparently, he won't be there beyond the following morning. They can make what they like of it.'

His words drift in and out of my head.

I wake to a sweet feeling. Before I can work out why this should be – my old room – the enormity of the day and what is before me takes its place . . .

Yesterday, Father left at first light, with little said at breakfast. I set to clearing and cleaning the table, ready for the spread. I made a fruit cake, then took the money Father had set aside and went down to the butcher's for a tongue, to augment our own cured ham, and to the baker's for a white loaf. Neither shopkeeper would accept remuneration, the butcher closing my outstretched hand in his two and shaking his head, the baker's wife telling me it was the least she and her husband could do to honour the memory of my dear mother. On the way home, I was stopped many times with similar expressions of condolence.

Full though I was with thoughts of Mother, nothing prepared me for the shock of seeing her coffin, so large in our small living room. It rested on Father's chair and two others, all but blocking the way through to the scullery. Father was making final arrangements with Will Sturgess. When he had gone, I tried to find the words for Father's craftsmanship: the burnished oak, the restrained yet gracious ornament, his signature on a masterpiece he would have given anything not to have to create. Neither of us could speak, so I went upstairs and took off the sheets from my old bed and Father's, first shaking from his counterpane the imprint of the coffin shell, blurred by my tears.

Since the day was fair, I washed and mangled the sheets and hung them out, then put clean sheets on Father's bed and mine, which I shall share with Hilda. Father and I ate bread and cheese, after which he fell asleep. In the afternoon lull, I wrote my letter of acceptance to Leonard Pritchard. It felt an odd thing to be doing, as if I were speaking for someone in another life. I felt emotionless, and tried to bring Leonard once more to my mind's eye, but somehow his vitality was missing. I hoped my letter would not convey my inner state, but would be taken simply for the formality it was.

I brought in the sheets, thankfully almost dry, and hoisted them to air on the pulley, with a mental note to put them away first thing next day. Just before I scrambled eggs for supper, Mrs Jepp called with a fruit cake far superior to mine, a large Dundee whose concentric rings of polished almonds shone in the lamplight. She said she would come and help me in the morning.

. . . It is still dark, yet there is a quality about the darkness which tells me it is time to get up.

Mrs Jepp arrives as the clock strikes nine. She has brought an extra packet of tea for which I am very grateful. I have the feeling, judging by all who crossed to stop me yesterday, that there will be quite a press of people here after the service.

By half past ten, we have the best tea set ready on the dresser with the glasses, the plates on the table, food under cloths: Mrs Jepp's dainty sandwiches, neatly arranged; my less accomplished ones; the two fruit cakes echoing this pattern. She melts away as Father reappears wielding a flagon of beer he has been drawing from the keg he keeps at one end of his shed, brewed for special occasions. He goes upstairs to change into his best dark coat. I am already dressed in a neat black skirt – truly second-hand, Phyllis being the first.

I step outside. It is a clear winter's day, the sky blue and the sun shining with a warmth worthy of springtime. Just the kind of day on which Mother would have wrapped her warm shawl around her and sat in front here on the bench. I test it for dryness and, as a tribute to her, sit down to enjoy, as she would have, the sunlight on my face and the scent of winter jasmine next to me on the wall. I close my eyes.

Ticking wheels. Voices. 'Poor thing, she's probably exhausted.' Hilda. I jerk awake. Joe and Hubert are wheeling their bicycles up the path. Hilda and Phyllis are already beside me, Dot, Ralph and Jack following behind the machines. Dazed, I stand and let my sisters embrace me. Phyllis gives me a proper hug. Jack and Ralph also hold me for a moment. Joe and Hubert nod acknowledgment as they take their bicycles round to the back. When they return, we stand about like a flock of crows just landed, too engulfed in our own sorrow to attempt conversation. Then, Joe and Hubert, who are holding saddlebags, sit down on the seat and each bring out an identical round of fish-paste sandwiches and bottled ginger beer with which they have been provided by the kind staff at the station buffet.

'There is food afterwards,' I tell them.

'But we're starving,' Joe says.

'We've just cycled twelve miles non-stop.'

'Yes, I'm a bit peckish,' Ralph says.

Father comes out to join us, holding a black top hat which completes his sombre elegance. 'Don't get up,' he says to Joe and Hubert, who have now unwrapped twin slabs of glistening Genoa cake. 'H'm, more fruit cake,' he adds, 'as if there isn't enough.'

'*Is* there – more than enough?' Ralph asks.

I offer them all a slice of my humble effort which, at Hilda's insistence, they eat standing up outside so that the crumbs will not sully their clothes. 'Or Rose's floor,' says Phyllis, who shares my lack of charity for housework. 'I don't know how you can eat.'

'Nor me,' echoes Hilda.

Jack has carried a satchel of lemonade bottles, made up by Dot. 'I didn't want you fussing over tea,' she says to me.

No sooner have they finished, than we hear the dreadful clop and creak approaching up our lane. Father goes to greet Will Sturgess and his son, Luke. The mare, used to her role, stares vacantly ahead but when she hears my father's voice something seems to pass through her to him as she looks his way. 'Not today, old girl,' he says. Will Sturgess mounts the hearse.

Father hands me his hat and I fetch mine. Then, the six men go inside. When they come out, they have the coffin on their shoulders. We hand them their hats and they put them on like soldiers going into battle. Their faces are set rigid as they pass slowly down the path. I turn away, and catch sight of Hilda and Dot, similarly turned, hands to their eyes. Phyllis is holding herself, staring at the ground. A tear splashes at her feet. She swipes her face. I am drawing great gulps of breath as I try to control my brimming eyes.

We all have to mine our own reserves as we fall in, Dot and Hilda, Phyllis and I, behind the men and follow the hearse, firstly down our little lane, then out into the road and through the town where the market is almost over. I find that if I fasten my eyes on Dot's astrakhan collar, I can keep control but, even so, I cannot fail to notice the dark blur of movement on either side of me as every stallholder doffs his cap.

I survive the service and the burial by employing the same technique of pinning my eyes to something ordinary. In the packed church, the wooden board above the pulpit displaying hymn numbers. At the graveside, the raised pattern of small jet beads on the back of my clasped gloves. The sun shines. I like to think it is a blessing.

At home, our sorrow is held in check by business. The house is, as I had thought it might be, full. Father and the boys serve beer to the men. We are kept busy with plates, teacups, kettle and teapot. At first the mood is sombre, with many expressions of heartfelt sympathy offered to all of us together and as individuals. As time passes, though, anecdotes begin. The first laugh is heard, Father's, as he affectionately recalls how Mother would call him her Jack-in-the-Hedge when he came home with wood shavings in his hair. Conversation begins to flow. The need to serve our guests has eased. I realise, with a lurch of apprehension, that this is the moment when I must speak to Phyllis. I catch her sleeve and nod towards the open back door. We walk outside where Joe and Hubert are standing proudly by their bicycles talking to Dr Jepp. 'Mine came from Howes of Cambridge,' he says as we pass. We walk on, out of earshot, round to the side of the woodshed.

'You look dreadful, Rose. There's really no need to be scared, if it's about coming back with us. You'll soon get used to it at Sawdons.'

Her compassionate look is too much for me. I burst into tears and blurt out everything about the bookshop job, from the chance meeting with Leonard Pritchard on the day of Mother's death to Father's favourable impression of him and disposal to agreement.

While I have been speaking, Phyllis has been chewing her lip. Now, she says, quietly, 'You could have told me.'

And I realise I should have done that. On Saturday, when I came back to relay the news of Mother's funeral, and Phyllis said goodbye to me in the garden, I should have detained her from her duties just for one moment. I should have trusted her. 'I'm so sorry –' I begin, but there are footsteps.

'Sorry about what, Rose?' Joe has come over, closely followed by Hubert. There is no sign of Dr Jepp.

Hubert glances at the three of us. 'What's all this about?'

I can't help looking at Phyllis, but her face is stony – shocked, probably. In my hazy imaginings of how I would present myself to the family today, I had somehow thought that Joe and Hubert could simply be told later, when I was already settled in my new position. Another ill-judged idea on my part.

'Come on, Rose. We haven't got time to hang around now, so spit it out.'

Behind Joe, while he is speaking, Father comes across to us. I can see he has grasped the situation. 'The guests have left,' he says, 'let's go inside.'

'But we need to —' Hubert begins.

'Yes, and I must take everyone back soon, but this won't last long,' Father says.

There are not seats for everyone, so we all stand.

'Rose has something to tell you,' Father says.

All eyes are on me. The clock at my shoulder adds its insistent beat. I am surprised at how cool my voice sounds as I give them the bare bones. It is probably because I am completely drained. When I say I won't be working at the Hall, Hilda gasps, Dot looks disapproving, Phyllis non-committal. Jack and Ralph both look as if they'd like to be pleased for me.

'A shop assistant? You must be mad!' Joe says.

It feels like a slap across the face.

'You've never even worked in a shop,' Hubert adds, frowning.

'She will get training,' Father says, but I can hear the waver in his voice.

'I think Rose would be good in a bookshop,' Jack ventures, ever loyal. 'She reads a lot of books.'

'She'd have to sell the things, not read them,' Joe says with disdain.

Hubert is shaking his head as if I have lost my wits. 'There's always going to be work for a good domestic, but a shop assistant . . . well . . .'

'That's true,' Dot chimes in. 'Very good position – the one you're set on giving up, Rose. Think about it.'

'I have,' I say, beginning to feel angry, but not wanting to show it in case it makes matters worse for me.

Father clears his throat. 'I've thought about all this, too, but I did

41

like young Pritchard when I met him. That's why I gave Rose my permission –'

Joe cuts across him. 'Father, if I may, I really would urge you to think again.'

My heart plummets. I stare at Joe, askance.

'It isn't just the job. I'm sorry to have to raise this subject in present company, but you know what these women's hostels really are.'

I am incredulous, can feel the others' acute anxiety.

'Yes,' Hubert chips in, 'she wouldn't be safe.'

'Well, Leonard Pritchard assures me that it is not the case with this one. In fact, I'm invited to meet the landlady and visit the bookshop,' Father says, but I can see he is rattled.

'Then, there's the traffic,' Joe says. 'She isn't used to it.'

'Yes, we do have motor cars, you know,' says Hubert.

'If she gets run over, who'll be responsible for her?' Joe adds.

Incensed at being discussed as if I were not present, I say, 'If I get run over, none of you will have to be responsible for me.'

Father says, 'Don't be silly, Rose.' He sounds worried. I have not helped myself.

'Surely, it's not too late to put a stop to this foolishness?' Hubert says. 'They don't know any of this back at Sawdons. She can take up the job there as planned and tell this Pritchard fellow he can keep his offer.'

There is a moment's silence as we each take this in. I dare not speak for fear of bursting into angry tears and blurting out something which will make me look stupid and childish. I suddenly remember what it was like when Joe and Hubert were boys at home. One evening in particular comes to mind. Phyllis and I were reaching the climax of one of our Uncle Bottomley stories by the fireside, yelping with laughter, when Joe's voice carried above ours telling our parents it was 'time those little girls went to bed' and Hubert agreeing. Though Mother and Father made light of the admonition, the mood had been broken. We did, shortly after, go to bed.

'I think Rose is old enough –' Jack begins, but gets no further. Joe rounds on him, Ralph weighs in on my side, and soon the boys are all speaking at once, the situation not helped by Hilda's contribution, 'She might meet a learned gentleman', which Hubert dismisses with, 'Not on that side of town she won't. It'll be all women from the training college.'

'Oh dear,' says Father, 'this is all too much.'

I am riven to hear him use those words again on my account.

The boys fall quiet. Phyllis takes her hands from her ears.

'You see, Rose,' Joe turns to me. 'Look what you've done. You've upset Father *and* Phyllis.' He sounds triumphant.

Phyllis stares at Joe.

'She got you the job at Sawdons and you've let her down. How do you think she feels?'

Phyllis says, 'She feels you should accept the job at the bookshop, Rose. By golly, she would if she had the chance.' Phyllis's eyes on Joe are blazing.

Jack says, 'I agree.'

'So do I,' says Ralph.

There is silence.

Joe says, 'To think, a solemn day such as this and we end it in discord.'

Father says, slowly, 'Yes, God forgive us, we're all forgetting Mother. What would she want for Rose?'

Suddenly, there it is: the unquestionable answer – Mother, who had made sure we could read and write, who had wanted us all to have an education as a stepping stone out of a life of drudgery. I have only to glance at Joe and Hubert's faces to know that Mother has won the argument.

Phyllis says, as if to make sure everyone's got the message, 'Mother would say: chamber pots or books, Rose? She'd tell Rose to seize this opportunity.'

'That's right,' says Jack, and Ralph gives a vigorous nod, Hilda and Dot offering less effusive ones.

'Very well,' says Hubert and, after a moment, 'So be it,' says Joe. They start putting on their bicycle clips.

Father turns to me, 'What Phyllis says is true. It's your life, Rose.

43

I'm willing to let you go. You do still want the job at Pritchard's bookshop?'

I look at all the people who love me, framed by all the things I know and love. I think of living in a town I hardly know, surrounded by strangers except for two brothers, the least like me of any of my family and who would prefer me not to be there. Then, I think about Leonard Pritchard and how exhilarating I found his discourse on the poets. I can see his face clearly now, his dark, intense eyes full of light. 'Yes,' I say, 'I would like to take the job.'

Chapter Four

As the light fades, I can feel frost forming in the air, see Sable's breath against a lamp-lit window. Jack springs down and takes her head, talking to her gently as the rest of us climb out of the cart. Ralph squeezes my shoulder, mouths 'Good Luck' before turning to Father, who is standing still as a stone, staring at the ground. Neither speaks. Then Ralph steps forward and touches his arm. Father raises his eyes and nods, as if in reassurance. It is an act of release, and Ralph's face relaxes slightly as he takes his leave.

Dot approaches Father next but, as Phyllis and I do, turns at the sound of footsteps from the house. Her usually sweet face stiffens almost imperceptibly. Leonard approaches us. 'I was looking out for you.' He walks straight up to Father and clasps his hand. 'Again, my deepest sympathy —' including us in his gaze, 'to you, sir, and all the family'.

'Thank you, Mr Pritchard.' Father looks relieved, as if these fitting words confirm his image of Leonard.

'Perhaps we may speak a little later, Mr Alleyn, Rose,' he says.

Father agrees. Dot crosses between them without looking at Leonard, takes Father's hand in both of hers and says goodbye.

So now at Jack's suggestion, we are in the tack room, the nearest place where we can hold a private conversation. Jack has brought a hurricane lamp and hung it from a long nail aslant on one of the beams. Its meagre light glints on brass snaffles and casts exaggerated shadows on our tense faces. Jack has gone to tend to Sable. The smell of polished leather is comforting. I try to smile as I pass across my letter of acceptance, but I am nervous. What if he has changed his mind? As if reading mine, Father says to Leonard, 'I hope you'll be pleased.'

Then the atmosphere changes with the smile which breaks across Leonard's face. 'Welcome to Pritchard's – purveyor of quality books. We should have some champagne.'

'I'll just go and get some,' says Phyllis. 'Will the 1865 *Veuve Cliquot* do? There's a whole rack of it in the wine cellar.'

For a moment, it feels as if she isn't joking, but Father and Leonard are laughing, and then Father is asking about the arrangements for Saturday.

'Ah, I've been thinking,' says Leonard. 'Working on the assumption that you would accept the position, Rose, and given our discussion on Sunday, Mr Alleyn, I wonder whether you could start a day early, this Friday, that is.'

Father looks as surprised as I am.

Before either of us can answer, Leonard says, 'It's the official opening on Saturday, you see, and it would be most advantageous to give you a full day's training first.'

'Well, I could . . . couldn't I, Father?' My heart is racing.

Father is sucking his teeth. 'It all depends when I can have the mare. It would mean taking you over on Thursday, wouldn't it, Rose?'

'Oh well, I'm sure I'll manage –'

'I've had a thought,' Father says. 'Sturgess said I didn't have to worry when I brought the mare back because she isn't needed for a couple of days. So, yes, Thursday morning would be convenient.'

'Even better,' says Leonard.

Father still looks exercised. 'What about . . . you know . . . you said this Mrs – what was her name – was expecting Rose on Saturday.'

'The room is empty now,' says Leonard. 'I checked. Mrs Fuller will be delighted to accommodate Rose as soon as she can come. She looks forward to meeting you both.'

I feel scared and excited at the same time.

'Very well,' says Father. 'You'll have to give me directions. It's near the station, isn't it?'

Now comes the part from which, over the past two days, my mind has shied like a frightened horse.

Father goes to talk to Jack. 'I'll be here if you need me, Rose,' he says as the three of us enter the house.

At the end of the shadowy passage are two lights. One is on the wall by the back stairs and the other is a strip of light under the kitchen door.

'I'll say goodbye until Thursday morning,' says Leonard, 'at Pritchard's Bookshop,' and he grasps my hand before he leaves us. I feel its pressure.

'Come on,' says Phyllis. 'No one's going to harm you. Not with me here.' She opens the kitchen door, firmly.

We are confronted by a curious tableau: Mrs Gilliatt, a black pillar at the far end of the table, Mrs Brandon, the cook, bobbing to her and seeming to be thanking her, very happy. Dot stands behind her looking, despite her florid birthmark, drained. All three now turn at our approach, and I know from their faces that this little scene has everything to do with me.

'I'm sorry, Rose, I was so upset, I –'

'That will do, Dorothy. I believe you wish to speak to me, Rose,' says the housekeeper in a hard voice.

I make myself meet her flinty eyes. 'I very much regret, Mrs Gilliatt, I shall be unable to take up the position of between-stairs maid.' She says nothing, but I have decided not to elaborate, merely concluding, 'And I regret the inconvenience that this has caused you.'

When she realises I have nothing more to add, she draws herself up. 'Well, Rose, I hope you do not live to regret your decision, because there will be no second chance. And now, I have dinner for twenty guests to supervise, minus one maid. I shall be obliged if you will allow me to get on with it. You may leave.' She sweeps to the door, which Phyllis opens for her, and is gone.

I knew it would be difficult, but I have hardly time to feel the stinging words. A hand touches my shoulder. 'You have done me such a favour, Rose.' It is the kindly voice of Mrs Brandon, smiling as I turn, bewildered. 'My granddaughter worked her way to upstairs maid in another household, but they're going next week as missionaries and will employ some of the native people. Mrs Gilliatt has agreed my Becky can have your job.'

So, really there was no need for Mrs Gilliatt to scold me – except her own.

I am glad for Mrs Brandon's granddaughter, and tell her. Then, I say goodbye to Dot, restored to something like her sweet good humour. Phyllis comes with me to the back door. 'I'll be with you in spirit,' she says, reading my mind. In the shadows, unobserved, we give way to the emotion of the day and of the moment and hug each other tight. 'You'd better go. Father'll be getting frostbite,' she says. We wave goodbye.

Jack has brought Sable round and is talking with Father, the mare's head between them. We all say our farewells, Jack accepting my hug, then Father and I are up on the seat, Father arranging the crocheted blanket which Hilda insisted we should have. He snaps the reins on Sable's back and Jack makes clicking sounds, encouraging her to trot. As he slips behind us, he raises his arm as I raise mine, and then we are out of the courtyard and the clatter of hooves on cobbles becomes a dull drumming as we leave by the tradesmen's dirt track. I settle against Father, feel the rough wool of his overcoat, smell, on the blanket, the scent of last summer's lavender pressed in the linen chest.

The next thing I know is that the cart has stopped.

'We're home, Rose.'

I open my eyes and we're in our little lane, the moon etching the branches of the bare trees above us against the sky. There are stars.

'Good, you're awake, then,' Father says. 'You go on in. I won't be long.'

I climb down and cross the meadow, Sable's soft footfalls on dead leaves and the creak of the wheels diminishing to silence.

Our cottage is bathed in silver light. In the kitchen, our winter curtains are lit up by lamplight, the window a square of gold. I feel a lump starting in my throat. Suddenly, in the trees behind me, close by and loud, comes the female owl's silly squeak, *too-whit, too-whit, too-whit*, repeated again and again, as if she is laughing at me. I don't know whether to laugh with her or cry.

Inside, everything is tidy, cosy and welcoming, Hilda fashion. She has made us a supper of lentil soup, a round each of sandwiches using the last of the white bread, delicately sliced, and the tongue, and she has cut three slices from the remains of Mrs Jepp's Dundee cake. The teapot stands by the gently steaming kettle. Father will be well looked after, if proof were ever needed.

I spend a quiet day with Hilda, which we both enjoy. She gives me her valise, as I don't have one. 'Well, I shan't be needing it – I hope,' she says. It does not take long to pack. We bring it downstairs and I quickly slip in, amongst the rolled clothes, my Bible given me when I was confirmed and, at Hilda's insistence, Mother's book of poems, for as she says, 'Father's not going to read it, is he? And I'm going to renew my subscription at the library. See if they've got the latest novel by that Mr Hall Caine.'

After we've eaten and cleared up, the three of us sit round the fire. Hilda keeps us all from brooding by recounting incidents from her life in service. In view of our early start tomorrow, we soon go up to bed.

'You used to tell us stories, do you remember?' Hilda says, when we are snuggled up together.

'So I did,' I say. 'I don't think they were very good.'

'You were only little. We liked them anyway.' She yawns. 'You could tell me one now.'

'I'm tired.'

'Oh, go on.' She yawns again.

'All right, then.' Now, I'm yawning. 'Once upon a time,' I say, slowly, 'there were three teacups hanging on hooks on a dresser. The first teacup was very beautiful –'

Hilda's breathing is slow and even. '. . . still listening . . .' slurred. '. . . and was made of bone china so fine . . .'

Deep and regular breathing.

'. . . it was . . .' I whisper, 'just like you, Hilda.'

No answer.

I close my eyes, wondering how I would have described the other teacups.

We are seated once again behind Sable's broad back, the valise between us like an armrest and the cart empty. 'There's a wood yard, if I remember rightly,' Father says. 'On my way back, I'll see what they've got and what they're charging.'

The sun which has been veiled by milky cloud since we started finally breaks through. I feel its warmth on my back as we travel west, bare winter fields on either side, the occasional red brick farmhouse flanked by black wooden barns. We come to Hadle Street, the place which stands between Markly and Widdock, soon passed through. It seems even smaller than our town.

As we leave its last, straggling cottages behind us the river, which has been an unseen presence marked by willows running beside us somewhere to the south, now comes into view glinting between water meadows on which rough-coated cattle graze. There is an adjective for such meadows but it eludes me now and, although I push the consequent irritation to the back of my mind, it continues to buzz there like a dying fly.

'Not long now,' Father says.

We have already said 'Good morning' to a couple of carters going the other way. Now we pass a trap, two individual riders and a wagon stacked with sacks of flour. The road twists into a gentle climb and there, as we breast the hill, is Widdock laid out below us, smoking and steaming in the pleasant winter sunshine. The rich fragrance of roasting barley hits us and I can pick out the distinctive shapes of the cowls which crown the kiln roofs of the many maltings for which the town is renowned.

We come down into the valley, pausing to let more wagons

leave a tall modern flour mill which looks like a factory. We pass a plot of land divided into strips, bare now except for rows of cabbages, then a pub, The Angel, with its yard and patch of grass where workers might sit in summer. Now, there is a row of cottages to our right. To our left, at right angles to the road, several rows of cottages run down to the river which has suddenly come very close. I can see the dark sails of barges. After another pub, The Barley Mow, we are entering the town proper, the river blotted out by the towering wall of an immense malting. We have to stop and let out two drays which take the road in front of us. Slowed by their pace, we gain our first sight and sound of the High Street, full of shops and other impressive buildings. There are carts, traps, bicycles, people on foot, and a level of noise to which we are both unaccustomed.

Father is looking slightly tense. 'Cross the river, he said . . .' he murmurs to himself.

So, we turn our back on the High Street and follow the two drays up to a bridge, where men in flat caps are leaning on its cast-iron railings, looking down onto the river. I glimpse, on either side, barges packed in together. Besides the idlers on the bridge, there are working men everywhere. We can hear their shouts coming up from the decks and see them on the towpath, loading sacks or going about their business in the street. Father looks troubled. The butterflies in my stomach, which I have been feeling since we first set eyes on the town, have turned into a heart-clenching sensation much more akin to fear. This is all so unfamiliar to us. Yet part of my apprehension arises from the knowledge that, if he should chose to do so, Father could still change his mind about the wisdom of my employment here. He glances at me but, as luck would have it, I am smiling. He looks relieved. He need not know that my apparent nonchalance stems from personal satisfaction. I have just recalled the word for water meadows: riparian.

The two drays peel away onto the London road, and we dip down into a busy little street of shops with, at its end, the railway track with level crossing gates. My heart jumps. Was this why my brothers

51

were so against my coming here? Being so close to where they both work, I might be a nuisance.

The scent of fresh-baked bread from the baker's on the corner makes me hungry. Two customers are chatting outside, their bread baskets on their arms, and the shop seems to be staffed by women. A woman outside the next shop, a greengrocer's, looks up from placing in a vase burgeoning stems of bright yellow blooms like sunbeams. 'Cornish daffodils,' she says, smiling, not unkindly at our wide-eyed wonder.

Father touches his cap to her. 'Good morning, ma'am. Can you tell me if there is a bookshop, Pritchard's, about to open here?'

'Turn the other way and you'll see it, sir,' she says.

Father thanks her. I am already looking at the opposite side of the road, ashamed of myself for my involuntary reaction: disappointment. In my mind's eye, I had summoned gracious premises: bow windows on either side of a black-and-white tiled path to the shop door which would open with a tinkling bell. Pritchard's is altogether smaller, the door opening directly onto the street, the windows modest, but at least it has two of them, and the lettering on the cross-board is elegant as well as clear. And here is Leonard, looking sincerely pleased to see us. 'Good morning, Mr Alleyn and Rose. Welcome to Pritchard's.' My anxieties evaporate.

Father hitches the reins and gives Sable her nose-bag. Then, Leonard holds the door open for us. 'You've come at just the right moment. I've been cataloguing and shelving since first light.'

Two lovely scents assail me. The first I know well from Father's shop: wood, from the new bookshelves which line three of the walls and from the counter. The other scent, I realise, emanates from the ranks of books themselves. It has an inviting freshness about it, reminding me of newly laundered linen. I am quite overcome with a sense of affirmation. For a moment, I cannot speak.

'I'll take you both up to meet Mrs Fuller and see your room, Rose, and then I thought, you and I between us can probably complete stocking the shelves before dark. Tomorrow, I can show you the ropes.'

'Yes, yes.' I am smiling and nodding in an idiotic fashion.

'But you both must be starving. Come through to the sitting room. I've got the kettle on and I went across earlier and bought some pies. I thought we could have an early lunch.'

My stomach growls quietly as if in response. Hoping it will not give me further cause for embarrassment, I hurry across to summon Father, who has been moving around the room not seeing the books but the shelves upon which they rest. 'Nice piece of oak, that.' He runs his hand along the counter as we pass through the shop. 'Good work altogether.'

Leonard opens a door at the back of the shop, and we walk into as agreeable a living room as anyone could wish for in a family home. My heart warms to it straightaway. An open range, with kettle on a hot-plate, is flanked by two armchairs. One is a buttoned library chair in leather, the other a slightly smaller but deep-seated chair upholstered in plush velvet.

'It's a bit worn, I know,' says Leonard, following my gaze, 'but when I knew you were coming, I wanted to find you something comfortable, so that you can rest properly during your breaks.'

'It's lovely.'

'And the colour – well, it had to be yours, didn't it?'

I tentatively stroke the soft pile. I cannot stop smiling.

'Sit down, Rose, try it out. And you, sir, take the other chair. I'll make some tea.'

While Leonard moves about with the kettle, chatting to Father about our journey here, I take in the rest of the room. A small but adequate back window has new nets and lined curtains in a heavy fabric of wine red, as is the rug beneath our feet. Under the window is a small gate-legged table, one side folded down and with a dining chair tucked in neatly. Beyond another closed door must be the scullery. I cannot discern anything outside because the sunlight is too strong. Behind me, opposite the hearth, is an alcove made by the stairs. It contains a table on and under which are cardboard packing cases, stamped *'With Care'*. On the other side of me from Father is a full bookshelf, some of whose titles have already caught my eye, the firelight playing on gilt-embossed lettering: *Treasure Island*, *The Black Arrow*. These must be Leonard's boyhood library.

'You may borrow any book you like,' he says.

I blush. I hadn't realised he was looking at me, but he is smiling as he passes me tea and then a warm pie on a plate which I balance on my knees. 'Perhaps I could read during my breaks,' I venture. 'You've made it very cosy here.' I would feel uncomfortable about taking one of Leonard's books away with me. Besides, what I said is true. I cannot imagine a more comfortable reading room. The danger, for me, might be that I would forget the time.

'And practical,' says Father, busy keeping his mutton pie over the plate, as he takes a mouthful of the delicious filling. 'No wasted space.'

'Thank you.' Leonard, who has pulled out the dining chair to face us, looks thoroughly pleased to hear our praise.

The pies are gone in no time, and Father starts to slap his leg and look concerned. I know he is thinking about Sable and about his journey home.

Leonard rises. 'If I may ride with you, I can quickly introduce you to Mrs Fuller, sir, and then you will know that Rose is in safe hands from dawn to dusk.'

Thus, I find myself up on the cart seat once more, pinioned between Father's ample thigh on one side and Leonard's altogether bonier one on the other. I stare straight ahead, my valise clamped on my knees. Neither man seems to notice my discomfort.

'Malting is the major industry, of course,' Leonard is saying. 'Malting in winter and the brickfields in summer, I expect you knew that.'

'Now you come to mention it,' says Father.

We have left the High Street behind us and are passing another huge malting, its roof punctuated at one end by several brick kilns topped with white cowls. In front of it, drays are being loaded and unloaded. I see a man march out of one door and in through another, carrying the flat, square shovel, used for turning barley. It is a scene of great activity, the burnt toffee smell of the malt all-pervasive. On our other side are a long row of cottages, probably built to house the malting workers. This is New Road, I read from its sign. Soon the reason for that name becomes clear. The small cottages giving straight onto the street are replaced by new houses, set back in front gardens. As the road begins to climb away from the town, the houses become less uniform. Many have Gothic features, but here is one styled as if trying to look like a big country cottage with a deep-eaved roof. Here is another looking like a palace from a foreign land, perhaps Italy. Some of them have their own small drives. At last we come to a board with the words: Apple Tree House written on it. There is a sturdy apple tree behind the sign raising bare, ivy-clad branches to the sky. Under the house name is written in smaller but still bold script: Hostel for Women. I feel a twinge of apprehension and excitement. Leonard nods to Father's questioning glance. We turn into the little drive.

The house is not one of the largest in the street but, by our stand-ards, it is handsomely proportioned. Although only possessing a single frontage, it has three tall sash windows in an imposing bay, replicated at first floor level. A black and white tiled porch supports a room above it with a single window. A rather elegant front door, painted midnight blue, displays a large panel of stained glass in the most beautiful design of birds and foliage. Close to the bell-pull is a note: 'If no reply, try studio in back garden.'

'More than one string to her bow, Mrs Fuller,' Leonard begins, by which time someone, a woman but clearly not a maid, is coming to the door.

'Ah, Leonard. And you must be Mr Alleyn and Rose. How d'you do? Come in, come in.'

We step into an imposing hall. For all its length, I gain an impression of lightness, spring-green wallpaper in a delicate floral pattern.

What sort of person had I been expecting? Someone like a school teacher? No one like this, her reddish-gold hair escaping from the onion of a low pompadour, her flowing and, I am sure, un-corseted gown, a more flamboyant version of the style which Mother, of necessity, took to wearing. A firm handshake. 'Will you take tea?'

Father starts to clear his throat, but Leonard answers. 'We've just had some thank you.'

'And I shall have to be leaving soon,' Father says.

'Of course. I'll show you the room then, and we can all go about our business.'

'I'll wait here,' says Leonard.

We follow Mrs Fuller's tall figure along the hall to the staircase, whose runner picks up the floral theme in subtly deeper shades of green, red and blue, the same pattern as the front door rug and the drugget, which stretches along where the corridor narrows beside the stairs, presumably, to the kitchen. I cast a sideways glance at Father to see what he makes, so far, of Mrs Fuller. Hers is just the kind of forthright manner for which he rebukes me and which he tells me is unladylike. I am somewhat surprised, therefore, but relieved to see that he is wearing a respectful face. This expression deepens as we go upstairs and he takes in the polished mahogany handrail and delicate carved balusters, painted ivory. Looking down into the hall, I am aware of large paintings, and have a sense of rich, swirling colours and bold figures, but the light is not good enough to make out anything further unless one were to stop in front of them and really look. The stair wall, too, is hung with pictures, this time smaller, some of them pencil sketches.

We turn at a bend in the stairs and advance to the first door on the landing, which Mrs Fuller opens. 'Here we are, Rose. The young lady who will share this room with you, if you like it, doesn't arrive till Sunday, so you may choose your bed.'

I am astounded at the size of the room, which I am to share with only one other person. There is a fireplace in the outer wall and in the back one, a window. This is a tall house with high ceilings, it seems. From where we are standing in the middle of the room, I can see trees and the backs of houses and gardens in another street. It is an altogether pleasing prospect. Again, the walls are papered in a lovely floral print. Whilst Mrs Fuller and Father are agreeing terms, which seem very reasonable, I make my easy choice and take the bed which is slightly nearer to the window it faces and to the fireplace, though the fire is neither laid nor lit as, Mrs Fuller explains, this is entirely our responsibility making a suitable contribution for the extra coal. This room, although large, has good thick rugs and, being in the well of the house, is likely to be warm. The two beds look well made up, with thick winter quilts. 'I am sure I shall not need a fire,' I say.

We return along the landing, through a doorway into a small space with three more doors before us. Mrs Fuller gestures towards the door ahead. 'That would be the maid's room if I kept one, but it's a guest's. And here,' she opens the two other doors, 'are the bathroom and lavatory'.

This is luxury. I am speechless.

As we go downstairs she tells me, over her shoulder, I shall have to discuss the bathroom rota with the current five other girls. 'There are four young women who keep factory hours. I will introduce you this evening. Your companion, like you, will be working in a shop.'

While she is speaking, Father is making faces at me to indicate that I have done very well here. I am relieved when we rejoin Leonard, who is studying a painting of an elderly, white-haired man with a kindly, interesting face. It is so full of animation that I imagine he could step from the frame into the room.

'High tea will be at half past six,' says Mrs Fuller, 'though I can keep it warm for you if necessary.'

'No, I will bring Rose back in good time for that,' says Leonard.

Father looks gratified that I will be accompanied from the shop.

'You'll have to bear with me, Rose,' says Mrs Fuller. 'My cook has eloped.'

We all make sounds of consternation. 'How dramatic,' Leonard says.

'It's all to do with the Ibbots and the Hobbses,' Mrs Fuller says. 'These are two big families in the town, who apparently hold some longstanding grudge.'

'Like the Montagues and Capulets,' I say.

'Exactly so.' Mrs Fuller's keen smile also takes in Leonard. They both seem pleased at my contribution. 'Well, you can guess what happened. My cook was a Hobbs and her Romeo an Ibbot. It was the only topic of conversation in the shops this morning. Meanwhile, I shall be Chef.'

I embrace Father, and we alight at the High Street, waving to him as he goes in search of the wood yard. He looks, as he turns briefly and raises a hand, as content as he can be in the circumstances. He no longer needs to worry about me.

Leonard and I cross the bridge, where men are still lolling gazing down at all the activity, and then we are back in the shop, the winter sun coming round to lighten everything.

'The trouble with an early lunch,' says Leonard, as we hang our coats and hats on hooks beside the scullery door, 'is the yearning for another one at normal lunchtime.'

I think of the bread and cheese wrapped in a cloth in my coat pocket, and wonder whether Father has stopped yet to have his.

'I'm ready to work, if you would like,' I say which, after all, is true.

'Excellent. Let's finish this job,' says Leonard. 'But don't be afraid to ask if you need a break.'

We seem to develop a rhythm, Leonard on his side of the shop, me on mine, both making the odd remark but working largely in a companionable silence the quicker to complete the task, so that the only sounds are the *clonk* of a block of books placed on a shelf, then *chock-chock-chock* as we neaten the line of them. I know I must be strict with myself not to become absorbed by their subjects which would greatly extend my knowledge in such areas as history, geography and English literature. I allow my mind to dwell on something curious which I have noticed happening to me this afternoon.

It is almost like shock, but without the unpleasantness. I am out of the habit of being, for any length of time, in the company of men who are not family. Male height and movements, voices. It is slightly unnerving and makes me recall how, when I was little, I used to shrink against my mother's skirts when the grocer, twirling closed a brown paper bag of broken biscuits, would put it in her basket and then bend down and tickle me under the chin, whilst telling her that I had lovely eyes or some such nonsense. I found him frightening enough, poor man, but nothing like the fear engendered by the knife-grinder, when his swarthy face appeared at our back window. I grew out of it, of course, and what I feel this afternoon here with Leonard, who is neither threatening nor a stranger, bears no resemblance to those childhood experiences. It is the novelty of him affecting me, I conclude. I feel my spirits being lifted.

Suddenly, we've finished and it is mid-afternoon. Although the brightness has gone out of the day, Leonard says, 'Let's get some fresh air.'

We cross the river and walk down into the long High Street, busy with every kind of shop, from the forage stores, with its bales of corn and bags of seed resting up against its frontage, to the iron and brass founder with his display of malting shovels. We walk on, and the High Street gives way to a pleasant market square. The town is much bigger than I thought.

'There's more to it beyond this,' says Leonard. 'This is just the beginning of the favoured side.' We turn right at the end of the High Street into a wide road which rises to cross the river. On the near side is a parade of smaller shops, a sweetshop and tobacconist, a newsagent. On the other side of the road I glimpse a green swathe behind decorative iron railings which looks as if it might be a municipal park. At the end of the shops is a crossroads. Set back from this thoroughfare is an imposing modern building. Leonard stops and gestures towards it. 'That's the public library. I see our bookshop and the library not as rivals for custom but as complementing each other.'

I rather like 'our' bookshop. I thank Leonard for showing me where it is, as I want to join as soon as I can.

'So do I,' says Leonard, 'but I think that's enough exploring for today. I don't want to tire you out completely.'

We turn and walk back. As we approach our end of the town, the subtle change of character in the premises is noticeable. 'If you don't mind my asking, would you not have preferred your bookshop to be in the High Street or beyond?'

'No, actually, and I don't mind your asking,' says Leonard, 'because I'd like to spend the rest of the afternoon discussing my plans for the business with you.'

I feel honoured, and I try to tell him so.

'Well, it's only fair that you should be included.'

Over tea, seated in our own armchairs but sharing my bread and cheese, Leonard tells me that he chose this town because, hard though it was for him to believe when he carried out his research, there was no modern bookseller. 'There's an old chap on the west side – yes, the favoured side – who deals in second-hand books and has a few bound editions of the classics, but he carries few current titles and his poetry is non-existent. The station bookstall offers what you would expect: popular fiction and some travel guides. I knew I had to set up quickly before someone else spotted the opportunity. I hope that being placed here, close to the station, we will catch the discerning rail passenger. Furthermore – and this is what I hope will make the difference – I have secured a contract with the training college which opens in September. I am to be their official supplier. All we've got to do between now and then is make ends meet.'

He says this in a jokey way, but I don't care to think about the alternative. 'It all sounds very exciting,' I say, and mean it.

'Exactly.'

We are both smiling. There is one thing, though, which has been troubling me intermittently for quite a while. 'I think, from now on, I must call you Mr Pritchard, otherwise it will seem disrespectful.' I do not add that people will think, hearing 'Leonard', that we are two assistants. They might well ask when 'Mr Pritchard' will be back.

'Yes, I have been thinking about that,' says Leonard, 'and I suppose you're right, but let's think of it as a kind of game. I am Mr Pritchard and you are Miss Alleyn on the shop floor, but we can revert to first names here.'

'As long as we don't become muddled,' I say, meaning myself.

'I'm sure we can manage it,' says Leonard. 'It'll be like the informal thou in Shakespeare. Did you know that in France and Germany – and Argentina, where they speak Spanish – they use the two forms of "you", polite and familiar, as a matter of course. Strangers who have become friends agree to use the friendly version.'

'Goodness,' I say, and then, 'but do they revert? That is what we would be doing here.'

'In a situation such as ours, undoubtedly.'

'Oh well, if all those foreigners manage it, I suppose I can,' I say.

'That's not all they manage. Every noun is either masculine or feminine. In German, they have neuter, too. Three different forms of "the".'

'So,' I say, slowly, 'the table . . .'

'In French is *la table*, feminine, in German, *der Tisch*, masculine.'

I can hear Father's comment, *thank goodness we are English*, but it is intriguing. 'Would you read me some French and German writing one day?' I say.

'I can do better than "one day".' From his bookshelf, Leonard picks a slim volume, and produces from his inside pocket a case from which he takes a pair of spectacles with slim steel frames. I notice that his eyes, which I had assumed were brown, are in fact a very dark blue, almost navy. He reads what sounds like the most beautiful poem, though I understand nothing of it except the melody of the French language. It is called 'Les Roses de Saadi' by a female poet, Marceline Desbordes-Valmore. 'Another day, I'll read in German. But it's time I escorted you to your new home, and you can start here fresh tomorrow at ten.'

We put on our coats, hats and gloves and step outside, Leonard locking up. The sky is streaked with gold, reflected in the river. The evenings are drawing out, the evidence cannot be denied, and neither can the corresponding lift in my spirits. As we walk, the lamps in the High Street come on, making the night seem darker by contrast. I think how, in our field at home, I would still be able to distinguish the path to our gate quite distinctly, and our garden.

61

Dawn and dusk are a time I like to walk out. I am relieved for the future, though, when I shall surely have to go this way alone, to see gas lamps marching up the length of New Road.

'Are your lodgings near here?' I ask, as we walk.

Leonard chuckles. 'You've seen my lodgings.'

I am mystified.

'I live at the shop. I suppose, eventually, I might move out but at the moment, I prefer to save my money until I know we are comfortably in profit.'

'But . . .' I imagine him returning to that empty building between other, probably empty, buildings. 'Aren't you lonely?'

'Not at all. I can go for a meal at an inn if I want to, but I haven't yet. I learnt to cook for myself in South America. I'm in no hurry to be a lodger and have to make small-talk across the dining table. There will be plenty of opportunities to meet people when the shop opens.' He laughs. 'I expect I shall be glad of my own company. And I shan't want for intellectual stimulation, shall I?'

'No . . . ?' I say, uncertainly.

'I mean, you, Rose. I've got you to talk to.'

I feel extraordinarily elated.

Chapter Five

The gas lamp flowers into a soft light. I know, from working at the solicitor's house, that if I were to tug again at the ring attached to a chain the light would become brighter, but this is quite enough for my needs. It doesn't take me long to hang my few clothes in the large wardrobe. It pleases me to tuck my Bible and Mother's book of poetry neatly in the drawer of my bedside cabinet.

In the bathroom, I wash my hands at the tap marked HOT, though the water is still tepid by the time I've finished. As the adjacent lavatory's tumult abates, I realise I am not alone in the house. I tell myself these town-folk must become inured to its embarrassing self-advertisement. The voice I hear below me is in what I guess must be the kitchen. This is confirmed by the metallic scrape of pans on a hob and the ring of a utensil. I take the voice to be that of Mrs Fuller, though I am by no means certain, as whoever it is speaks only now and then. If there is another present, that person is keeping quiet.

I step into a big room. A long table and six chairs are to my left under the window. To my right, seated in a rocking chair by the range, is Mrs Fuller. All at once I take in her flowing style of dress and the way she is leaning back against the cushions with her face slightly lowered, as if she has nodded off in the middle of doing something. I stand, still holding the doorknob, helpless to prevent a great building wave of heat which breaks in wrenching sobs.

Her head jerks up. 'Rose . . .'

I collapse into her arms, while she murmurs, 'there, there . . .' I let the sobs come. Eventually, they turn to hiccups.

'I'm – hic – sorry . . .'

'Sorry for what?' She holds my arms, looking directly into my eyes. 'For showing that you loved your mother? Yes, I know, Leonard told me, and I'm glad he did.'

'She was alive this time last week,' I say, and I see her, dozing by the fireside, legs supported by a footstool, head tilting towards her soft bulk. I feel fresh tears but, with great, shuddering breaths, manage to restrain them.

Mrs Fuller is still holding me without embarrassment. 'There's nothing shameful about grieving, Rose. It can be difficult in public, if grief overtakes you suddenly – and that does happen, I know, but here you are amongst friends. You can always come and find me, in the house or in the studio. Don't be afraid.' Her eyes have a glint about them. 'I do understand.'

I feel calmer now and try to smile. Mrs Fuller smiles. 'You sit there.' She indicates an armchair opposite her rocker. 'The others will be in before long, but I think we just need a moment's quiet.'

I begin to look around me at this large yet welcoming room, my attention drawn to another little armchair opposite mine and made, I imagine, for a child. In it, as if woven together, are two sleeping cats, their fur a bright patchwork. Mrs Fuller gives them a fond glance.

'They're brothers. The ginger-and-white one is Morris and the black, white and ginger is Ruskin. I met William Morris once, you know, at one of his public lectures. Inspiring man! He had a big, gingery beard and whiskers and a mane of tawny hair. When I met John Ruskin, he was gingery too but going grey. He had a big beard and whiskers, both white. He was an impressive public speaker. I should so have loved to have had him as my professor, but we had a disagreeable man, Edward Poynter. I wouldn't have called any cat of mine after him. Besides, it would have sounded like a dog's name.'

I think about the cats who live in our outbuildings keeping down the mice. Those are small, fleeting tabbies too nervous to set foot inside our cottage. 'Morris and Ruskin seem very contented.'

'They weren't earlier. I told them I had to concentrate on feeding humans. We had quite a disagreement. I lost.'

We hear the front door open and shut and voices in the hall, hurriedly ascending the stairs.

'That will be the Thurlow sisters. The other two won't be far behind them.'

Mrs Fuller rises and moves to check the contents of a large saucepan on the range. It feels homely and yet not homely, of course. In order to avoid dwelling on the thought, I offer to lay the table.

'Would you? You'll find a cloth and mats in the dresser drawer, cutlery in the table drawer, this end. Lay for six, nursery fashion. Oh, and a soup spoon next to the fork.'

I place the silver in the only way I know, knife and fork either side of the place mat, with the soup spoon, as directed, and a dessertspoon across the top, which must be right, as Mrs Fuller nods encouragement. To think – our family eats as if we were still children!

We hear the front door again and further voices. There is movement and noise upstairs. Before I can thank Mrs Fuller for the information that there is an outside lavatory, the door handle turns. In come two neat, glossy-haired girls who look rather alike.

'Rose, this is Meg and this is Winnie.'

Each flashes me a welcoming smile, extending her hand. 'Pleased to meet you.'

The door opens again to admit, I'm told, Jenny Bridges, who has silvery-blond hair drawn back into a black velvet bow. 'How d'you do, Rose.' Her smile is shy, but I feel warmth in it.

'I take it Priscilla –' Mrs Fuller begins, but the door is opening.

'I'm here. Good evening.' The final lodger slides in and closes the door quietly behind her. 'You must be Rose.' Her smile, too, seems to invite friendship. Our hands barely have time to touch. Mine feels overheated against her cool one. Winnie ushers me to the front of the queue, 'because you're like a guest'. 'Make the most of it,' says Meg, as I take a warmed dish from the stack on the hob and receive two ladles of what appears to be a meaty vegetable broth administered by Mrs Fuller.

'Where should I sit?' I ask, as I begin to move with my full platter.

'Next to me,' says Priscilla.

We stand behind our chairs for a grace, said by Winnie.

Mrs Fuller, seated at the top of the table, says, 'This is *Pot au Feu*, literally "pot at the fire".'

'Like a sort of hot-pot?' I ask.

Our landlady says she thinks that probably all cultures have these basic dishes which are similar. 'We'll eat it French style, the broth first the meat afterwards.'

Thickening the broth of parsnip, carrot and other root vegetables is what appears to be seed pearl tapioca. A scoop of barley would have added flavour and thickening without being so cloying, I can't help thinking. If this is French cuisine, it isn't to my taste.

'It's true, then?' says Priscilla, as Mrs Fuller cuts the string on the brisket of beef and shares the meat between us. 'The cook really has eloped?'

'That's what *we* heard,' says Winnie.

'I'm afraid so. I shall place an advertisement in next week's *Courier*, but in the meantime it'll be more dishes from *Cuisine Traditionelle et Nouvelle de France*.'

'Lovely,' says Priscilla.

I look at her, but her head is down as she attacks the beef. I notice that her thick hair, drawn back into a roll at the nape, is matt. With no discernible shine, it is the colour of smoke.

'Be glad I didn't choose *cheval à la mode*,' says Mrs Fuller, dryly. 'Horsemeat!' Above our squeals and groans, she tells us that the book of recipes was one her mother gave her as a souvenir from the Paris *Exposition Universelle* of 1889. 'What with having to translate the French, then all that chopping of vegetables, I'm utterly exhausted.'

'Haven't you got a *Mrs Beeton*?' Meg asks, her earnest, open face showing that she only means to help, not to be critical.

Mrs Fuller seems to be debating her answer. 'I did have.'

It isn't long before the others remember, with gasps of shock, that she was using it to teach the cook how to read.

'Good job she didn't take this, too,' says Priscilla, lifting her spoon.

'We all know that Bella came from the most unpromising of backgrounds,' says Mrs Fuller. 'Whilst I don't condone the theft, if that is what has happened, I will say that she longed to be a chef in a grand hotel. Whether she does or doesn't achieve that aim, I'm sure the ability to read and write will help her wherever she is. If she can continue to teach herself by using my *Mrs Beeton*, I cannot wish her anything other than well. And, as you rightly comment, Priscilla, she did not steal the silver.' She rises and goes over to the range oven.

There is a short silence. Then, Priscilla scrapes her chair back and addresses me. 'We have to take our dishes through to the scullery ready to wash them, but we leave the pots and pans in soak for the cleaner in the morning . . . No, Rose, Mrs Munns would think we were taking her job away from her if we did all the washing up.'

We come back from the cold dark room into the warm glow of the kitchen, where an apple crumble waits on the table. We take our dishes from the dresser shelf and sit down. The crumble has an odd, sunken look about it. 'Oh! Bother!' Mrs Fuller claps a hand to her forehead. 'I forgot to add the sugar.'

'You could ask Mrs Munns to do the cooking,' says Priscilla.

'She has far too much else to do,' says Mrs Fuller.

There is Bird's custard in a jug. We all help ourselves.

'H'mn . . . I was so afraid of letting it burn, I don't think I heated it long enough,' says Mrs Fuller. 'I can taste the cornflour.'

This is true, but the stewed apples in the crumble are full of flavour, sweet with a hint of sharpness. I ask if they are from the tree which gives the house its name. They are.

I learn that Meg and Winnie pack pills and jujubes at a big factory which also produces food for invalids and babies. A good employer, they both agree, and expanding. Jenny and Priscilla also work at a factory, but a smaller one, a family business making toothbrushes.

'Delicious,' says Jenny, after the meal. 'Thank you, Mrs Fuller.' We all echo her.

'Let's have a game of beggar-my-neighbour before bed,' says Priscilla, jumping up for a pack of cards on the mantelpiece.

Mrs Fuller, who has been briefly absent, returns with a violin case and music stand, which she sets up in the middle of the room under the light. 'I belong to a string quartet, Rose. I must rehearse our next piece.'

She tells me the name of the composer which makes me think of distant dogs. Nothing could be further from that sound than the soaring flourishes which fill the room after she has tuned her instrument and practised scales. Everyone is clearly used to this musical accompaniment, but I am captivated and have to be nudged to attend my hand. I am glad when my cards run out so that I can listen to the music. Jenny is listening, too, I think. The word 'sublime' comes to me. I watch Mrs Fuller's arm moving, the delicate crook of her wrist, her pursed brow and sometimes closed eyes. Under the light, her hair is spun with gold threads. Eventually, she seems to return from whatever place her music took her. She smiles at us. I realise I have been staring, as if entranced.

After cocoa, made by the sisters, Mrs Fuller reaches for a large black saucepan which could be the double of the one we have at home. Suddenly, she looks worn out, older than I had thought her, as she lifts down from a shelf a large glass jar of porridge oats. I make the excuse of collecting everyone's cups on a tray, saying goodnight to them as they leave the kitchen. Light spills into the room as Mrs Fuller comes back from the scullery with the milk jug.

'I wonder . . .' I begin, but now I feel presumptuous.

'Go on,' she says.

'I wonder whether you would like me to make our porridge for the mornings. I've been doing it for years and we were a big family, so I know . . . how,' I end, lamely.

'I should be delighted,' says Mrs Fuller. Smiling, she looks almost young.

I come to in darkness and, for a moment, cannot think where, in the wide world, I can be. Then I hear scurrying footsteps along the landing, muted voices outside the bathroom. A little later, there are footsteps on the stairs, the kitchen door opening and closing.

The distinctive voice of the grandfather clock confirms my feeling of what the time must be with six muted, yet throbbing notes. It is supremely comfortable here in my new bed where the sheets have not been sides-to-middled. I am happy to stay out of the way until the factory girls have all left, since their routine is to cut it fine. In next to no time, the front door opens and bangs shut with finality. The house is still.

In the kitchen, the scent of breakfast lingers though the others have cleared up thoroughly. There is enough porridge left in the saucepan for me and for Mrs Fuller and water nearly boiling in the kettle which I move onto the hob. I am alone except for the cats, Morris completely occupying the little armchair, curled round with one leg dangling from the seat, Ruskin draped rather ostentatiously on the armchair where Mrs Fuller seated me after my emotions overcame me. Hearing that she is up, I look around, spot the teapot and make enough for two.

When she enters, she is wearing a full-skirted dressing gown of purple velvet belted with a sash of turquoise thread. Her slippers are little boots of the same material. 'Good morning, Rose, how did you sleep?' She waits, concerned for my reply, pleased and relieved when it is positive, delighted to accept the tea I have just poured. 'I usually take it back to bed but, do you know, I think I'll stay here and eat breakfast with you, if it doesn't put you out – or off.'

'That would be lovely.' I take my cup and bowl to the table. 'Ruskin does look very handsome, the way he's stretched out.'

'That's why he does it. See, he's smiling at your compliment.'

Indeed, it could be true. 'And Morris looks endearing.' As I speak, the cat raises his head and gazes at me dreamily before returning to his slumbers.

'They seem to know it's Friday. They're waiting for the fish man to call. We will have whiting tonight, as it's in season, and kippers tomorrow.'

I voice a growing thought. 'Would you like me to peel some potatoes, Mrs Fuller?'

'Do you have time?'

'I have at least an hour. I could make a jam tart, too, and bake it before I go.'

'I'm overwhelmed. I'll fetch the ingredients and scales.'

'I don't need scales.'

I am just washing my hands in the bathroom when I hear quite distinctly from the room below: '. . . jam tart? I was going to do that!' and Mrs Fuller's less forceful tones in some kind of soothing reply. I hope I have not offended Mrs Munns.

I return to my room, put on my outdoor clothes and slip as quietly as possible downstairs. The stained glass of the front door is alive with sunlight casting reflections of soft green, yellow and blue from its square panes. In the middle is a roundel, depicting an elegant white swan on a lake framed by rushes. There are two letters on the doormat. I pick them up to place them on the hall stand, but both are addressed to me. I recognise immediately Phyllis's cursive script and Hilda's more careful hand. I put them both in my pocket and let myself quickly and silently out into a sunny, busy morning.

I have allowed far more time than I need for this walk, but I'd rather be early than nearly late, so I do not dawdle, especially passing the men on the bridge. Fortunately, they seem absorbed in the traffic on the river below, but I keep my eyes firmly ahead. Father gave me a little money so I stop at the baker's and buy a pork pie which Leonard, Mr Pritchard, may share with me if he wishes or keep his half for later, if I haven't been overcome with greed. They are brisk but friendly women who serve me, and the shop is rich with the smell of baking, which I have to steel myself to ignore. I see, from the corner of my eye as I pass the greengrocer's and am about to cross the road, small heads of celery, locally grown. It is a reasonable price and by the look of it, sweet and white. This, I cannot resist, so I go inside and exchange names and pleasantries with the assistant, Kate, whom we met yesterday.

As I approach Pritchard's Bookshop I see that, in each window, the board announcing the opening date now has a flash diagonally across it: TOMORROW. As I wait for my employer to unlock the door, I feel suddenly shy but also excited. *You can do it, Rose*, a voice seems to say to me.

Mr Pritchard gives me a brief tour of the shelves, which I try to commit to memory, whilst resisting the urge to lose myself in book after book. Even a dictionary would have me enthralled with its outlandish words. Next, my employer shows me the cash drawer under the counter and gives me a key, which I shall secure in my deep pocket. 'It's probably best to keep the drawer locked until you need to use it.' I agree. He shows me the sales ledger, the customer receipt pad and the order book. He has a comprehensive list of publishers with their addresses and their stock lists. These will be kept for reference at the counter. I learn that *The Bookseller* magazine is, as Mr Pritchard says, like a Bible. It contains everything we might need to know about the world of publishing, including each month's list of newly published books. 'And if there's any query which I can't answer, odds on you'll find what you're looking for in there. Or, if not, we can write to the magazine and ask them. They are enormously helpful. Take the next hour or so, Miss Alleyn, to get to know the magazine and the layout of the shop. That way, if someone comes in and asks you for a particular title, you will know exactly where to direct him – or her, of course.' He starts opening new boxes of books. I sit on one of the two high stools behind the counter with *The Bookseller*. I become absorbed in all its titles.

After tea we play at shops, as Mr Pritchard puts it, with me as shopkeeper and him as a series of customers: equable, curt, unsure of a book's details, knowing only its subject matter. I manage, he says when he is back being himself, to treat each with professional courtesy and efficiency. I also learn how to count back change. I rather enjoy my new-found skill.

'Now it's my turn,' he says. 'It will be good practice for tomorrow.'

So, I come in as a shy young lady who has to be guided round the fiction shelves until she recognises an author's name. 'That's the one,' I cry.

'You're rather good at this acting game,' says Mr Pritchard. 'Think of another one.'

I rack my brains. Then it comes to me. I draw myself up as tall as I can and approach the counter slowly with a pompous gait and voice: 'Good afternoon. Ay should be oblayged if you would gade me —'

My employer bursts out laughing.

'Ay was about to say . . .' I begin, but I am laughing too.

'Black mark to me,' says Mr Pritchard. 'I should have controlled myself, but where on earth did he come from?'

I tell him about Uncle Bottomley.

At one o'clock, he asks me if I will be at ease alone here while he visits the bank to collect tomorrow's change float and my wages. He will lock the shop door. I am perfectly content and settle down to eat my half of the pork pie (so savoury) and celery (so sweet) whilst reading the two letters from my sisters, which have been at the back of my mind throughout the morning. They both, it turns out, have the same purpose and bear yesterday's date.

Dearest Rose,

Just a quick missive to wish you all the very best for Saturday. (I thought I had better write today in case you leave for work before the post on Saturday.) Everything is well here. I hope all is well with you.
   Love from

Hilda and Father
XX

Dear Rose,

I am writing today to make sure my very best wishes, echoed by Dot, Jack and Ralph, attend you and Leonard at the opening of Pritchard's Bookshop on Saturday.
   Life goes on as usual here, though I miss the occasional chat with your employer, tell him. I should not complain. I am currently reading

an interesting new magazine, 'Design in the Home', which is delivered upstairs and never touched.

As you know, we are not supposed to receive letters, so don't bother to reply.

Thinking of you with love,
Phyllis
XX

In their differing ways and for differing reasons, the two letters move me almost to tears.

By the time I have composed myself, Leonard has returned. I know I shall feel better for a walk, so beg his leave to do so, which he gives gladly, saying it's a good idea to get out in the sunshine even if the air isn't exactly country-fresh.

I find myself retracing the path which we took yesterday, along the High Street and on through the market square to the park and the public library. Yes, I may join, says the librarian, provided I can show him two posted letters addressed to me as proof that I live in Widdock. He looks as if he expects me not to have the documentation on me but of course, as luck would have it, I do. His manner seems to change then. His assistant will have my tickets ready by the time I have chosen up to six books!

I realise I shall need much longer to get to know the library than I feel I have today. I choose one book for now, my favourite, the novel I wish I had brought with me from Mother's bookshelf: *Jane Eyre*. Slightly embarrassed, I present my solitary offering at the desk, but the young woman stamping it looks relieved. She hadn't finished writing all my tickets, so she'll keep the remaining five together for me when I return the borrowed book.

Leonard congratulates my enterprise. 'I must join, too. Here's the money for these two days, plus a week's wages in advance, so you can pay Mrs Fuller and meet any other expenses you might have.'

I tuck the envelope into my deep pocket.

It is now time to dress the two windows. Mr Pritchard removes the board from the one on the right, and replaces the notice simply announcing the opening tomorrow with one which gives that information but whose main message is as follows:

THINKERS OF OUR TIME

Mr William Philpott continues his course of lectures
for a further twelve weeks commencing on
Wednesday the 24th January at 8 p.m.
in The Assembly Rooms
BOOKS ON HIS READING LIST AVAILABLE HERE
Also available, the book of Mr Philpott's previous lecture series:
The French Revolution and its Aftermath

Mr Pritchard has the reading list and the relevant books in a box by the window. He invites me to make a pleasing arrangement so that the titles will catch the eye. 'Take your time,' he says. 'Browse, if you wish.' There are names of which I have never heard. Two, however, thanks to Mrs Fuller, I do now recognise. A book by William Morris on Socialism is beautifully printed but its contents are formidable. Another draws me as much by its evocative title as by the name, John Ruskin. I open *The Stones of Venice* on a chapter named, I gather, after a place: '*Torcello*: . . . Seven miles to the north of Venice, the banks of sand . . . knit themselves into fields of salt morass . . . a plot of greener grass covered with ground ivy and violets . . .' I come to with a feeling that time has passed. Mr Pritchard is arranging books in the other window. I follow his example.

Afterwards, we walk outside to inspect our handiwork. We nod to each other.

'Both windows make an artistic composition, don't you think? As well as displaying the books to best advantage,' Mr Pritchard says.

We walk across to the window with which he has been occupied. I read its new notice.

FOOD FOR THOUGHT AND ENJOYMENT

A book of poetry by Shelley catches my eye, as well as a compendium of Shakespeare's plays. 'Be thinking, what books you would like to put in this window.' My mind goes blank. We walk back inside. It comes to me that, when studying the books in stock this morning, I was intrigued to find one with maps of Britain showing how the earth is made up of different layers of rock many ages old.

'Yes, Geology, good idea,' says Mr Pritchard.

I manage to go straight to the shelf and bring it over. This gives me time to think of other suggestions. I had leafed through an anthology containing some of my favourite poets, John Clare and Elizabeth Barratt Browning amongst them. I find this and then round off my selection with Charlotte Brontë's *Shirley*.

'Excellent choice,' says Mr Pritchard, when I have displayed them in the window. He turns to me with an almost-amused smile. 'I expect you have guessed that there is more to my opening this shop than wanting to make a decent living, though it is that too.'

'I understand it is . . . your heartfelt wish,' I say.

'It is indeed.' He pulls out one of the two stools behind the counter for me and stands facing me, his back to the window. 'It's true that like you I love books, so I couldn't work with more congenial goods – and goods are what books are to me, things of goodness, not just items in a bill of lading. I feel that reading is a way into a finer and less restricted life, a life of knowledge and truth, and the beauty of art and nature. I feel a thirst in myself to discover more and more through the medium of the word. But we live in a world of men and women as well as ideas and words. I want to meet other people who will be drawn, if my hopes for this new enterprise are fulfilled, to visit our premises and perhaps little by little turn our small shop into a meeting place of like minds, a centre of human spirit.'

While he is talking I have been keenly taking in every twist and turn of his meaning, and trying not to be distracted by my happiness that he includes me so freely as a partner and confidante.

'Do you think this might become a kind of gentlemen's club?' I ask him, uncertainly. I do not think I could maintain the illusion of sharing responsibility for a place in which well-dressed strangers make themselves comfortably at home, discoursing about books they stand holding open or reach down from the shelves I have carefully arranged.

'A club, yes, but not only for gentlemen. For gentlewomen too and working men and women, and for children of all sorts and conditions, if it comes to that. I mean it to come to that. Of course, the prosperous burghers of Widdock will be our freest-spending customers and perhaps our most numerous, at least before the College opens. And with them we shall find conversations arising out of our stock – our goods, in the best sense – which will be meat and drink to you and me.'

I must look doubtful, feeling that I might easily become reticent in such company. A look of sympathy crosses his face, but then he smiles again. 'Never fear, Rose, you will soon find yourself conversing with the best of them.'

I can feel the colour in my cheeks, but Mr Pritchard seems not to notice, such is his ardour.

As he goes on speaking the sun, in its final glory, lights his dark hair giving it coppery glints, giving him a glowing aura matched only by the fire from within him. 'We cannot give formal schooling and free time to those who must labour from morning till night in farm, factory or domestic work. But for those who have at least learned to read, and who have a little free time, we can put their feet on the lowest rungs of the ladder we ourselves have climbed.'

In the kitchen, I find Jenny mashing potatoes. The door opens admitting Meg and Winnie, followed by Priscilla. Mrs Fuller drains her beans and I fry the floured and seasoned fish very lightly. The course is a success. All the jam tart and custard vanishes, too.

'Tomorrow, I'll buy Swiss buns for pudding,' Mrs Fuller says.

'We can make the Sunday lunch, can't we?' Jenny suggests.

We all agree. 'And if the joint is large enough, we can have cottage pie on Monday,' I say.

When we have cleared the dishes, it is time to pay Mrs Fuller this week's rent, after which her copy of the *Courier* is spread out on the table while she rehearses and we pour over its pages to find out what's on in town tomorrow night. The general consensus is for the pantomime.

Suddenly, the moment has come. Mr Pritchard turns the sign to 'Open' and unlocks the door. He looks extremely smart in a suit and tie of navy, which accentuate the colour of his eyes. Immediately, the shop seems full of people, though there's probably no more than half a dozen at any one time. All morning we are busy. I maintain a level head – just, making sure I go through all the procedures I have been taught.

There is a goodly spread of people, many gentlefolk, mainly men but some women, I am pleased to see. I am introduced to a greying man with sharp blue eyes: Mr Philpott. 'And will you be coming to my lectures, Miss Alleyn?'

'They certainly sound fascinating,' I say, and Mr Philpott seems to take this as assent, releasing me from his intense gaze.

When he has moved out of earshot, Mr Pritchard says, quietly, 'If you are concerned about the cost, Rose, I will sponsor you.' He brooks my incipient protest with a finger to his lips. 'It will be my pleasure.'

Mrs Fuller comes in, browses and chooses. Between the two of them, they have my attendance at the lectures arranged. I am truly grateful. 'And I suppose I'd better buy another Mrs Beeton, if you have one.' I go to fetch it.

Already, it is time for our lunch break. I hurry to the park with its swans on a pond, the air laced with the burr of malt.

In the afternoon, there are working men like the one who stands twisting his cap while he waits for me to write out his receipt. This man has given up his precious family hours because he believes in all the things of which Leonard spoke with such conviction. I hand him his purchase in a strong brown paper bag and he almost glances away, this man who must be twice my age. Something just makes him look enough to catch the corner of my smile. His wary eyes soften. He gives me back an uncertain smile, takes the bag, nods and leaves. I see him through the window, beginning to walk away. His shoulders relax, his head goes up.

Here are Meg and Winnie, Jenny and Priscilla, interested in getting the measure of the place – and my employer. Mr Pritchard is glad to show Meg and Winnie the Science section. He patiently shows Priscilla what we have on self-improvement. Jenny is leafing through a biography. They leave at last, regretting that they cannot afford to buy. 'By all means let them come and extend themselves. Besides, they brought in other customers who did make purchases.'

At closing time, 'Today has exceeded my expectations,' says Mr Pritchard, as he locks the takings into the safe. 'Of course, it's all a gamble here until the College opens.'

There is, nonetheless, a sense of quiet euphoria. 'While you go to the panto, I think that I shall treat myself to dinner at The Railway Hotel.'

Widow Twankey is full of jokes which clearly mean a lot to his local audience. There are rousing choruses whose simple words are printed on boards held up so everyone who can read may join in. Although exhausted, I do not fall asleep because we all have indigestion from the kippers we had for tea. Meg and Winnie discreetly pass along a packet of scientifically proven pills from their factory. We each take one. It tastes like peppermint to me.

I fall into bed, and know nothing further till morning.

I take it upon myself to put the joint in and make a rice pudding with a scrape of nutmeg across the top, just as Mother and Dot would have made it, all of which will be ready when we come back from church. Jenny prepares vegetables, working quietly beside me.

Meg and Winnie leave for the Friends' Meeting House.

'That's how they got the job at Hallambury's,' Priscilla comments. 'All Quakers there.'

Jenny, Priscilla and I go with Mrs Fuller, resplendent in an elegant hat with a crimson feather, to St Saviour's, the parish church, which is further than the new church built halfway down our road. 'But the services are shorter,' Mrs Fuller has pointed out, 'the choir is better and the architecture is beautiful.' The church is quite like our own at Markly. I have never really thought about its appearance and spend much of the service doing so, when I am not being prodded by Priscilla who is evidently bored.

Luncheon is an enjoyable event. Meg and Winnie describe their Meeting to me. I like the idea of sitting in a quiet, white-washed room, thinking and speaking only when one is moved, but I am torn. I love the music of our service and the sense of joining in with words which are so familiar they are part of who I am. There is comfort and solace in it. I can feel my emotions rising again and move to clear the table. Mrs Fuller gives me an enquiring look, but I tell her I am well.

We clear up everything, mindful of Mrs Munns' extra work tomorrow, wash-day. I must remember to strip my bed.

I hurry to my room, anxious to write a quick note to Hilda and post it. I relate briefly the events of yesterday and tell her, for something else to say, that I might be embarking upon a course of lectures. As I leave my room, Priscilla is coming out of hers.

'Have you got a beau, Rose?' She nods at the envelope in my hand.

I correct her misapprehension.

'Can I join you for a walk?'

I experience a sinking feeling. Knowing that this evening I will be sharing a room, I should have liked some time alone, simply to think. How can I refuse, though? I smile.

We walk down towards the town.

'How long have you lived in Widdock?' I enquire.

'Long enough.'

I find it difficult to think of anything else to say. Soon we are approaching the new church. Mothers are collecting little tots from Sunday School. Their mistress stands at the door of the church hall to see them on their way.

'Look at her – hatchet face,' says Priscilla.

It is true that the young woman has an unfortunate cast of features. I wish I hadn't smiled at the remark. I hope the teacher was too far away to hear – and see.

I realise we have walked down to the bridge, where no men linger today as it is Sunday. There is a pillar box nearby and I drop my letter in it. While I am doing so, Priscilla is gazing across the road.

'Let's go and see if your employer's at home,' she says, and heads towards the bookshop.

I am horrified.

She presses her nose against the window, peering in. 'Oo-oo, Mr Pritchard,' she calls in a silly voice, rapping on the glass.

I turn and head for home, hearing her laughter behind me.

Priscilla has not followed me, thank goodness. I race up to the sanctuary of my room.

On the floor by the other bed is a valise. On the bed is a pair of gloves and a hat with a big tartan bow.

Chapter Six

'Hello, Rose, this is Lettie who will share your room with you.' Mrs Fuller is sitting stroking Morris. She looks tired.

I scarcely have time to take in a black-haired young woman with bright, dark eyes, before she is leaping from her seat to take my hand in both of hers.

'Rose! I had a best friend called Rose, so it must be a good omen. She had lovely, curly fair hair.' Her use of the past tense hangs in the air for a moment, as does the obvious contrast with my hair. 'You work at a bookshop, don't you? Do you like it?'

'Yes, I do. I've only just started but –'

'I'm starting at Gifford's tomorrow. Ladies' fashions and window dressing. I got that job because I used to dress the windows at Madame Clara's – that was the name of the dress shop in Staplebridge. Do you know Staplebridge, Rose? No? I'm not surprised. Where do you come from? Tell me all about yourself.'

Mrs Fuller rises, placing Morris gently beside his brother on the little armchair. 'I'll leave you two to become acquainted.'

I tell Lettie everything about my family which might be of interest to her, and receive genuine sympathy for my bereavement. I learn that she, too, comes from a large family and must earn in order to send money home. Although her father has steady work at an iron foundry, he suffers from an affliction of the lungs which increasingly confines him to his bed. All are worried that he will lose his job.

I begin to cut up the leftover roast to make a cottage pie for tomorrow, Morris and Ruskin rubbing round my legs.

'The cook *eloped*? Fancy! How romantic.'

Without stopping talking, Lettie willingly peels potatoes, scrapes carrots and helps me with the onions when I am blinded by tears. She is quick and deft.

Meg and Winnie are back from First Day School, the Friends' name for their Sunday School. I hear their quiet voices in the corridor, 'thee-ing' and 'thou-ing' to each other which they have told me is normal amongst Quakers. Jenny returns from wherever she has been. My head is reeling. I make the introductions, then go through to the scullery to feed the cats with the scraps of meat Mrs Fuller has said that they may have. Above their chirruping and purring, I can hear Meg, answering Lettie's questions about the sisters' work at Hallambury's, and Winnie revealing that they are the daughters of a pharmaceutical chemist in Harwick Ford.

'I know Harwick Ford!' cries Lettie. 'I come from Staplebridge. We've probably passed each other in the street.'

'We were allowed to dust the carboys in the window,' Winnie says.

I imagine her behind those three mysterious stoppered bottles, running a cloth down a swan neck and gazing into the iridescent liquid depths of each: yellow, green and purple.

From a young age, she and Meg became familiar with the names written on the drawers of the dispensary and, as they grew up, would sometimes help their father in much the way they are employed now, wrapping or bottling the pills and powders which he, or their older brother, Fred, would have measured out. Fred has passed the Society's examination to become a pharmaceutical chemist. The shop is now called 'Thurlow & Son'.

Lettie makes some kind of comment about this which I do not hear because I'm rinsing my hands at the sink.

'Hallambury's are looking for more office staff to handle orders and answer customers' enquiries,' says Meg. 'We were wondering whether to put ourselves forward. We wouldn't be in charge, of course, but our knowledge might be useful.'

Jenny's 'Good luck' is lost as the kitchen door opens, heralding

Priscilla. The introductions start again. I see her peering into the bookshop window, calling out in that silly voice. I feel very tired, half inclined to stay out here in the cold scullery with the chewing cats.

As I re-enter the warmth and brightness, Lettie is saying: 'Ooh! Do you stick the bristles in the little holes?'

There is a fraction of a moment in which Priscilla shoots an unsmiling look across at Jenny who, glancing up from making tea, meets it. Meg and Winnie, preoccupied with toasting fork and butter knife, miss this but Lettie's brows knit slightly before Priscilla answers, 'No, we're on the clerical side.' She walks over to the dresser. 'I suppose there's none of that marble cake left.'

'We ate it all, didn't we? Let's have this toast,' says Winnie.

But Priscilla, pulling the lid off a large tin, gives a cry of delight: 'Gingerbread! Look!'

'Well, there we are,' says Mrs Fuller, who has come in on our pleased expressions, 'I think that's Bella's way of saying sorry she left us in the lurch.'

'We've been talking about the cooking situation,' says Winnie.

'Yes,' says Meg, 'Rose, you could be our permanent cook, couldn't she Mrs Fuller?' The others, even Priscilla, all take this up. 'We'll help you, Rose. We don't need another cook.'

'You must only do this if you feel you can cope without jeopardising your real job,' says Mrs Fuller. 'I have till Tuesday to place an advertisement in the *Courier*, so think about it carefully in the meantime.'

I can see how hard she is trying not to appear too anxious for my acceptance. I say I can't see why I shouldn't. The others cheer.

We take our plates to the table, where three will have to sit down one side, an extra chair being brought in. 'Sit next to me, Lettie,' says Priscilla, 'and you sit on the other side, Rose.'

I smile, of course, but recognise a momentary sinking feeling.

We all become quiet and attentive over the dark, sticky gingerbread, whose flavour is just the right balance of mellow treacle laced with crystals of fire.

Mrs Fuller tells Lettie and me that the way everyone usually spends the remainder of a Sunday evening, before an early night, is in reading to herself. 'It doesn't have to be the Bible but something positive, I'd say, to set us up for the working week. Anyone who has nothing suitable may borrow from me.'

We all come down with our bibles. I bring my anthology of poems. Jenny has a smaller one. Winnie and Meg have *The Quaker Poets of Great Britain and Ireland* by Evelyn Noble Armitage. We four are pleased to share with each other and with Lettie and Priscilla. I am impressed with the Quaker poets, many of whom are women. Mrs Fuller has some poetry books by William Morris, beautifully printed, and illustrated with sinuous drawings. I hear Lettie turning the pages, poring over them. Priscilla, when I glance up, is not reading but watching her. I look down at the page in front of me, but have the sensation that her eyes are now on me.

Cocoa-time comes and is over. Mrs Fuller says she's going to bed, reminding us to put out any laundry with our sheets. Winnie and Meg follow after a short interval, then Jenny. Lettie wants to check her outfit for the morning. I tell her I'll be up as soon as I've made the porridge.

Priscilla lingers by the door. 'I know what your Mr Pritchard does on a Sunday afternoon.'

I try not to look as tense as I feel. Did her stupid summoning bring him to the shop door? I am appalled.

'You'd have found out, too, if you hadn't run away.' She smiles. 'Good night, Rose.'

I finish my task and go upstairs, my mind in turmoil. Did she speak to him and, if so, what did she say? Heaven forbid that he might have thought I put her up to it.

Lettie is in the bathroom when I enter our room. I try to put Priscilla's mischief out of my mind and concentrate on getting myself ready for tomorrow. I am in my nightdress, brushing my hair, when Lettie comes in. She takes off her dressing gown and spreads it across her bed. On the chair next to it are her corset, drawers and stockings, neatly arranged for the morning.

'Ooh, I like that.'

I straighten from brushing my hair down in a curtain in front of my face. It stands out around my head. I follow her gaze to my bodice, laid out for the morning.

'The thing is, you can get away with it. There's nothing of you.'

'My mother thought up the design – for herself, and there was more of her than me. We all had one when we grew up because it was more practical and comfortable than stays.'

'I hate mine, but I have to do something to keep these under control,' Lettie giggles, butting herself under her nightdress.

'A dart in the right place – a couple of strong French seams – that's all it needs,' I say, only half attending to her.

'Could you make me one, *please*, Rose? You can sew, can't you? I mean, use a sewing machine?'

I am rather taken aback. I think of Mother's whirring treadle. It is as if I feel the cloth running under my fingers as my foot keeps the rhythm pounding along like a cantering horse. I find myself smiling. 'Yes, all right.'

'Oh, thank you, thank you. It'll be such fun. When we get in from work tomorrow, you can measure me, and then we'll make a pattern . . . I've brought my portable Singer.'

Suddenly, I am almost dropping with tiredness. I make a point of kneeling down by my bed. Lettie follows suit and we say our silent prayers, then climb between the sheets.

'Rose? Are you awake?'

'Not . . . really . . .' I let myself drift.

'She's a funny one, that Priscilla. Did you see the look she gave Jenny? Rose?'

It is easy to keep quiet. I just hear Lettie as she says, almost to herself, 'I mean to get to the bottom of that.'

The pattering mouse-footsteps on stairs and landing, the bark and bellow of the lavatory nudge me from sleep even earlier today, I sense. When the front door opens and shuts with finality, I can already hear Mrs Fuller moving in her room next to ours, so I stay put, drifting, as she walks along the landing to the bathroom. Lettie sleeps on through all, the soft rise and fall of her breath reminding me of home, the childhood sharing of room and bed. I take deep breaths myself. When I feel steadier and I know the bathroom to be free, I get up.

Lettie has asked me to wake her, as she is a heavy sleeper. When I return to our room, I gently shake her arm, which is crooked above her head, resting on her fanned out black hair. 'Lettie.'

She groans. I repeat the operation and she slowly wakes, rubbing her eyes, but speaking already: 'Oh, Rose, that was such a lovely dream. I was having a ballgown made – can you imagine? Apple-green watered silk, it was. The dressmaker was just asking me about the trimmings.'

Pang! The grandfather clock's subtle note cuts short her musings.

'What time is it?' She swings her legs out of bed.

'That must be a quarter past seven.'

'Oh, goodness!' She grabs her toilet bag and runs, the door resounding behind her.

We both end up going downstairs together, I carrying my dirty laundry and Lettie her hair tongs, which she proposes to heat at the range, so she can do her fringe.

'Would you like me to put a bit of bounce into your hair, Rose?'

'No, thank you.'

We meet Mrs Fuller in the hall. She explains that she has had her breakfast and is going upstairs for her 'digestive pause' before Mrs Munns arrives, when they will change the beds. 'She's supposed to come at eight o'clock, but she's always early.'

Lettie starts straight away. There is soon a smell of hot metal and crimped hair. She stands in front of the mirror over the mantelpiece, tweaking her fringe into a resplendent frizz, which sets off her dark eyes. I make tea and eat my porridge. It comes to me that I could buy vegetables to augment tomorrow's meal, bubble-and-squeak, and if we have custard on the remains of gingerbread tonight for pudding, I am almost certain there are bottled pears in the larder which would serve for tomorrow's pudding. Mrs Fuller will not have to go down to the town at all, unless she chooses,

86

on this busiest day of the week at home. I suggest this to her when she returns.

'Well, if you're sure.'

We are both looking at my list when a figure passes the window and enters. 'Good morning, Mrs Eff, if it is. There's a nasty wind blowing.'

'Good morning, Mrs Munns,' says Mrs Fuller.

I take the list from her hand, but the cleaner has seen it. Before Mrs Fuller can introduce us, Mrs Munns says, 'Don't tell me – Rose.' Her grey eyes, level with mine, assess me though she offers me a brief smile in response to my greeting. She puts down her big wicker laundry basket. 'And this is Lettie, then.'

Lettie jumps up from the table where she has just finished breakfast. Her spoon rattles against the bowl. 'Oops. Oh dear!'

This seems to amuse Mrs Munns, her weathered face creasing into another, broader smile. 'No harm done, dear,' she says, hanging up her hat and coat and stuffing her gloves in the pockets. She begins immediately to roll up her sleeves. Although she is slightly built, her arms are well-muscled. She gives an impression of energy and wiry strength.

Lettie pauses as she takes her crockery through to wash. 'Can we do anything to help?' She looks at Mrs Munns and at Mrs Fuller. 'We could put clean sheets on Rose's bed.'

Mrs Fuller glances quickly at her cleaner. I, too, wonder how this offer will be received.

'Bless you, that's very kind, my dear, but you're all dressed up for work,' Mrs Munns smiles.

'That's right,' adds Mrs Fuller. 'We can manage. Off you go. Good luck, Lettie, and to you, Rose.'

Lettie leaves so as to give herself plenty of time. I follow her example shortly after since, besides my other errands, I have to go to the post office with my letter to Hilda. As I slip down the stairs, Mrs Fuller and Mrs Munns are in Meg and Winnie's room. I am level with the door which is not completely closed. I hear the movement of a bed and the cleaner's voice: 'What a bonny girl that Lettie is.

Lovely manner, too.' Mrs Fuller's voice murmurs some brief assent. I do not linger to hear Mrs Munns's assessment of me.

The cleaner is right about the weather. That chill easterly wind I have known all my life is a reminder that though January may be about to depart, this is still winter. I am glad I remembered my muffler. My hat is well secured. I dig my gloved hands deep into my pockets.

I don't have long to wait at either post office or baker's.

'I've barely exchanged two words with anyone this morning,' says Kate, rubbing her hands encased in fingerless gloves, before she weighs my carrots and parsnips. 'Everyone's hurrying to get home.' She follows me out of her shop.

'*They* don't seem to mind the weather.' I nod towards the men on the bridge.

'You know what they say about that lot? Warts on their chests from all that leaning!'

Laughing, we say goodbye. I turn towards the bookshop. To my surprise, Leonard is rearranging his part of the display in our joint window. He has an open newspaper in his hand and is about to place it in the space which he has cleared, but he catches sight of me, puts it carefully down and comes to the door to let me in. As he says good morning, his face looks full of kindly concern.

'Good morning, Mr Pritchard. Has something . . . happened?' Suddenly, I feel chilled through to the marrow.

'Don't look so worried, please, Rose. Come through and have some tea. You're early, you have time.'

When we are in the sitting room, Leonard turns to face me. 'I have to tell you – John Ruskin has died.'

I catch my breath. I think about how I lost myself reading his *Stones of Venice*. It is as if someone who might have become my friend has passed away.

'I knew you would be sad, but I felt I couldn't keep it from you,' says Leonard. 'There's a fine obituary in this morning's *Times*. You may care to read it. I bought a second copy so I could put one in the window and group his books around it. I am not in favour of

88

excessive use of black, but I shall probably drape a black band over the corner to draw attention to it.'

'When did he die?' I ask.

'On Saturday, St Agnes' Eve. In his home in the Lake District.'

I cannot speak. While we were busy enjoying our opening day, Mr Ruskin's life was drawing to a close on the coldest day of the year or so it is said, all the more so in the Lakes, I imagine. This sorrowful thought will not leave me. I can feel that familiar heat, shortness of breath and the constriction in my throat.

'Rose . . . ?'

I hear a movement and know he mustn't comfort me or I will break down. I lunge for the back door, his hand brushing my sleeve as I blunder past. Outside, the cold whipping my cheeks helps me regain my equilibrium. I take steadying breaths and, gradually, begin to look about me. I am in an enclosed yard, reached from the street by an arch wide enough for a cart to pass. At the far end, laden washing lines are strung across from one building to another. Two small children are playing with sticks in the dirt. They are both wearing coats too big for them, whose fabric has worn to a thin, colourless sheen. I suspect that these garments cover very little else in the way of clothing, as I catch glimpses of bare leg. One child has on his feet the remnants of socks, the wool unravelled and quite worn through at toe and heel. The other's feet are bagged in newspaper, tied round his ankles with filthy string. From inside one of the buildings comes the thin, high wail of a baby. The easterly wind gusts, bringing with it an unwholesome smell. A woman comes out of another tenement, pours slops down an open drain, gives me a sour look, and then goes in again. I return inside myself, trying not to let my thoughts wander onto this new and somewhat troubling ground. I must present myself as a reliable employee, in control of herself. I smile at Leonard's apprehensive face and brook his solicitous enquiries by telling him I am perfectly able to start work immediately.

I help him, by going outside the window and reporting back, to make an arresting display centred upon the obituary, and flanked by Mr Ruskin's volumes. The upshot of the tribute is that we gain an interesting range of customers. Those who have not yet bought their books for Mr Philpott's lecture course are now spurred on to do so. Those who have no real intention of purchasing anything at all see this as an opportunity for discussion or, in one or two cases, discourse about society in general. These latter, to a man, conduct their conversations entirely with Mr Pritchard, of course, which is only to be expected. Writing receipts or quietly restocking the shelves, I am learning all the time. I am gratified on behalf of my employer that, although he is less than half the age of most of them, his is the greater breadth of knowledge. It is not delivered in a boastful way, but implicit in everything he says, as is his more expansive outlook. I know that I have found another new home.

The morning passes quickly. At one o'clock, Leonard goes out, turning the sign to 'closed'. I eat my pie and immerse myself in the other copy of *The Times*, finishing the obituary, from which I gain a strong picture of the remarkable Mr Ruskin. Other news is not so edifying, particularly about the war in Africa.

Leonard returns with glowing cheeks, saying that he enjoyed his brisk walk to the public library, which he too has now joined. He shows me three books of poetry, all by local people, past and present. While he eats his pie I look through each volume, interesting either for its verse, its illustrations or for its presentation. I remember to tell him about Winnie and Meg using thee and thou, and I ask whether he has come across *The Quaker Poets of Great Britain and Ireland*.

'I'm aware that there is a strong tradition of Quaker poetry. But tell me about this book, please.'

I start to describe it, and find myself becoming animated. 'Even the first poet in the book, Bessie Adams, I found interesting. Her descriptions of nature seem . . . fresh and real. I think she must be someone who has lived in the country.'

'Or someone whose eyes and ears are practised in responding to the world around her. And in conveying what she sees and hears, and smells and touches and tastes, so that the reader shares her experience.'

'I see what you are saying,' I say, slowly. 'I suppose that is what being a poet is.'

'Exactly so.'

Leonard's dark eyes are alight with interest, so I go on. 'There's also a funny poem for children by her — about why a certain major can get away with things for which they would be reprimanded. It's very . . .' I search for the word, 'wry. And there are short biographies about each poet as introductions to the poems themselves.'

'Well, you've certainly sold the book to me. We must have a copy. Perhaps, this afternoon, you'd like to order one from the publishers.'

Outside, the day looks bleak, so I decide to stay indoors by the fire for the rest of our break. 'I've done the shopping already, this morning.' I indicate the bag of vegetables next to my chair and explain my new role at Apple Tree House.

His brows knit a fraction. 'Do make sure you're not being taken advantage of, Rose.'

'Mrs Fuller wouldn't do that,' I say with the certainty of truth. 'And the others have all said they'll help.'

'I'm glad to hear it,' says my employer.

Thinking about yesterday brings to the forefront of my mind something which the events of today have successfully obscured. Now it returns to worry me. I decide that there is nothing for it but to learn the truth. 'Did you have an enjoyable Day of Rest?' I ask, hoping that my question doesn't sound too studied, bracing myself for the worst that Priscilla may have done which, surely, will rebound on me.

'I did, thank you.' Leonard stands and stretches. It is almost time to return to the shop. 'It wasn't exactly restful, but it was very enjoyable. I bicycled down the towpath beyond Chesford in search of an Eleanor Cross.'

'Oh, I've heard of them.' I try to recollect. 'Isn't there one in London?'

'That's right. There's a series of them, a king's commemoration of his queen.'

'Was it Eleanor of Aquitaine?'

'No,' Leonard laughs. 'She was a very different kettle of fish. This was "The Queen of Good Memory", Eleanor of Castile.'

He starts towards the door to the shop, then turns. 'Oh, and when I was wheeling the bike up from the path at Bridgefoot, I met your fellow hosteller – what's her name, Prudence? No, Priscilla.'

My heart is banging.

'The one who pretended an interest in self-improvement. I am, as you know, the first to share an enthusiasm for a subject with some-one who wants to learn, but I felt with her . . . well, no matter.'

'I hope she didn't detain you,' I say, carefully.

'No, no, she merely bade me good afternoon. I responded and remounted, which she took as her cue to walk on, I'm relieved to say.'

And I am relieved to hear it.

The afternoon falls pleasantly quiet for a spell. Mr Pritchard takes from the shelf a book of essays by John Ruskin called *Unto This Last*. He says that he doesn't want to pre-empt what Mr Philpott may have to say in his lectures. 'But I think this concluding sentence is, actually, a fitting introduction to them: "The entire purpose of a great thinker may be difficult to fathom, and we be over and over again more or less mistaken in guessing his meaning; but the real, profound, nay, quite bottomless mistake, is the fool's thought, that he have no meaning."'

This, in itself, though to my ear oddly phrased, is an arresting thought. I like Mr Ruskin's honest manner. He must be – have been – an inspiring teacher. I enjoyed listening to Mr Pritchard who has, I realise, a lovely voice, warm and pitched at just the right level of deepness.

'Would you like to read anything, Rose?' My employer asks, so I fetch *The Stones of Venice*, and find the passage about Torcello which so engrossed me.

I am just concluding, when a figure passes the window and enters. We both straighten up. I return the book to the shelves.

'Good afternoon, sir,' Mr Pritchard says.

The other nods, but does not speak. He is an older man with what were once fine features. He turns immediately to the bookshelves but, rather than looking intensely at one section as I have seen other customers do in search of a particular volume, he seems to drift slowly round the room. I turn from my shelving task as he passes me and notice his expression, as if he is sharing some kind of joke with himself. His eyes, behind his spectacles, give the impression of being colourless.

He has now done a complete circuit of the shop in this perfunctory way.

'Do you need any assistance?' Mr Pritchard asks. He addresses the would-be customer by his name, which sounds like Quinaper. There is something vaguely familiar about it.

'So, you do recognise me, Pritchard.' A thin, dry voice, well-spoken in a lazy way.

'I wasn't sure when you first came in. Do feel free –'

'Oh, I shall, don't worry,' the gentleman replies, 'but I've satisfied my curiosity. A comprehensive stock, I'll grant you that.' He moves to the door and turns. 'Monday is always quiet. You'll probably find it more economic –' he glances at me, 'to make it a day off.' He opens the door and pauses. 'Don't forget, Pritchard, all our fellow *tradesmen* are looking forward to meeting you tonight. The George. Eight o'clock sharp.'

As soon as the door closes and our visitor has passed the window out of sight, Mr Pritchard groans. 'You can guess who that was – my rival, if such he can be called.'

'What a horrible person,' I say, and now I remember the elegant shopfront in the better part of town – and the double-barrelled name, spelt Quinn-Harper, but pronounced as one word, without the H. What traps the gentry set for ordinary folks!

'I'm not upset by him,' Mr Pritchard says. 'I have only to remember that he is forced to work rather than doing so for love of books and learning. He squandered his family's wealth, I gather. When he opened, his stock was the library he'd inherited.'

I am shocked.

'Oh, and rest assured, Rose, I have no intention of closing on Mondays – nor of being intimidated by him or anyone else this evening at the Chamber of Trade.'

I tell him I'm glad, but I'm thinking about the similarity with Sawdons and how one of the owning family's ancestors gambled their London residence away. All their best paintings, so the story goes, were snapped up by Catherine the Great.

In the afternoon, a few more customers come in to buy their course books. These are, by their looks, gentlemen and women of middling years. Between five o'clock and six, an assortment of people begin to appear. These, for the most part, are smartly dressed men who could work in offices further down the railway line or even in the City of London. There are one or two manual workers and, I'm pleased to say, a couple of young women of about my age, both of whom buy course books. Not everyone makes a purchase, but Mr Pritchard was already pleased when he went to bank the day's takings after tea-break. These additional monies, which he places in the safe, prove the wisdom of his opening hours, and I tell him so. I also make myself tell him that he need not walk me home, as he has a busy evening ahead.

'All the more reason to get a breath of fresh air,' he says, darkly. 'Besides, I enjoy this end of our working day and seeing you safely behind the door of Apple Tree House.'

As we walk towards New Road, briskly, for the air is cold, Leonard asks me how I shall spend the evening. I cannot tell him that if Lettie has her way, and enough newspaper can be spared its usual function, I shall be cutting a pattern for a supporting undergarment. I say that there won't be much time after we've cleared the dishes and I have prepared tomorrow's meal, which is true.

A sharp easterly breeze flickers across our faces. Leonard says, gently testing how I will react:

'St Agnes' Eve – Ah, bitter chill it was.'

He nods. I smile: 'The owl, for all his feathers, was a-cold.'

'The hare limped trembling through the frozen grass.'

'And silent was the flock in woolly fold.'

It is exhilarating to step out under the stars, reciting a poem which is clearly a mutual favourite. We manage four stanzas, as I have learnt to call verses, with barely a hesitation. As we approach Apple Tree House, we are concluding stanza five. I have to admit to being relieved that this forms a kind of natural break although it is, of course, the threshold of the poem as we 'turn, sole-thoughted, to one Lady there' 'Whose heart had brooded all that wintry day' (my line next) 'On love and winged St Agnes' saintly care' 'As she had heard old dames full many times declare'.

We are now at the gate. For a moment, the poem resonates in the air between us. Neither of us seems able to speak. I feel almost giddy with relief at having spoken the word 'love' in front of a man without showing my embarrassment. Perhaps Leonard is relieved to have avoided the next stanza, which details St Agnes's pastoral care of virgins who carry out particular rites on her night.

'That was wonderful, wasn't it?'

'I feel uplifted.'

We still seem to be slightly dazed as we say goodnight.

Chapter Seven

In the kitchen, I find Mrs Fuller and Lettie. I seem to have interrupted some kind of joke. Lettie looks guilty, her hand flying back to her mouth after she has greeted me. Mrs Fuller is wearing a wry expression. On the table in front of her is a copy of today's *Times* newspaper.

'Oh, Rose, I feel terrible,' says Lettie, 'being relieved it was a man that died, not a cat, God forgive me.'

'I said she could have the newspaper to cut up, but I wanted to keep the Ruskin obituary. That's where the confusion started,' says Mrs Fuller.

'It gave me a nasty turn,' says Lettie. 'I'm fond of Puss and his brother already.'

'Oh, I think I see.' I can't help smiling, but it comes to me that this time last week I would have been no more knowledgeable than Lettie.

Muddle and chaos seem to be this evening's theme. There are several conversations going on over dinner. I tell Jenny of my day, though she says little of hers. Lettie repeats with pleasure her response to my enquiry as we laid the table: yes, she enjoyed her first day at Gifford's, where she has been given a ladies' window to dress with spring fashions. Meg quietly compliments me on the cottage pie. Winnie picks this up. 'You haven't had second thoughts, have you, Rose?' I reassure her.

'What are we having tomorrow?' Priscilla asks and, when I tell her, pulls a face. 'Though I'm sure you make the best bubble-and-squeak in the world,' she adds, with a smile.

Discussion of favourite foods reaches ridiculous heights, strawberry trifle with a syllabub topping being Jenny's crowning contribution. Mrs Fuller taps her spoon against the side of her dish and, in the hush, reminds us all of Mr Philpott's lecture on Wednesday. Inspired by discussion of John Ruskin, Lettie says she'd like to go. Jenny opens her mouth, but Priscilla speaks first, the others reluctantly agreeing with what she says. Their long factory hours make attendance an impossibility. They'd all be nodding, especially if he drones on, says Priscilla.

'That's a point,' says Lettie.

I feel tired myself, after we've cleared away, but do not have the heart to put a damper on Lettie's eagerness to start work on her bodice. Meg and Winnie are absorbed in writing letters, which activity Priscilla clearly finds more interesting than the clock patience she has set out on the table. Jenny is hidden behind the remaining pages of *The Times*. Mrs Fuller opens her music stand under the light and tunes her violin. She has a rehearsal with her string quartet tomorrow evening. Lettie, also under the light, stands in her chemise trying not to flinch at the cold steel of her big, dressmaking scissors which I am guiding up her side and under her arm, cutting an ample dart. It is a tricky procedure.

Mrs Fuller's bowing arm flashes past the corner of my eye, followed by a screech of strings. Lettie jumps, tearing the newspaper and stepping backwards on to Morris's tail, the cat giving an aggrieved yowl, not unlike the offending chord, as he scampers to the scullery. We all try to resume but, in the limited time before bed, I am not pleased with my handiwork so far. I can barely concentrate as Mrs Fuller rehearses her dissonant piece, which she tells us is '*avant-garde*'. Priscilla has forced Jenny to abandon current affairs in favour of a loud game of Snap, much to Meg and Winnie's annoyance, though they are far too courteous to complain.

In the midst of the cacophony, Leonard comes to mind. I wonder how his evening is progressing at the Chamber of Trade. Far more soberly than ours, I imagine. As Mrs Fuller puts her instrument away I find that, after all, I have enjoyed the evening. We go to our

rooms. I fall asleep to Lettie's grandiose plans involving the manu-
facture of bodices for sale. I dream of a line of them dancing to a
raucous tune.

I wake because I am cold, my nose feeling quite frozen at the tip,
feet so chill that even with knees drawn up inside my nightdress I
cannot warm myself.

It is warm, though, in the kitchen. The others are long gone.
There is only Lettie, curling her fringe, the two cats wrapped around
each other on the little armchair and me, eating the porridge which,
last night, I almost forgot to make. A fine cook I would have turned
out to be!

Lettie is looking forward to getting on with her window-dressing
project. 'Have you got something nice to do today, Rose?'

I want to say of my new employment, 'It's all nice,' though nice
is too limited a word to describe all its facets, like cut-glass catching
the light.

At the public library I noticed, with fresh eyes, how neatly the
books are shelved, their spines aligned with the front edge forming
vertical, parti-coloured strips from top to bottom of each bookcase.
The practicality of this arrangement is clear. There is less damage to
the binding of the book when it is pulled from the shelf because it
has not been dragged forwards. Also, the titles are clearer for the
prospective reader to discern if the books are not lurking in shadow
halfway back.

So I tell Lettie about my self-appointed task of tidying, with
which I start the day, bringing all the books into a perfect straight
line as if standing to attention at the border of the shelf. I like the
atmosphere of calm reflection, the soft shuffling sound as I adjust
them, authors' names greeting me like old friends or new acquaint-
ances I am only just beginning to recognise.

'That'd drive me mad,' says Lettie, 'the silence. I must fly.'

After she has left, Mrs Fuller comes in while I am planning a
menu for the rest of the week. We will have gammon tomorrow,
then macaroni cheese, before the week draws to a close with fresh

fish on Friday followed by smoked on Saturday, ending with Sunday's roast. We sit and talk it over. She seems pleased. It's all harmonious. A small part of me remains in that cosy room as, wishing my old black coat were thicker, and huddling into my muffler, I face into bitter sleet.

I step out briskly, giving 'The Eve of St Agnes' a private performance in my head. This is a wonderful tonic which carries me, as if by magic carpet, to the baker's, where one of the assistants points out Scotch pies whose crust alone would tempt the taste buds without the knowledge of a beef mince filling rich with gravy. I purchase two, say goodbye and cross the road to the bookshop.

Mr Pritchard is at the counter, engrossed in paperwork. I hesitate before knocking on the glass of the door, almost feeling I shouldn't interrupt him and, indeed, his smile is that of someone coming back from being absorbed. How well I know that situation when reluctantly wrenched from the world of the book I am reading to deal with what sometimes seems a duller world. We exchange greetings.

'As you can see, I'm rather busy with orders. When you've hung up your coat and hat, perhaps you would shelve these new books which I've checked in, please. They are replacements for the course books we've sold so far. Do ask if you need help.'

I go through to the back of the shop. For the first time since I started my new employment, I feel slightly anxious. Mr Pritchard seemed unusually brusque. *Don't be stupid*, I tell myself, *he's being business-like*. I come through to the shop again and start the task which needs my concentration but is not difficult. I tidy the shelves as I go.

The town hall clock strikes ten. Mr Pritchard puts down his spectacles, goes to unlock the door and turns the sign. He glances in my direction and catches me looking up. He gives me what I have to call a perfunctory smile and returns to sit at the counter. For a moment, my wits desert me. I hope he does not notice me pausing in my work. He looks different. Two short lines have sprung up between his brows. It is his eyes though . . . I catch myself shivering in this sunless room. His eyes, which are usually a dark, dark blue now seem opaque, like slate. Perhaps he isn't well. It would be like him not to want to inflict his ills on anyone else. *Would it? What do you really know of him? Get on, get on with the job in hand.*

I will my attention not to stray, and actually manage to absorb myself so that time passes unnoticed. I jump at the clatter of his boots as he leaves his seat. He strides across the shop to the back, shuts the door sharply behind him, leaving silence ringing in my ears. I hear the back door slam. He *must* be ill. I understand his reticence, but if only he'd let me help. I could run to the chemist's. He is back, saying nothing, almost flinging himself onto his stool, riffling through papers, snatching up a pen. I hear the nib scratching across paper and it comes to me with a cold dread: this is not illness, it is anger. What on earth has happened? Do the accounts not tally? Is it something to do with me? I can feel my heart knocking against my chest. I have to know the worst.

'Mr Pritchard,' my voice is dry as dust.

He fixes his attention on me. 'Yes, Rose.' His face is drawn. His eyes, behind his spectacles, have no light in them.

'Is everything in order?'

Before he can answer, a customer enters – a spry, elderly gentleman. It becomes clear fairly quickly that, despite a good deal of circumlocution including admiration of the bookshop, he has a purpose. Would Mr Pritchard be prepared to display for sale some copies of his published booklet upon the local fauna and flora? I find that I am holding my breath. All the while, Mr Pritchard has been perfectly civil, and the old gentlemen is so bound up with his discourse and objective that he notices nothing untoward, but I can feel the tension in my employer. I keep my eyes pinned on the title in front of me: *Sartor Resartus . . . Sartor Resartus . . . Please let this end harmoniously, whatever happens.*

'May I?' asks Mr Pritchard. I hear the pages turning. 'Leave a dozen, sir, and we'll see what happens.'

The author seems content with the arrangement that Mr Pritchard should take a small percentage of any sales. He will come back in a month's time. I am limp with relief, though after the door has shut, I hear Mr Pritchard sigh through his teeth and slap the booklet down on its pile. 'I can't imagine a vast new audience for this publication – one which hasn't bought it already over the years. Now then, you asked me something, Rose.'

It is as if my mind has become a void. I cannot speak.

'What's the matter?'

Yes, what is the matter? I feel a tick of irritation, which prompts me, but I must be careful and courteous. 'I felt that . . . something was wrong. You seem . . . displeased, and I wondered –'

'You must forgive me, please, Rose, while I learn to maintain a more professional persona. The fact is that when I went to buy my food this morning, the experience confirmed a growing feeling I have had since actually living here in Widdock – or rather a feeling I've been *made* to have at the butcher's, grocer's, fishmonger's – of being out of place in that kind of shop. I am angry with myself. This is the twentieth century, I shouldn't let out-dated social attitudes affect me. Do you understand?'

I am floating on a cloud of personal relief. 'Of course, I do, Mr Pritchard. It would be . . . almost as if I entered a public house and ordered a drink. But there is a simple solution, provided you don't consider it a denial of your principles. Give me your shopping list. I've ample time –'

'Good God, Rose, you've taken on enough without being chief cook and bottle-washer for me, too.'

A customer enters. Mr Pritchard turns to greet him – which is just as well. I face a bookshelf, though it is a blank to me.

The rest of the morning is busy enough with customers for course books and other enquiries. There is not a moment to allow for further private conversation. Mr Pritchard is thus occupied and I continue shelving and tidying, but slowly, as if numbed. I surprise myself by being able to answer someone's question in a normal manner.

At one o'clock, Mr Pritchard has his hat and coat on by the time I'm back from the privy, washing my hands at the sink.

'I must get some fresh air – have a walk,' he says. 'See you later, Rose.'

The day is dank and cold or I'd have gone out, too – in a different direction. I pick up Mr Pritchard's newspaper, but it is full of the war in Africa, which is not going well. I try to eat my rather large Scotch pie. What should have been a lovely treat is just too much. I cut it in half unequally and put the greater portion on a saucer. There are no children playing outside in this weather. Feeling self-conscious, I walk down the yard. Before I can knock on the worn tenement door, it opens. The scowling woman regards me and my offering for a second, then snatches the pie and shuts the door. Walking back, I feel a slight lessening of anxiety and manage to eat the other half with a cup of tea. All the same, I can't help wondering – have been doing so all morning – whether Mr Pritchard thinks my work here is suffering because of my being cook at Apple Tree House. Perhaps I have been foolish, thinking I could cope. I shall have to bring the subject up. If this is the cause of his – yes – bad mood, then I must relinquish that other role. This is my real job, the one I already love. The thought makes me very sad, though. Can this be the only root of his displeasure?

As his footsteps resound under the arch to the yard, I can't help bracing. He enters the sitting room. I see immediately that he is himself again. His brows have lost that frown and his eyes are back to their remarkable deep blue.

'Is there any tea left in that pot?' He smiles.

I tell him there is but my smile back is a moment slow. I am still taking in his restored spirits.

He flops down in his armchair. 'I must apologise for my ill humour this morning, Rose. You do still want to work here, I hope.'

He remains smiling, but is this his way of introducing the topic uppermost in my mind? My mouth feels stiff as I speak. I have to force the words out. 'It is I who should apologise. I should never have taken on the job of cook to the detriment of my employment here. I'll give it up –'

'What on earth are you talking about? You clearly manage both admirably. And while we're on the subject or near it, yes please, I have swallowed my principles. For the meantime at least, I should be very grateful if you would shop for me to save me the embarrassment of being thought out of place in a woman's world. I suppose you don't know someone who would do my laundry?'

'I . . . I think I may.'

'I knew it. You are wonderful.'

If I weren't already seated, I'd have to sit down. I feel faint with relief.

'There is half an hour before we open the shop again. That should be time enough for me to tell you what happened last night at the Chamber of Trade.'

I raise a hand. 'Please, it is your business –'

'No, I want to Rose, if you'll let me. It'll help me to consign it to where it belongs.'

As Leonard speaks, I imagine the upstairs room at The George, with its meagre fire, and the introductions, formal yet welcoming which dispelled, to some extent, the chilly atmosphere. 'The meeting was about to start when Quinn-Harper entered the room, followed by a man I recognised, which gave me a bit of a jolt. He was a business associate of my father's. On the few occasions I had met him, I didn't take to him. He nodded in my direction. As the two men sat down, their heads bent together and I saw Quinn-Harper's mouth tighten into a smirk at something the other man, Bledington – I recalled his name – said in his ear as the Chairman addressed the meeting, presenting me again for the benefit of the two latecomers.

'There wasn't much on the agenda, it being so soon after Christmas. They were all pleased with their profits – up on this time last year. I gathered that Bledington has recently acquired a large malting in Widdock. I got the impression that they want to know Mr Hallambury's plans for extending his pharmaceutical site still further. This was all news to me. There was joking about the town being swallowed as if it were one of his pills, but he's a quiet man – or he's keeping his cards close to his chest and won't be drawn.

When I first came to Widdock it was summer. I saw families strolling and picnicking on those water meadows surrounding his site. It suddenly struck me that they might be under threat. I couldn't help mentioning that I'd assumed they are common land. I realised immediately that I'd struck upon a contentious issue. Already, I had made my presence felt in a way I had not intended. The meeting closed after that, anyway. I was on the point of turning for home when Mr Simpson, who runs the hardware store, clapped me on the back and said that it was customary to go downstairs for a drink. Much as the only thing I craved was my bed, this was a friendly gesture which it would have been impolite and unwise to repel. He bought me a pint of stout – my father's old company. I was sorry to see Quinn-Harper and Bledington join us at the bar.

'The talk touched on families, in a perfunctory way, then someone asked Mr Simpson if he'd be kind enough to send his man to come and fix the shop door which was sticking again. A discussion began about that. I am out of the habit of barley-drinking. I was joined in the Gentlemen's Room by Bledington. "I didn't expect our paths to cross again," he said. I would have matched his cool tone with "Nor I", but he went on, "Your father built up a tidy business, Pritchard, for you to take over, and here you are playing about with books. It grieves me, I have to tell you." "I'm certainly not playing about," I began, but he cut across me. "We already have one respected bookseller in the town, we don't need two."'

'That sounds like a threat.' I am appalled. 'What did you say?'

'I was tempted not to answer at all. I thanked him politely for his opinion and walked away.'

'No wonder you felt angry,' I say. I don't add *and intimidated*, which I can imagine being the case.

'The anger came later – as you saw, more's the pity. At the time I was shocked. What I would *never* tell any of those men is that, when I came to examine my father's books, after his death, I found that the business was *not* in good order. He'd made some unwise investments. Even had I not have wanted to do so, I would have been forced to sell up to pay his creditors. The sale of his house gave me just enough to set up here. None of the Widdock traders seems to have caught wind of any of this, thank goodness. Fortunately, when I returned to the bar, the group was dispersing, so I was able to make my own farewells. As I walked to the door, the Chairman slipped me a note in a conspiratorial way. He had a well-meaning smile on his face, but by this stage I could barely take in the meaning of words spoken under his breath. All became clear, though, when I read the note at home. It bore the name and address of lodgings. What the Chairman had murmured more than once included the word "respectable".'

'Oh, dear. But I thought you'd determined to stay here. With the arrangements we discussed about shopping and laundry, that would be feasible, wouldn't it?'

'In the meantime, certainly, but I don't know what to think regarding the future. It hadn't occurred to me that there was anything unrespectable about a man looking after himself. But being eccentric in the eyes of the town is one thing, being a laughing-stock another.'

'I understand your – dismay,' I put it, 'and your dilemma.' What I don't understand is how, although his worries have not vanished, the mood which had consumed him this morning has dispersed completely. We spend the afternoon in affable work and discourse with customers.

When Leonard escorts me home, his mind is already turning towards Mr Philpott's lecture tomorrow evening. I think I am able to sound as eager in my responses but, try as I may to concentrate, *my* mind feels numbed as if the freezing moisture, with which the air is laden, has somehow entered my head, blanketing my brain. It is a sensation which has been creeping up on me all day.

Alone in my room, before dinner, it comes to me that I am disappointed in Leonard. It feels shocking to admit this, almost like a betrayal, but by whom and of whom? I thought he had a sunny disposition which would prevail at all times, not that I had got as far as imagining him in a difficult situation, let alone one which might give rise to anger. I certainly would not have imagined him allowing such an emotion to rebound on me. But isn't this the point? *You can imagine all you like*, I tell myself, *but what do you really know of Leonard Pritchard? You have worked with him for five days, and had barely met him before that.*

Why should it matter, anyway? The solicitor I worked for had an unpleasant temper, but if Cook or I had the misfortune to encounter him on one of the days when things weren't going well for him, we merely laughed about it afterwards in the cosy privacy of the kitchen. We did not take it to heart. *That's employers for you.* And here's the rub: I have been thinking of Leonard, I realise, in the same manner as I would of my brothers, rather in the easy way I might think of Jack, if he were someone who shared my interest in books. I see now that I have been casting Leonard as my friend, albeit an older, better-educated one. He is not my friend, though. I must remember this. It will help me to maintain an appropriate distance, as befits an employee. From now on, I must think of him to myself only as Mr Pritchard.

Perhaps it is fortunate that I am not allowed the chance to dwell on my decision.

'Thank goodness,' says Mrs Fuller, when I enter the kitchen. It could almost be a reproof.

I had completely forgotten, for the moment, that she is going out tonight for her rehearsal. She wears a pinafore over her smart dress, has the frying pan already heating and a pan of water on the boil. We hurriedly prepare the parsnips and carrots I have bought. 'If they're not ready when the bubble-and-squeak is, we'll have to have them afterwards,' she says.

There is barely a moment to give attention to the still figure in the armchair to the side of the range. Lettie is pale and drawn, hunched over a small hot-water bottle swaddled in her shawl. She has all our unspoken sympathy, of course, for the regular affliction all we women have to share.

Jenny lays the table. Meg and Winnie are seated in their places, heads together, pens poised over paper until the kitchen door opens when they swiftly clear away.

'At it again,' says Priscilla. 'Are you both writing to the same fellow?'

The sisters glance at each other.

'Oh, don't tell me you *are*,' says Priscilla.

'Of course not,' Winnie says. 'We're simply practising our hands.'

Priscilla snorts. 'And why might that be?'

'Please come and collect your plates,' says Mrs Fuller. 'I'd be grateful if we can conduct this meal briskly. And we'll be in the same mode tomorrow night, when Rose and I are going to the lecture.'

Despite this attempt at a diversion Priscilla manages to elicit, during the course of the meal, the information that Winnie and Meg are due, tomorrow, to sit a test which will determine whether they may work in the administrative section of their company. Mrs Fuller, declining a bottled pear, rises, wishes them both well and leaves behind her a trace of Palma violets.

We tidy up. 'I know what would help you two,' says Priscilla. 'Let's have a spelling bee.'

Lettie, back in the armchair, groans. 'I'm going to bed.'

'Oh, come on, it'll be fun,' Priscilla says to the rest of us. 'I'll start if you like. Ask me to spell a word, Jenny.'

'Disagreeable,' says Jenny.

Priscilla narrows her eyes, but correctly spells the word without comment. She turns to me. 'Separate.'

I spell it.

'Yes, that's right. I always get the middle mixed up with "desperate", but that's with an "e", isn't it?' She looks at us all for confirmation. 'Now you ask someone.'

I turn to the sisters. 'A word which might be useful: receipt.'

They both smile. Winnie gestures to Meg, who answers, spelling it correctly.

'"i" before "e" except after "c",' Winnie adds. She turns to Jenny. 'Confirm.'

'Too easy,' says Priscilla, before Jenny can open her mouth.

Jenny spells it, nonetheless.

'Rhythm,' Priscilla says to me. 'Don't get it mixed up with rhyme.'

'I won't.' I spell it. 'Though I can't imagine it'll crop up much in correspondence.'

'Correspondence – that's a good word,' says Priscilla. 'Two "r"s isn't it? . . . a-n-c-e.'

Winnie and Meg glance at each other, clearly disconcerted.

'*ence*,' I say. I can feel a beat rising inside me.

'That's what I said,' says Priscilla. 'I've got a good one for you two: accommodation.'

'I don't know whether I want to –' Meg begins.

'I'll do it, then,' Priscilla cuts across. 'a-c-o –No–a-c-c–'

'For goodness sake, be quiet! You're not helping Meg and Winnie at all!' The loud words pour out of me. Everyone gasps. I am alight with anger. My heart banging. Priscilla looks as if I have slapped her in the face. She makes a little noise as if she would speak, but I pull my chair back and stand, trying to control the shake in my voice. 'I've had enough, I'm going to make the porridge.'

Behind me, chairs scrape. 'I think, perhaps, an early night . . .' Winnie murmurs.

'We're all tired,' Meg adds.

'I meant it kindly.' Priscilla has found her voice, a sullen one. 'You know that, don't you?'

Meg and Winnie are through the door. There is a hair's-breadth pause before Jenny says, 'It's getting late.'

'That's true,' says Priscilla, rising. 'We've all got long days tomorrow – well, some of us have.' She sounds like her normal self. 'Oh, and I forgot, so have you, Rosy-posy. Must rush back to get our *delicious din-dins*, eh? Before you go to "*Stinkers* of our Time".' She titters.

Jenny gives a weak smirk, but glances at me as if sorry. I return it briefly as she leaves the room. Priscilla seems to have some kind of hold over her, and I'm certainly not going to make matters worse for her by taking umbrage. I have caused enough upset for one evening.

Now there is just myself and Priscilla, who is about to leave, too. I take a deep breath. 'Look, I'm sorry I shouted at you. It was just –'

Priscilla raises a hand as if to dismiss me. 'I don't care. Just as well Mrs Fuller wasn't here, though. She doesn't like disharmony. I'd watch it, if I were you. Goodnight, Rose.' She smiles and leaves the room.

I finish the porridge and go up to bed. The weak light from the landing as I open the bedroom door shows me that Lettie is asleep. Her face looks carved in pain. I try to say my prayers, but my mind keeps replaying the scene in the kitchen. I cannot believe I allowed myself to be provoked. I should have controlled my anger and found another way of influencing what happened. I have probably made a subtle enemy of Priscilla.

I lie in bed, my mind in turmoil. It comes to me that I can hardly criticise Le – Mr Pritchard for failing to control his emotions when I am guilty of exactly this shortcoming, albeit differently expressed. I must, as Priscilla said, watch it. I have to be careful in my own behaviour here at Apple Tree House and maintain my reserve when at the bookshop.

Suddenly, I feel very tired and miserable. I think of home, Hilda and Father, and wish I were there. I would be tucked up with Hilda. Father would be snoring gently in his room across the landing. How I miss them! For the first time since arriving here in Widdock, I feel alone in spirit. Is this new situation, one which I brought upon myself, turning sour? Will it become, if not drudgery, a daily penance? *Mother.* I speak, but softly. *What shall I do? Please help me. Mother . . . Where are you?*

Chapter Eight

MARGATE – In the small hours of Sunday morning the Margate lifeboat No.2, known as the *Civil Service*, was launched in reply to signals of distress and proceeded to the Shingles Sand, ten miles NNW of Margate, where she was just in time to rescue the captain and crew, five in number, of the Carnavon schooner, *Picton*. The vessel, which was from Shoreham with vitriol, had gone ashore the previous night in the blinding snow and was unable to make her signals seen, although only a mile away from the *Princess* lightship. Eventually the signals were discerned by the *Tongue* lightship and communicated to Margate. The cargo of vitriol became damaged and set fire to the ship before the crew left her, and the lifeboat, which lay alongside while the men endeavoured to pump out the ship and subdue the flames, also sustained injury. The rescued crew include Captain Anson, the mate, Carvil, two ordinary seamen named Christensen and Thorkelsden and the boy, G. Smith, a native of Shoreham. A dog was also saved and the men were able to rescue their kits.

I let the newspaper rest in my lap. Whilst we slept in our beds and the soft flakes fell, coating our familiar landscape with a whiteness at which we, when we pulled back the curtains next morning, exclaimed with delight and anticipatory pleasure, all around our coasts men were fighting for their own lives and battling to save others'. I think about the ship's boy, G. Smith, and wonder how old he is. Not too old to want his mother at a moment such as this as she, poor woman, surely prayed for him on such a night oblivious, thank goodness, of how close he was to death. He must have felt very alone and frightened with the men no doubt yelling in their native tongue, trying to save themselves and their boat on the plunging seas. Perhaps he simply did not have time to feel afraid, there being too much to do. I hope that was the case. And the dog, was it his? I find myself profoundly glad that the dog was saved.

I pick up the paper again and read that the Ramsgate lifeboat was out, too, saving the crew of the ketch, *Sunbeam*, struck by the blizzard – a sunbeam put out. I imagine the four men, safe and warm at, we are told, The Sailors' Home. From Scotland to Wales, all across the land, deep snow fell with, I read, three-foot drifts in Manchester. In London, as early as Saturday evening while we were tucking into bloaters, omnibuses were queueing back behind the famous bridges, their horses quite unable to mount the treacherous slopes.

Under the heading *Skating*, I learn that the ice was 'in splendid condition' for the National Championship at Littleport, which I take to be somewhere in the Fens, and a Reuter telegram from the International Championships at Davos dated the tenth of February says that, despite slight snow and a strong wind, two world records were established by the same man, one P. Oestland. He must be just as exercised, I shouldn't wonder, in keeping his pride at bay. I imagine how exhilarating it would be to race on an expanse of firm ice.

Father made our skates, of course, which we had to share between us, strapping them to our boots. Of the three robust pairs, large, middle and small, the size approximating adult also had iron blades. This made the pair attractive for their better speed but, since the blades had worked a little loose over the years, they required an expertise which after a while became an irritation. Those of us not taking a turn and tumble with everyone out on the ice would have no difficulty keeping the younger children happy, playing with snow or testing one boot, then the other, at the pond's edge: finding our balance, hazarding a slide. Jimmy, in thick coat, cap and scarf – only his

111

rosy, laughing face bare to the morning's keen brightness. My eyes prick. I hear Mr Pritchard's footsteps under the arch into the yard. It is the end of lunch hour. Rising, I breathe deeply, regain control and am ready to offer him an enquiring smile as he comes in through the back door.

He removes his gloves and splays his hands to the glowing fire. 'Oh, that's better. I think it's going to snow again.' He starts hanging up his coat and hat. 'Let's go through, I'll tell you what happened.'

In the shop, he lights the lamps. Outside, swollen, sulphur-tinged clouds are banking. He is probably right in his prediction. I have an order I can follow up, which is fortunate. It stops my mind from dwelling on the anxiety of these last twelve days of snow showers. We have already noticed a marked decline in customers and the inevitable effect this has on sales. In view of last weekend's forecast for substantial and continuing snowfall, everything has been cancelled in advance by post and noticeboard. Tonight there will be no meeting of the Fabian Society, to which Leonard – Mr Pritchard – has been only twice since purchasing this bookshop. It was there that he and Mrs Fuller met. I had been about to join. The string quartet will not rehearse this week. Mr Philpott, with regret, has postponed Wednesday's lecture saying that, although we'll be one week in arears, he'll give two lectures at the end of the course, in the week before Easter. (*'Two hours!'* says Lettie. 'There will be a refreshment break, he promises.' 'I should think he does. I'd need to be resuscitated.')

Mr Pritchard comes through and looks both ways down the almost empty street. 'Well,' he says, turning to me with a rueful smile, 'as you can imagine, Rose, although today was technically the day for agenda items, the Chairman had other preoccupations, chiefly, directing more cinder-spreading so that if his yard freezes, his two lads will still be able to get out on their bicycles and deliver the orders. I get the impression he does rather well from snow and ice. People who can afford to do so stock up a bit. At least that put him in a mood genial enough to see me.'

'Oh, that's good.'

'Don't let's get carried away, Rose. To be fair to him, he treated me seriously. We sat down in his office, he listened and noted what I said, but when I'd finished he gave me what you might call a tired smile. "You are not the first businessman in Widdock to step forward with a moral conscience, though your alacrity does you credit," was what he said.'

'Well, if you're not the first, then why hasn't something been done?'

I found Mr Pritchard, this morning, helping to clear a path through the yard so that his neighbours might spare their inadequate footwear as far as the road to the station, where it is their custom to try to sell matches at a price cheaper than that of the station kiosk. He is no stranger to poverty, having spent his school days in London, and I know that there are families in Markly for whom our family's circumstances would seem the height of comfort. Neither fact lessens the sense of shock one feels upon the realisation that many of the yards and courts of Widdock are full of people living in the most abject and insanitary conditions. Surely, this cannot be all their fault? This was the thrust of Mr Pritchard's argument, the touch-stone for an anger, whose signs I now recognise, which could not be assuaged until he had taken the action he is describing.

'The Chairman said, of course, that technically it's a parish coun-cil matter though, of course, the churches and the businesses are very concerned. It's a question of what can practically be done, given that there will be no financial return and that, therefore,' Mr Pritchard assumes a slightly patronising tone, '"it would be like throwing your money – your hard-earned money – into a bottom-less pit. This is where the discussion usually falters, but I'm perfectly willing to give the matter another airing at this month's meeting, so I'll have The Poor of Widdock added to the agenda." He showed me his notes, as if to prove it. Then he stood up and shook my hand. I suppose I should be as pleased as he believes I ought to be.'

'Do be. You are reminding them that the topic is important. He didn't ask about your accommodation?'

'I think he had too much on his mind. I would have told him, if he'd asked, that Mrs Waterson has no vacancies, thank goodness. Now you kindly do my shopping and Mrs Munns my laundry, I feel I am no longer a cause for speculation in the town.'

We settle to our respective paperwork. By four o'clock, without one customer, Mr Pritchard suggests that we commence our study of the poets, for which purpose we have adopted Monday afternoons since, as Mr Quinn-Harper correctly pointed out, it seems to be a quiet time. I have been introduced to poetry in French and German, Italian and Spanish. Now it is the turn of English poetry, once more. This being so, I have been invited to contribute, much to my trepidation.

'What have you to read me, Rose?'

Mr Pritchard calls me by my Christian name when no customers are present. I am still resolved to maintain a more professional approach particularly in the shop, customers or not. It is hard, though. I tend to avoid addressing him at all, which seems discourteous. Thus, I am doubly flustered. 'It's been a difficult choice,' I begin.

'I see you have two books there. Would you like to read a selection of poems?'

The glint of humour in his eyes, curiously, gives me courage. 'I think I'd like to read two, please.'

'Excellent. Go ahead.' He settles himself on the stool next to me, behind the counter.

Outside the window, flakes begin to fall again.

I turn, first, to Eliza Cook whose poems I have known since I could read and before that, when Mother read them out to us. I try not to think about Miss Cook's most famous poem, *The Old Arm-Chair*, made even more poignant since my mother, like the one in the poem, is now dead. I've chosen to read *Snow*, of course. We knew it all off by heart. How we loved to recite it with Mother. I am unsure how Mr Pritchard will react, though, as I have a feeling he will not condone the poet's depiction of the urchins, 'how happy are they/To welcome the first deep snowy day./ Shouting and pelting – what bliss to fall/ Half-smother'd beneath the well-aim'd ball!' These are a far cry from the poor mites who live in our yard. Nevertheless, I still like the portrayal of snow 'In his velvet robes of stainless white' and 'the hills with glittering diadems crown'd'. Most of all, I like the fact that the poem is rousing, a celebration of the wonder of snow. As its final line says: 'Hurrah! then, hurrah! for the drifting snow!' I put everything I can into reading the poem. Behind my voice as I read are all these thoughts of grief and of joy.

'There is no need to look so apprehensive, Rose. I know you're thinking that I shall criticise the poem as sentimental and idealised, but who couldn't respond to its jubilation in the sheer pleasure of snow?'

Relief floods me, my cheeks flaming as much, I'm sure, as they were out in the fresh air yesterday morning when we all set to on the blanket of pure white which had held us spellbound an hour earlier. Mrs Fuller came out and offered a gentleman's cloth cap and muffler for our completed snowman, her kind smile tinged with sadness. I tell Mr Pritchard about our return to childhood.

'So you missed church?'

'Almost, by the time we had dried our boots and blacked them.'

Mr Pritchard laughs. Then, he tells me a little about Eliza Cook's life: how she educated herself, had her first volume of poems published at the age of seventeen and was a poet all her life until illness overcame her. 'But she wasn't just popular,' says Mr Pritchard, 'she really was quite radical. Do you know her *Song for the Workers*? No? It's all about a decent life for working people. She wrote it in support of the Early Closing Movement, of which I am in favour. You, too, I imagine.'

I confess that I haven't thought about it. 'I am perfectly happy,' I say, blushing again for no reason.

Sensing my embarrassment, 'Let's hear your other poem,' says Mr Pritchard.

'It's by Mathilde *Blind*,' I pronounce the word carefully, hoping I have remembered aright Mr Pritchard's pronunciation of the letter d. The poet was of German origin.

'Well done, you're a linguist. Do you know, I almost chose Blind myself. Admirable woman. Socialist, feminist, atheist – sorry, Rose. Do go on and read the poem.'

> '*A Winter Landscape* by Mathilde Blind
> All night, all day, in dizzy downward flight,
> Fell the wild-whirling, vague, chaotic snow,
> Till every landmark of the earth below,
> Trees, moorlands, roads, and each familiar sight
> Were blotted out by the bewildering white . . .'

When I have concluded the two stanzas, Mr Pritchard asks me what I make of the poem. He requests, as it is unfamiliar to him, that we should both read it through again to ourselves. He draws his stool up next to mine. I move the book over. As I read, I am aware of his physical presence beside me, a kind of masculine density. He still has the smoky, icy scent of the outside world about him.

'It seems to me,' I say, when we have both looked up from the page, 'that when she uses words like "chaotic" and "bewildering", she feels snow to be something outside the order of the world, almost threatening.'

Mr Pritchard is looking at me intently, and I wonder whether I have somehow misread the text. 'Exactly,' he says quietly. 'Anything else you'd like to add?'

'Well, when she speaks about the "lamentations" of the wind seeming as if "death must swallow life, and darkness light", she has a very different view of snow from Eliza Cook but then, in the second stanza, when the snow storm ends and the moon comes out – I like that line – "like a flame the crescent moon" – she sees the beauty of the landscape, "Earth vied in whiteness with the Milky Way, Herself a star beneath the starry sky." In a way, she seems more thoughtful – though that can't be so – Eliza Cook must have thought hard enough –'

'I agree,' Mr Pritchard cuts in eagerly. 'The Cook poem feels more spontaneous. There's certainly less exuberance and more craft

116

in the Blind. They aim for different responses. Your understanding of both poems is first rate. Award yourself a tea-break.'

When I return, Mr Pritchard is standing by the window.

'It's still snowing,' he says. 'If it begins to settle, you should go home.'

'But it's not even four o'clock,' I say, 'and I'd like to hear you read after your tea.'

'In that case, I'll dispense with tea and read straight away. Then, we'll reassess the snow. I've chosen Ralph Waldo Emerson. He's American.'

He reads *The Snow-Storm*. His sonorous voice and the beauty of such images as 'the whited air' which 'Hides hills and woods, the river and the heaven, /And veils the farmhouse at the garden's end' have me captivated. We read it through again to ourselves, but then I have to comment upon what is, perhaps, my favourite phrase: 'the housemates sit/ Around the radiant fireplace, enclosed/ In a tumultuous privacy of storm'. It is as if the poet had seen into the heart of Apple Tree House.

'Yes, I thought you'd like that,' says Mr Pritchard.

We both comment on the personification, as with the previous poem, this time of 'the north wind's masonry' as he 'curves his white bastions with projected roof/ round every windward stake, or tree, or door'. I like especially, 'A swan-like form invests the hidden thorn'. How vivid! Again, as with the previous poem, the theme of savagery comes through, 'his wild work' and 'the mad wind's night-work'. But the poem ends on a note of elation: 'The frolic architecture of the snow'.

'The poem doesn't rhyme, though – well, not much.'

'It doesn't have to, Rose. Just think about *Paradise Lost*. In fact, John Milton had some pretty scathing things to say about rhyme.'

'I suppose what this poet – Emerson – wanted was to sound more natural, with the lines running on.'

'Exactly. It's called *enjambment*, by the way.'

'But it still has a kind of . . . grandeur. You know it's a poem.'

'Well said.'

He closes the anthology and goes to look out of the window. Outside, the afternoon is made darker by the golden lamplight which falls on another book, formerly hidden by the larger one. I recognise it, a notebook with a marbled cover. Sometimes, when I return from lunch, Mr Pritchard is reading it and making amendments to what he tells me is his morning writing. It occurs to me that perhaps he wishes to do so now in private.

'It's stopped snowing,' I say.

'Yes . . .' he sounds unusually hesitant. 'I suppose I *should* let you go.'

I am at a loss to know what to do for the best.

He strides over to the counter. 'Rose, would you mind if I read something of mine to you? Then, we will lock the shop and I'll escort you home.'

'Something of yours? You mean, a poem?' Soon I'll be losing count of the times I've blushed today, but this time it's with delight. 'I'd be honoured.'

'When I picked up the newspaper this morning, I started reading about the weekend's weather, and my eye was caught by the word "skating".' I don't interrupt to tell him that I had done the same. 'I was reminded of a poem I wrote some years ago. It wasn't satisfactory, and I'm not sure it's right now, but I'd like to try it out on you.'

I am seated once more. Mr Pritchard stands in a pool of lamplight.

'*Skating Alone*

The clean cut of my blades through the ice pleases my ear and makes
A thin powder beside the two parallel lines which I see
As I curve automatically into a figure of eight.
I admire the motif, repeat it again and again
Until the emotion released cools in the mist of my breath.
This frozen lake is grey, like the sky, except where my skates slice,
Leaving their trail with its ruffle of fondant adjacent.
Far away at the margin, trees blossom with snow, dots moving
Under them, muted. No sound can I hear but of my own making

Leaning into the lunges, or should I say slides, quickly now
As I follow the impulse to glide on down the river.
What if I follow my whim, let it take me on to the sea?'

His apprehensive face breaks into a smile when he sees that my smile is one of genuine appreciation. It feels strange for me to be the one saying well done, but I mean it. 'I'm full of admiration.'

'Don't be. I've been writing since childhood, so I ought to get some things right. I'm not sure it doesn't end too abruptly.'

'Well, it's certainly intriguing. The image of you is clear, though, and the beautiful descriptions.' I pick out some of them. 'It feels . . . as if you are portraying an agitated person,' I say, guardedly.

'I am. When I first tried to write this I was too close to the anger.'

He sits down across from me. I wait. There is just the whisper of one of the lamps burning raggedly.

'It was the morning when I had to confront my father and say that I would not be joining the family firm. He took it badly, as I knew he would.'

'I do understand.' I say no more for now, but this brings to mind my family situation, my father and my brothers, to the fullest degree.

'Do you, Rose? Many people – Bledington being an example, as I now discover – thought me ungrateful and undutiful.'

'You must have had good reason.'

'Oh, I did, believe me.'

I wait again.

'You see, it wasn't just that I found the work in his malting office boring.'

'And a waste of your education, I should have thought.'

'Oh, I expect I could have put up with that. The thing was . . .' He seems to be weighing up whether to go on. 'My father didn't just own maltings, he owned a public house as well in the East End of London. One Saturday afternoon, free time for older school boys who were allowed out till supper, I decided to go and have a look at The Dog and Whistle. I knew it wasn't all that far away, but I was surprised how quickly the neighbourhood deteriorated to the kind of streets I'd only read about in Dickens. I was soon being menaced for pennies. Just as I was beginning to worry that one of the shadows lurking in alleyways would jump out with a knife, I came upon the place around a corner. I'd heard the racket first, though, out in the street, a background swell of shouting. It was the other sound that almost stopped me in my tracks. Scarcely human.' He speaks in a tense, quiet voice, almost to himself. 'Then I did see. And wished I hadn't. How I wished I hadn't. I couldn't believe . . . Even recalling it now is painful.'

'Please, stop then.'

'Yes, I will stop. If I were to go on, you would be . . . shocked to the core. I need hardly add that the whole scene was fuelled by alcohol. For years, it haunted me that I had slunk away, horrified, and had not tried to intervene.'

'But you were just a boy. What would those men have done to you?'

'Rose, it wasn't just men. There! I see I've said more than I should have done already. You are quite right, though. The men would have made mincemeat of me. I realised that as the years passed. But you can imagine how I resolved to have nothing whatsoever to do with purveying alcohol to people such as those.'

'You are to be commended,' I say, meaning it, as I think about my grandfather and how hard my father had to work to restore the name of Alleyn.

'Perhaps. After that, of course, I was not welcome in my father's house. It was hard on my mother. I missed her, too. I had just left school. I got a job in a rather run-down London bookshop. I did that for about six months or so, which widened my education in every respect, but the two brothers who owned the shop were always quarrelling, to its detriment. I could see that there was no future there for me. Then I read a newspaper advertisement for a position teaching English in Buenos Aires.'

'Is that the capital city of Argentina?'

'It is. I had already learnt Spanish from another boy at school whose father was a government official in Gibraltar. I wrote to the

Principal of the school in Buenos Aires. We corresponded and he offered me the appointment. I think the fact that I could offer three other languages as well made the post mine. I sailed in the spring.'

'How old were you?'

'At that point, still seventeen.'

'Goodness!' My age, come June. And I thought Widdock a daring move.

My head is reeling with all I have had to take in: the scene witnessed as a boy which brought about the first courageous act, setting his life on a path entirely unforeseen. And then the second, self-willed, change of destiny, sailing to South America. My employer is a constant revelation to me.

He jumps up. 'It's past five o'clock, Rose. You have indulged me with patience and fortitude, and since no customer's likely to come in now, let's get you home while there is still light and before it freezes over which,' he peers through the window, 'seems likely.'

He is right. The pavement is already icy, the road little better. He takes my arm, but we still need all our concentration to keep upright.

In the kitchen, at Apple Tree House, I am glad to be moving freely and doing something which requires little thought, having already made the cottage pie. Whilst I am alone, I write my shopping list: porridge oats and tea – we consume bushels – and another nutmeg, if I am to make a rice pudding soon. I anchor the scrap of paper under the scales, something which has become a routine in order that Mrs Fuller can add to it if she wishes before I take it with me in the morning.

Lettie comes in and starts scraping carrots while I chop crosses into the stems of sprouts.

In answer to my question: 'Boring!' she says. 'I had to spend the afternoon tidying the haberdashery drawers. What about you?'

I tell her that we had no customers either and that, after we'd completed some tasks, we read poetry (not mentioning Mr Pritchard's own) to each other.

'You lucky thing! I'd rather read poetry than tidy drawers that don't need tidying.' While she is speaking all four others pile into the room, eager to share their snowy-day experiences and to quell their hunger. By the time Lettie has repeated her estimation of my good luck and Priscilla has commented: 'All right for some,' I am beginning to wish I had been more circumspect in my account.

How soon, in a town as large as Widdock, snow becomes sullied, losing all its glamour. How quickly, then, we wish it would go and take its inconvenience with it. Due to its malign omnipotence, I have already been denied a new chance to extend my education with what would have been the Fabians' topic for Monday's meeting, *Towards a Fixed Minimum Income*. Mrs Fuller's Tuesday-night rehearsal with friends did not take place yesterday. Tonight, I will not hear Mr Philpott deliver his lecture entitled, *Culture, Anarchy and the Arrival of Philistines: Matthew Arnold*. This evening promises to be a replica of the last two spent in playing cards, talking and going early to our beds. I realise that I have become restless. I am shocked at myself.

Mr Pritchard, too, has expressed his disappointment over the disruption of our intellectual pursuits. I had thought him largely philosophical about it but, all day today although not showing irritation, he has had something on his mind.

I return to the shop, following my tea-break this afternoon.

'Sit down a moment, Rose,' he says.

A fleeting chill runs through me as I do so.

'Don't look so stricken, you've done nothing wrong. I've been debating with myself whether to tell you about this.' He taps a single sheet of folded notepaper lying on the counter before him. 'In the end, I thought: forewarned is forearmed. You're aware today's St Valentine's?' He pulls a dismissive face.

The subject had arisen briefly last night, brought up by Lettie, but Meg and Winnie said they weren't concerned with courting, as marriage would mean giving up their jobs. I agreed. Jenny nodded and Priscilla, I recall, merely smiled.

Mr Pritchard pushes the paper across to me. It is a shock to see my own hand replicated.

Mine are red
Violets are blue
What about yours?
Will you be true?

I dare not speak. My anger is a slow beat marching up my body, constricting my throat and pricking my eyes. What convenient exemplars my shopping lists have been! She must have pushed this joke, as she would think of it, under the door on her way to work this morning.

Fortunately, Mr Pritchard isn't looking at me, but has picked up the page. He is smiling slightly, having put two and two together from my careful descriptions of the other housemates.

'You've got to give – Priscilla isn't it? – her due.'

I know what I'd like to give her.

'The idea's quite inventive, adapting the rhyme. Strictly speaking, of course, there should be an apostrophe – 'Violet's (the undergarments, presumably, belonging to her) are blue. Sorry, Rose, I didn't mean to embarrass you. I'd like to know whether she omitted the apostrophe for artistic reasons in order to retain the plurality, indeed the universality, of: "violets are blue" as in the original or whether such refinements simply didn't occur to her. I suspect the latter. Still, B+ for Effort, you can tell her.'

I still say nothing.

'Oh, and you can also tell her, if she thought I'd be fooled she's the one with delusions. Quite apart from the crudity of the humour you, Rose, would never be satisfied with a poem whose opening line scanned so badly. There should be two beats to the first word, as there is in the original rhyme. "Mi –ine" does not equate to "Roses". Tell her, if she's going to write doggerel, she must obey the rules of doggerel. D– for Attainment!'

Although I can't help but smile at Mr Pritchard's appraisal of this scrap of verse, I am beset by anxiety. Should I confront Priscilla in the way he suggests or would it be better to act as if nothing had happened? Why should I give her the satisfaction of knowing that she and her bag of tricks had been a topic of discussion?

As it turns out Lettie begins, immediately after grace has been said, to relate an involved incident about a ripped kid glove returned for refund, by a lady's maid, as faulty goods. Everyone in the shop, the maid included, knew this to be a lie but Mr Gifford, when called from his office, accepted the story because he didn't want to lose the custom of the gentry. This leads us to a heated discussion about rights and wrongs, which Mrs Fuller draws to a close because the noise is hurting her ears. She suggests that, when the meal has been digested, we might like to follow her example and put the same level of energy into dusting our rooms.

After this, Priscilla's enquiry, 'Did anyone get a Valentine card, then?' comes as rather a damp squib, quickly dismissed. There has been little post delivered to any of our establishments, it transpires, because of the disruptive weather.

'Certainly nothing of any importance,' I say, with a degree of emphasis. The others nod.

'No one in their right mind would venture out on such a foolish errand,' says Winnie in her no-nonsense manner.

I silently cheer.

'I suppose you're dying to tell us you got one,' says Lettie.

Priscilla just smiles.

'Next business,' says Mrs Fuller, rising to clear the table.

We all disperse to our rooms, thank goodness.

Chapter Nine

'How did you get on with that volume you took away last time?'

This is Mr Nash, who is a master at the boys' school. He has a lot of fluffy fair hair around a balding crown, which makes him look older than his thirty or so years. He has ice-blue eyes which twinkle, fiercely.

'I could have put eight and sixpence to better use,' says Mr Davidson, whom Mr Nash has known since boyhood, so we have learned, and whose voice fills the shop like a melancholic bell toll. He is the headmaster of a small school for boys, just outside the town. With his large, round eyes, beaked nose and lugubrious demeanour, he reminds me of an owl, hunched on a branch.

They start discussing the book in question, a recently published study of Spanish literature in Tudor England. I gather more of it was read here than I would ever have guessed, both in translation and in the original. Its popularity began in the time of Catherine of Aragon and continued through the reign of Queen Elizabeth who, it turns out, spoke several languages. What a clever woman she was!

'The pity is that there's clear evidence of erudition, but Underhill martials his facts so badly. I'd like to remind him how to present an argument,' says Mr Davidson.

'I'm sorry you found the book lacking,' Mr Pritchard says. He has been dipping into because of his interest in all things Spanish.

'Why don't you ask Pritchard to refund your money, Davidson? I'm sure he would oblige,' says the third of the men who always seem to find themselves together in our bookshop on a Saturday. His name is Mr Vance. He writes occasional articles for both national and local press. Once he had a book of poems published, so he has told us. His unblemished face, under a shock of black hair, could be mistaken for that of a younger man, but only for a moment. His dark eyes glitter as he looks from Mr Davidson to Mr Pritchard.

'Enough of your mischief,' says Mr Davidson. 'This chap, Rouse,' he lifts the book he has been holding to display its cover, *An Echo of Greek Song*, 'is, I can tell, the master of his subject. I shall enjoy returning to the original text and comparing his translation with my own. And it's less than half the price of the other.' He produces half a crown and searches in his pocket for the remaining shilling.

Mr Vance, in the meantime, has been casting a sardonic eye over a stack of slim, identical novels, placed for collection on the counter, but he crosses to see the book which Mr Nash has taken from the shelf. 'What have you there?'

'*The Complete Works of William Shakespeare, With Portraits of Famous Actors*,' Mr Nash reads from the cover.

'Aaagh – spare me!' says Mr Vance but joins him, as does Mr Davidson, saying, 'One really does not need –'

'You forget, Davidson, I used to tread the boards. I was a memorable Anthony.'

'That's one way of putting it.'

They become absorbed recalling performances, quoting lines. Mr Pritchard continues putting tickets with customers' names on them into the new novels. Business has been brisk since the snow disappeared in these last few days. Despite what now seems to be perpetual rain, people are eager to be outdoors and are glad to shelter in our bookshop when the downpour is at its worst. I record the sale to Mr Davidson, then look up as Meg and Winnie enter. I have told them about a new scientific memoir which, although far too expensive for their means, has caught their curiosity. When we open it, however, the account looks highly technical, even to their eyes.

'All right if you're keen on zoology,' I say under my breath, as we try to get the measure of it.

'Or palm-ology,' says Winnie, 'All this stuff about palm trees.'

'I'd rather have palm*istry*.' There's a catch in Meg's voice, and soon we're all trying to stifle giggles. 'It goes on and on.'

'Ladies, may we have a little hush please?' booms Mr Davidson in his headmasterly voice, which has the desired effect though I am cross, considering that his end of the room has hardly been a model of silence.

'What you're looking at is Volume Two,' says Mr Pritchard to Meg and Winnie. 'Wait until there is a selection from Mr Huxley's best papers. It will come.'

They thank him, say goodbye and leave.

'Why are they bothering their heads with all that?' says Mr Nash, his gaze following the two figures under one umbrella as they walk up the street.

'My friends are both scientists, sir,' I say, making sure I keep my voice light and free of the heat which threatens to gallop up into my mouth.

'That's put you in your place, Nash,' says Mr Vance.

I glance at Mr Pritchard, the heat now in my cheeks, worried that I may have overstepped my position but he says, equably, 'So, will you take the Glassford Bell, Mr Nash?'

'May I think about it, Pritchard?' He puts the book back on the shelf. 'What I really came for was another copy of *Savrola*.'

'Dear God! One's enough, surely?' cries Mr Vance.

'I know, I know. It's for my father-in-law. He has a birthday pending. I thought he'd already read it in instalments but apparently not, so I'm informed. He saw action at Sevastopol, so it's tailor-made. And before you say it, Vance – no, I can't slip him my copy. It must be unopened and entirely pristine. I have my orders.' He slaps a ten-bob note down on the counter.

Mr Pritchard gives him his change and I wrap the book.

'Tell me,' says Mr Vance, 'why did Churchill include a love interest? No females are ever going to read about his mythical country and its political upheavals.'

'Miss Alleyn has read it,' Mr Pritchard says, quietly, 'haven't you, Rose?'

Three pairs of surprised eyes fix me.

'I'd be grateful for your opinion to balance those of these repro-bates,' says Mr Davidson. 'I am number one hundred and thirty three on the public library's waiting list for the novel. Is my impatience misplaced?'

'Well,' I say, carefully, wondering what on earth they'll make of me, 'it's very . . . gripping, rather like a boy's adventure book.' (These rainy lunch hours I have taken, from his bookshelf, Mr Pritchard's boyhood copy of *The Black Arrow* which, despite the quaintness of the historical speech, puts *Savrola* in the shade.)

'Yes, yes,' Mr Vance interjects.

'But the characters seem . . . as if they are saying what the author wants said, if that makes any sense . . . ?'

'They are mouthpieces rather than being themselves,' says Mr Pritchard.

'And at the end of the book, I did become bored with all the descriptions of the stages of a battle and Savrola's lack of feeling about it all, it seemed to me.'

Mr Vance claps.

'Well said, Rose,' says Mr Pritchard.

'That's what he is, really, isn't he? Churchill, a soldier. Before he became a correspondent on the front, he was at Malakand and the Nile. First and foremost, he's a fighting man,' says Mr Nash.

'That's right,' says Mr Vance, with vigour, 'he's pugilistic. I met him once when I was lunching with my publisher. Do you know, he threatened to punch me? All over a chair.'

'Academic?' Mr Davidson looks almost wry.

'The point at issue was academic,' says Mr Vance with no suggestion of a smile. Anyway,' he squares his shoulders, 'I must go. I have to review the wretched thing for the *Courier.*'

Emboldened, I venture, 'I liked the old lady servant, though, a bit like a nurse. I think it's only fair to the author to say that.' I wonder how this will go down.

'Ah,' says Mr Vance, 'everyone likes his old nurse.'

'That's blatantly not true,' Mr Nash says, as the two men jostle their umbrellas from the stand and leave the shop.

Mr Davidson takes his and pauses, turning to us. He nods towards the unremitting rain. 'Couldn't be more unfortunate after all that snow. If it persists, I hope you'll have your sandbags at the ready.'

Mr Pritchard shakes his head fondly at the departing backs. He seems to enjoy the disputatious atmosphere. 'Trust him to leave us on a note of gloom,' he says, lightly, but I have glimpsed anxiety in his eyes.

A steady flow of customers has kept us unusually busy for a Monday. The pile of novels on the counter has dwindled rapidly and other orders, uncollected due to last week's icy pavements, have nearly all gone. There is hardly a moment when the shop is not occupied by at least one or two customers communing with the shelves in that little, slow dance which I have come to recognise, as a head tilts or a person moves closer to read a title, a movement I find comforting.

Guessing that our afternoon will pass as quickly as the morning, we use our lunch break to study a book of poetry, newly published in Great Britain, by a Spanish American whom Mr Pritchard admires, George Santayana, also a philosopher. We both agree that whilst the subject, Lucifer's fall, recalls *Paradise Lost*, the cadences are Shelleyan. The whole, if we had time to read it, would remind me, Mr Pritchard says, of *Prometheus Unbound*.

When I turn the sign to 'Open', a customer darts in, shaking his umbrella and exclaiming at there being no let-up. We should be rubbing our hands with glee because it certainly seems good for business. But if proof were ever needed of Fortune's Janus face, today would furnish it. I have never seen a river rise as high as The Blaken now is, swollen with meltwater from the land. The rain adds its measure as if cocking a snook at humankind, powerless to prevent what could become a disaster. The men on the bridge really do have something to discuss. All along our street, Holywell End, there is an almost palpable tension. Our shop will be one of the first to feel the effects should the river burst its banks.

Today, Tuesday, there are noticeably fewer customers. As with the snow, people are put off by the practical problem of trying to dry clothes. No one would go out except for necessities. Mr Pritchard has unearthed a substantial, if slightly decrepit, fireguard and we spread our coats and hats and place our boots on its horizontal surface. I have brought my shoes to wear indoors, a significant inconvenience in my shopping bag.

I glance up halfway through the morning and see, through the teeming windows, Kate's husband, Dan, dragging a sack to the front of their shop which is strangely barren with no greengrocery on display outside. I realise, with a little jolt, that this is not a heavy sack of potatoes. It is a sandbag.

My library books are due for return. As luck would have it, the rain eases around one o'clock, though the skies are leaden enough that no one would set foot outside without an umbrella. I force myself, rather than going through the town, to take the towpath so I can survey more of the river. I pass the baker's. They will be the first to suffer if the banks are breached. Then, surely, the water will come rushing down the incline into the rest of our street. This towpath will be completely submerged. I stop, heart beating wildly, trying to calculate. There can only be – an inch? – less than an inch before my conjecture becomes reality.

I stand in the centre of the footbridge at the other end of town. Ahead of me the water meadows are lakes right to the horizon, mirroring the glint of a lighter greyness in the surrounding deep cloud. Closer to, I see that at the old mill, the factory where Meg and Winnie work, water laps its little bridge. Soon it will be a causeway.

Drops are falling again as I hasten back through the town, having not delayed to choose more books. As I am about to cross our bridge, I notice a motionless figure down on the towpath where I stood earlier. He must have seen me because, when I am no longer screened by the men on the parapet, he raises his hat to me with what I feel to be a smug smile. It is Mr Quinn-Harper.

This evening, Wednesday, sees the delivery of Mr Philpott's lecture, postponed from last week. The subject is Charles Darwin and other scientific thinkers. Winnie and Meg were, exceptionally, to have come, but their boots are still wet from the trudge home from work and they are, as ever, bone-tired. I promise that I will relay to them as much of the lecture as I can remember. This is something which I have found myself undertaking on Thursday evenings, after the first three lectures, in response to Jenny's evident interest and her disappointment at also being too tired to attend. My task has not been made any easier by what Mr Philpott would call 'questions from the floor' which, in my case, are interruptions during the course of my account rather than waiting till the end. Lettie's enquiries are genuine. Priscilla is always, I feel, trying to trip me up and test the boundaries of my limited knowledge. After a brief introduction about The Great Exhibition and how it was regarded in terms of the principles of design, the subject of the first lecture was Mr Ruskin, whom I greeted almost like an old friend. I felt distinctly on home ground as I relayed to the others all I could remember, especially as Mrs Fuller was only too pleased to help me. There was less that she could contribute as additional material with regard to Mr Arnold and Mr Stuart Mill. I was very tired when I went to bed on those two Thursday evenings. Tonight's lecture will really stretch my intelligence and powers of memory.

It has rained all day, the lamps in the High Street showing us their slick reflections on puddles and drenched flagstones. We try to keep to one side of the street as far as possible so that we remain on the pavement. The road is mud.

'Tell me we're doing the right thing, Rose,' says Mrs Fuller, hoisting her skirts, as I try to handle mine with one hand and hold the umbrella over both of us with the other.

There are plenty of people, evident by their absence, who have thought better of tonight's excursion. Mr Pritchard has yet to arrive.

I feel a stab of worry. While I stayed in the shop, he spent the afternoon with Dan, Kate's husband, collecting sandbags from the Parish Council depot and forming them into barricades in front of the shop doors. But here he is behind Mr Philpott, who greets his meagre audience and thanks us for turning out on such a dreadful evening. Someone hisses, loud enough for all to hear, 'The hand of God.' There are murmurs of 'yes, yes, Darwin, that's right'. Mr Philpott is unflappable. By the end of the evening, having included a substantial appreciation of Alfred Wallace, a local hero, he receives his usual warm applause.

We discuss the lecture all the way to our parting at New Road, then Mr Pritchard says, 'It's going to happen, Rose. They say the river will breach its banks sometime in the early hours.'

I clap my hand to my mouth.

'Don't come to work tomorrow. There's no reason for you to have to wade through dirty water. And I won't be selling many books, will I?'

'I'd feel the same as you,' says Mrs Munns. I am chopping vegetables and boiling lentils for this evening's broth, while she is drying our breakfast crocks. 'I always think it's better to be doing something than sitting around getting mopey.'

It feels strange to be here in the house at this time of the morning when I would normally be out shopping and then at work. Meg and Winnie have left. A ferry will be instigated, if the mill bridge is under water. The whole day yawns before me, one in which I shall not be able to relax for wondering what on earth is happening in Holywell End and how Mr Pritchard is coping with it. I say as much.

'Show me your feet,' says Mrs Munns. 'Yes, I dare say I've got a pair of gum boots that'll fit you. Come home with me and you can try them.'

This is how I happen to be sharing my umbrella, though the rain seems to be stopping. Mrs Munns smells of carbolic soap, and her gum boots make a *wock, wock, wock* sound as she walks.

'There used to be meadowland between us and the town,' she tells me, 'before all these houses were built.'

As we climb the hill, past the last house in New Road, I see that where we are heading resembles a little village or hamlet on its own. There is a row of older cottages on either side of the steep street, with a public house in their midst. At the top of the hill, I glimpse open countryside.

'Here we are,' Mrs Munns pushes the door of the last cottage, which opens directly onto the street. We enter a small, neat room with a clean oilcloth on the table and walls which are bare except for an embroidered text, 'Blessed are the meek, for they shall inherit the earth', in cross-stitch. Although it is less comforting than my own home, 'without the grace notes', as Mrs Fuller would say, the damped-down range makes the room snug and there is something about it which tugs my heartstrings so powerfully that I am glad Mrs Munns has sat me down whilst she goes 'out the back'. By the time she returns, triumphant, I have mastered my emotion.

'These were my mother's when she worked in the brickfields. Oh, yes,' Mrs Munns says, with some satisfaction at what must be my surprised expression, 'women go to the brickfields as well as men in summer. Go on, walk around in them. See how they feel.'

The boots are a good fit.

'Well, I'll let you know if I ever need them, but as far as I'm concerned you can keep them.'

'Thank you very much, Mrs Munns.'

She bats my gratitude away. 'Mother would be pleased to see you getting the use out of them.'

'I hope I really can be useful.' I'm beginning to doubt my impetuosity. 'And I hope Mr Pritchard won't be angry that I've disobeyed him.'

'He won't be.'

'Oh! Goodness!'

'It happens every year, more or less,' says Mrs Munns, as we reach the top of the bridge. Today, it is noticeably free of loiterers. 'Pity no one thought to tell your boss before he took premises here.'

Holywell End is now covered by a muddy expanse stretching from the river footpath down the street and right across the railway tracks, stopping only at the rising ground beyond. A horse, whose cart is laden with a further supply of sandbags, stands in the middle of the road, his fetlocks submerged. I recognise two of the men from the bridge helping to unload bags. Another tries to hold the base of his wheelbarrow clear of the water as he trundles his cargo carefully so as not to cause a wash. We descend, stepping just as gingerly.

The baker's shop is, as I guessed, the first casualty of the flood, which must be more than a foot above its tightly sealed doorstep. But I'm sure I can smell baking bread.

'They won't stay closed,' says Mrs Munns, with cheerfulness. 'They're old hands at this lark.'

Further down the street, the water level is not quite so high but many shops stay shut and barricaded. Dan, though, has his door open and is standing on his sandbags looking out like King Canute defying the tide. He is not the only one displaying such bravado.

We hear Mr Pritchard's voice under the arch to the yard and come upon him building a defensive wall. I see he has found the galoshes which he said he'd bought in Buenos Aires. On the other side of his wall the ground is still dry, so far. Here an elderly man and the woman who accepted my offering of meat pie are attempting to help him. Their boots are worn, holes stuffed with newspaper. I take all this in as Mr Pritchard turns at the ringing note of Mrs Munns's 'Good morning.' He looks both exhausted and astonished to see us. 'Mrs Munns! Rose! I don't think —'

'This one to go on top here?' Mrs Munns ignores the protest, grabbing a corner. 'Many hands . . .' She looks at the rest of us. We all hoist the bag into place.

By the end of the operation, I have learnt much more of all our neighbours in the yard.

There's another argument out in the street. Tempers are frayed because it seems to some as if those in authority are not as exercised about our plight as they would be if were on the affluent side of town, premises which are not in such immediate danger as our own. That's what the row was about yesterday when the fire crew surveyed our street. Today, the cobbler's shaking his fist and yelling at one of the station flies for creating a tidal wave. 'Go round the other way, you so-and-so!'

'He's taking out his lack of fares on everyone else,' observes the postman, not lifting his dripping boots across our threshold, under which the water laps dangerously close. 'These will be your last letters from London till the flood abates. The tracks are covered. It's like that in places all down the Blaken Valley, so I'm told. And London Road's under water, so we can't send a coach through. We're cut off to the south and to the east.'

'To the east?'

'Yes, the Esh has breached over the road to Hadle Street and Markly.'

I feel odd. Shaky. The Esh is our river, a tributary of the Blaken. It isn't as if I'd harboured any thoughts of going all that long way home, but to know that it is as completely out of reach, as if it were another continent, unnerves me.

'You've been very quiet today, Rose. Are you sure you haven't over-exerted yourself?'

Mr Pritchard thinks I shouldn't have tried to help yesterday. 'If you aren't fully recovered, you must not come in tomorrow. It simply isn't worth it.' We have had hardly a customer.

I wake at the usual time, having slept soundly, untroubled by active dreams. I feel perfectly well. Besides, it is Saturday. How could I not go to work?

Though I still have on my gum boots, I walk down New Road free of an umbrella. At the bottom, I pause as a dray turns off in front of me towards the adjacent malting. Pale sunlight catches the brasses on the horses' harness. I can't help smiling. An old lady, coming out of the grocer's as I am about to enter, blinks at the light, smiles and returns my greeting, 'Good morning. Let's hope it stays a good one, too.'

I realise I have been hoping that the flood would have magically disappeared. But before I reach the top of the bridge, I can see the lake that is Holywell End. All the voluble talk amongst the lolling men, though, is that the water level has not risen, thank goodness. In fact, some assert, it may have dropped. And I remain cheerful in praise of human ingenuity. Although the baker's doors must remain firmly sealed and sandbagged, the heavenly smell of baking bread is drifting out from the upstairs windows where the baker's wife and her assistants are lowering loaves in roped baskets into which intrepid customers, shod like me, put their coins for hauling up.

It is not a usual Saturday. We sport our 'Open' sign because the water lies inches below the door sill, but only one or two daring souls step over our defences and stand on the mat in their waterproofs whilst we fetch their orders. Our usual trio do not look in today. It is as quiet as a Monday until we both look up at a knock on the glass of the door. Two young men stand outside unsure whether to enter.

'My goodness, it's my brothers!'

'Do let them in,' says Mr Pritchard.

Of all the times to come and visit, they would choose this! I have been to the station twice during the six weeks of my residence in Widdock, with the intention of letting my brothers know I am well and have settled in. The first time, there were such queues waiting to be served by the ticket clerks and such an air of frenzy in the office and on the platform, I doubted that my brothers would have been willing or able to converse with their troublesome little sister. The second time, neither Joe nor Hubert could be seen. I didn't want to ask for them in case they were engaged in something important behind the scenes, so I slipped away. They could have come to see me, I can't help thinking, but I banish the uncharitable thought and let them in. They are both wearing rubber Wellington boots to protect their smart uniform trousers. I wonder if these are railway issue.

I make the introductions. 'You're managing then,' says Joe, looking round with mild approval.

'Yes, thank you for your concern,' says Mr Pritchard. 'And you?'

'Ah . . . well . . . huh,' says Joe, 'that's why we're able to come and pay a visit on Rose, as she hasn't been to see us. No trains.'

'As a matter of fact, I *have* –'

'But, the news is that the tracks are proud again,' says Hubert.

'Oh, are they?' says Mr Pritchard.

'We're going to run an experimental train through,' says Joe. 'Exciting, eh?'

'All being well, a normal service should resume tomorrow,' says Hubert.

Joe slaps his hands together. 'So, we can't stand here, hob-nobbing.'

'Glad to know you're keeping well, Rose,' says Hubert, stepping through the doorway.

Joe turns before he leaves. 'Your rival must be making a killing. High and dry.'

'Actually,' I begin, my voice sounding strained as I try to control it, 'his stock is different –'

'Extended his range,' says Joe. 'That's what I've heard. Still, you look as if you're doing all right.' He waves his hand vaguely as he says goodbye, and closes the door.

'Calm down, Rose,' says Mr Pritchard. 'I'm not upset, though I understand, now, what you told me about them.'

'That's Joe all over. He has to come out with . . . a parting shot.'

'It's nothing. Quinn-Harper's got a board in his window, that's all: "Orders Taken For New Books". About time, too. Oh, and a board in the other window: "Buy your copy of *Savrola* here." '

Now that the trains are running again, Monday brings a flurry of delayed letters including one, from two school friends of Mr Pritchard's, written on Friday. They are both lawyers with business in Cambridge, so they will be passing through Widdock on their way. They have booked rooms at The Railway Hotel. Would Mr Pritchard care to join them there for dinner? Unless they hear to the contrary, they will present themselves at five o'clock on Tuesday, which is tomorrow.

★

I see, as soon as I step inside the shop, that Mr Pritchard is in one of his restless moods. His morning writing has been unprofitable and 'not worth reading out, Rose'. (He sometimes does read his poetry to me. I feel privileged.) I wondered whether he was on edge about meeting his old friends especially as Holywell End, though no longer flooded, still looks rather sodden and forlorn. It appears, though, that his lack of equilibrium emanates from last night's meeting of the Chamber of Trade. 'I've been co-opted.' He is to represent the Chamber at meetings of the Parish Council, the authority with powers to effect change. Here he can table for discussion, 'Sanitary Housing for Widdock's Poor'.

'That's progress, then.'

'I expect I shall have to sit through endless discussions about where to site another horse trough and whether raising the rate by a farthing to cover it will cause an outcry. Still, I'll treat it with an open mind. I shall soon be able to tell if I am amongst Matthew Arnold's Philistines or kindred spirits really wanting social change.'

Promptly, at five o'clock, Mr Pritchard's friends arrive and introductions are made. They both look prosperous, well fed and somehow older than their classmate.

'Lord! – We didn't know we'd be needing to build an ark to get here!' says Mr Huddleston.

They both laugh and Mr Pritchard expresses surprise at their description of the expanse of water-logged fields on either side of the railway track.

'They really are *water* meadows,' says Mr Darley.

They all chuckle and agree to meet in the saloon bar at half past six. I am glad that Mr Pritchard will be with his old friends tonight. It being Shrove Tuesday, my friends and I have planned a pancake party and, when I thought Mr Pritchard would be on his own while we were merrymaking, it caused me some anxiety. Now, I need not worry on that account.

Any concerns I may have had that Priscilla might contrive to spoil the atmosphere, are unfounded. She turns out to be the most adept at tossing a pancake which, with a strong flick of the wrist, she sends to a high and graceful revolution, catching it on its descent. 'Oh, yes, I'm fearless with a frying pan,' she says.

We stand about the range, eating pancakes as they come, and talking.

'I think sweet things are trickier to cook than savouries,' says Lettie.

'Mmn . . . I don't know. It's easy to overcook fish,' says Winnie.

Meg nods. 'And lose all the goodness in the poaching liquid.'

'Yes, but there's more work in a lemon meringue pie, isn't there? And more to go wrong. Swiss Roll – that's the worst. You manage to make the sponge. You spread it with jam, and then it all cracks to pieces as you try to roll it up. What do you think, Rose? Have you ever made a Swiss roll?'

And out of my mouth comes, 'No, but I've made a Russian wriggle.'

There is a split-second – and then everyone is laughing and it becomes a game. 'Have you ever made a Viennese whirl?' (Jenny). 'No, but I've made a Chinese whisper.' (Lettie). It is a game which quickly manifests its shortcomings. 'No, you can't have French horn – it would have to be a Frenchman horn,' which seems to be even funnier. Mrs Fuller, back from her string quartet rehearsal, puts her head round the door, smiles at our high spirits, and says goodnight.

It is time for us to clear up and make the cocoa. Winnie and Meg take our plates through to the scullery. I am at the table making porridge, whilst Jenny chops vegetables.

'Well,' says Priscilla, 'what are you all giving up for Lent?' She is leaning forward, laying out our cups and saucers.

Lettie is behind Priscilla's back, on her way to the range to fetch the saucepan. She turns and mouths, pointing both index fingers at Priscilla, 'Being nasty.'

The sound of crockery and spoons mask the two spoken words. I make sure my face shows no reaction as I mumble, 'I haven't really thought. . .', but I don't know whether Jenny's face disclosed anything.

Priscilla gives us a shrewd look as she straightens up. She turns round, but Lettie's reached the range and comes back with the saucepan to pour our drinks saying, brightly, that she'll try to give up sugar in her tea.

'And what about you, Priscilla?' I ask. 'What are you giving up?'

'Men.'

We all gasp.

'That shocked you, didn't it?'

It is true. In our lives, most of the time, we just get on with what must be done. There is little room beyond routine. That one blunt word has summoned an image of unknown figures lurking outside in the dark.

'I'm only joking. Drink your cocoa.'

Equilibrium is more or less restored, and we all part on affable terms.

As soon as we are alone in our room Lettie, feeling guilty, wants to know whether I think Priscilla guessed what she had said. I answer diplomatically and say goodnight. What I don't say, is that we all probably had a similar thought to the one which Lettie enacted, but we kept it to ourselves.

'How was your pancake party?' Mr Pritchard asks.

'Good . . . yes . . .' I say. 'How was your evening?'

'About the same as yours, I should think,' he says.

He must have picked up the note of hesitation in my voice, for which I'm sorry because it *was* an enjoyable evening, on the whole. I am debating whether to ask him more about his, when Mr Darley and Mr Huddleston appear and step inside. They have come to say goodbye.

'How's your head, Pritchard?' asks Mr Huddleston. 'Mine's cracking fit to burst.'

'He still managed a slap-up breakfast,' says Mr Darley.

They both look red-faced and robust.

'I'm none the worse for the claret,' says Mr Pritchard.

'A very fine one.' Mr Huddleston turns to me. 'You should have

140

seen him, Miss Alleyn, your employer. He was so animated discoursing about his blessed poets, he picked up the tail of his fish . . .' He begins to chortle at the memory, 'and started trying to cut with it.'

'He thought it was his knife,' says Mr Darley.

'I was the object of such hilarity,' says Mr Pritchard, 'they had to leave the dining room. While they were absent, I polished off the sautéed potatoes, which were delicious.'

'It was just like being back at school – the three of us in fits,' says Mr Darley. 'I do wish you could have seen us, Miss Alleyn.'

'And today, just think, my dear young lady,' says Mr Huddleston, 'if this had been a leap year, you could have asked the three of us to marry you and taken your pick.'

My cheeks are burning.

'Look, you've embarrassed the poor girl with your peculiar sense of humour,' says Mr Darley.

They've left the shop door ajar, and we hear the Town Hall clock strike its quarter.

'Time to go,' says Mr Huddleston.

They have to take a cab to the station on the other side of town, where they will board the train to Cambridge. They both wring Leonard's hand and slap him on the back. 'Capital fellow!' 'Until the next time!'

When they have gone, he says, 'Well, we won't see them again.'

I am surprised.

'They move in wealthy circles, Rose. It's clear I don't.'

I am unsure what to say. Mr Pritchard could almost be relieved. He goes about his work with what seems a lightness of spirit. Once again, I admire his ability to be completely self-contained. I might have given way to regret for a friendship which had run its course, but he nearly always has a positive outlook. He finds inspiration daily. Even so, I am delighted when he tells me, after my tea-break, that Mr Philpott has been in and, apologising for the shortness of notice, has invited Mr Pritchard to join him and his wife tonight for dinner.

★

'Talk about coincidence,' Mr Pritchard is recounting his thoroughly enjoyable evening, 'Philpott and I were at the same lecture by George Santayana, when he was at Cambridge. We could have sat next to each other. He's going to include him in the course.'

Although Mr Pritchard must be Mr Philpott's junior by at least six years, it sounds as if the two men are intellectually matched and that the evening was a stimulation to them both. I am profoundly pleased. They are planning a cultural trip to London, 'the galleries, the British Museum. Just to get to know the place again'.

I feel a fleeting pang, not so much for London, which I think would be beyond me, but for the enriching dinner table conversation.

'What are Mrs Philpott's interests?'

'Oh, she left us to it,' says Mr Pritchard. 'She isn't intellectual at all. Very pretty, though.'

He is wearing a look which Phyllis would say was 'bordering soppy'. I can hear Father's voice resounding in my head, 'There you are, Rose. There you are.'

I could spit.

Chapter Ten

'Hog's hair,' says Priscilla, matter-of-factly.

'Ugh.' Lettie wrinkles her nose.

'It is clean hair.' Jenny looks for a moment at Priscilla and then to me since I, too, am being addressed.

Lettie picks up the look and makes no more of it than I, other than that there is some private business between Jenny and Priscilla. Despite the fact that it is Priscilla who wishes to effect a sale to us, Jenny's intervention seemed almost like a plea.

'I didn't know you all had them,' I say, feeling slightly compromised.

'Oh yes,' says Meg, 'Mrs Fuller, too. I suppose we could keep them in the bathroom, but the basin would become rather crowded. We use our washstand.'

'What's the handle made of, bone?' Lettie prods the object in her palm.

'The thigh-bone of an ox,' Priscilla says.

'That sounds like something from the Bible,' I say.

'And how much cheaper do you reckon one like yours would be than the one at Collett's?' Lettie names the chemist's shop. I am reminded how little she spends on herself, putting away all she can spare to take home to her family against the dreadful day when, once again, her father cannot work.

'A penny off,' says Priscilla, 'and brand new, of course, not hanging about in Collett's window, gathering dust.'

'Can't Rose and I share one?' says Lettie.

'No!'

Winnie and Meg speak at the same time.

Their vehemence shocks us all. Winnie turns to her sister, opening her hand, letting Meg speak for them both. 'Infection. If one of you were to pick up a stray bacterium –'

'A mouth germ,' Winnie cuts in.

'You would almost certainly pass it to the other.'

There is a small silence while we all consider this literally unpalatable fact. Priscilla looks almost smug, as if the intervention of medical science on what might be called her side has not only proved her case but closed the sale.

It seems Lettie and I are in the minority. That Mrs Fuller has one is only to be expected but next day, as if secretly bidden to present itself for my inspection, I notice on a shelf in Mr Pritchard's scullery, one in a glass next to his shaving mug. Lettie and I succumb to the inevitable.

'The chatterbox', as Priscilla describes Lettie, has had to work late. With Mrs Fuller and myself going out and the others tired, our meal is a rather functional affair soon over. As if I needed reminding, Priscilla points out that tonight, Wednesday, is just the right occasion for me to employ my latest purchase before venturing into polite society. She doesn't put it quite like that. She's right, though. I shall be meeting Mrs Fuller's friends again and may be seated next to strangers. From the little off-cut box made by Father, I tip a pinch of salt into my half-glass of water. I use the mirror above the washstand in my bedroom for guidance. I suppose I shall become accustomed to these tickly hairs against my gums.

As I go on brushing, I cannot stop my mind from summoning the unpleasant turn of events last Saturday, when Priscilla produced the wretched things we'd ordered and calmly said she could only let us have them for a ha'penny off. They are a new line. 'Well, I'll have the old line,' Lettie said with some heat, only to be told that the ones we'd seen had been replaced. For a moment, she looked as if she would be having none of it but in the end she fetched her tuppence-ha'penny

144

and slammed it down, snatching up one of the two packages, the other being mine.

The exchange has left a lingering atmosphere. I wonder if the reason she has agreed, so willingly, to stay at work, taking a cheese sandwich for high tea, is not so much to do with trimming hats for her display, 'Spring into Spring', but because I shall not be back till nearly bedtime.

Our family, thankfully, has always had good teeth. As Mother would say, there's nothing like a crisp apple for cleansing the mouth or, in the depths of winter, little can beat crunching on a carrot or sweet-tasting parsnip. If I can't abide this tickly brush, I shall go back to the latest twig Father cut for me, as he has done for each of us which, with its split, flattened end, works perfectly well to eliminate the more reluctant morsels. I have cleaned it and placed it in the drawer in a laundered handkerchief. If Phyllis were here to see my newly purchased toothbrush we would laugh, especially in view of its handle, about its being a bone of contention.

At Apple Tree House I have my friends who are, roughly, my own age but at these evening meetings I attend, I realise I have another set of friends. I have to call them that because, although older, they treat me as another friend, call me by my first name and listen to what I say as if it mattered. In this respect, I cannot believe my luck. I am honoured.

It is dark now but as it is a clear night with stars and a sickle moon I notice how, as we cross into the better part of town, the silvery light graces streets of elegant brick houses with tall, airy windows, front doors with fanlights, some with imposing steps and wrought-iron railings. The shops are double-fronted, with generous bay windows. Here I have to stop myself from thinking about that other bookshop and its horrible, undeserving owner. Down that path lies ruination of the spirit and, besides, I love our vibrant side of town and all that's been achieved at Pritchard's Bookshop.

'I believe this to be the oldest Friends' Meeting House in England,' Mrs Fuller tells me, breaking off from chatting with Miss

Robertson, who plays first violin and who joined us at the bottom of New Road and with Mr and Mrs Cooper. They live in an imposing house near here. We had to wait whilst grandchildren were kissed goodnight. The string quartet meets in the Coopers' house, the most practical gathering point, since it is Mrs Cooper who plays the cello. These three confirm the veracity of Mrs Fuller's assertion about the age of the building.

We have come to a weathered brick wall with a door, standing slightly open, through which purposeful figures, mostly gentlemen of course, are entering what turns out to be a pleasant, paved courtyard. At the back stands a double-gabled, high-windowed building in whose porch people are moving slowly forwards to enter. This must be where Winnie and Meg come every Sunday to sit in communal silence.

Suddenly, there are greetings all round and hands being shaken. We join Mr Pritchard and Mr Philpott waiting to go in and chatting to Mrs Neale (viola). In their hats and high-heeled boots, the four women are not much shorter than the three men. For a moment, I feel as though I don't fit in, but Mrs Cooper takes my arm, 'Come on Rose, I hope you've brought a cushion or a padded bottom.'

I see what she means when we are inside. The square room is whitewashed and unadorned, with a wooden post holding up the gallery. The seats are plain wooden pews, most of which are taken. If this small room had craved a respite from its habitual silence, it now has one. We realise we cannot find a seat all together. Mrs Fuller's hat, with its nodding feather, goes ahead of us. Mr Pritchard leans towards me. He is looking at three empty seats to the side, 'Perhaps, we –' but Mrs Cooper surges forward, pulling me with her. I see Mrs Fuller mounting to the gallery. I glance back at Mr Pritchard and meet his brief smile, but his sleeve is being tugged by Mr Philpott, who is urging him to take one of the three seats. 'May I join you?' asks Mr Cooper, and the men fold straight into easy, animated conversation.

Mrs Fuller leans out from the gallery, nodding and smiling. Miss Robertson and Mrs Neale are already on the stairs. Mrs Cooper calls up, 'We're coming'. I have noticed that these four striking women have drawn many a pleasant 'good evening' from the assembled company and several looks from those with whom they aren't so well acquainted, not all of such looks entirely friendly. This last attitude, though, is not as prevalent as at the Wednesday lectures which garner a wider cross-section of the town's population. Nonetheless, encountering it makes me shiver inside.

I am on the end of a row, the quartet having gone ahead of me. The door is being closed, the guest speaker who will introduce tonight's debate, '*From Labour Representation Committee to an Independent Labour Party*', is stepping forward to address the room. There are footsteps on the stairs and a whispered enquiry. I smile and gesture to the empty space beside me. The young man smiles back and takes his seat.

Last month, in spite of all the worry about flooding, Mr Pritchard was excited about one thing, which he passed on to me from his newspaper, namely the formation of the Labour Representation Committee founded by the Trades Union Congress. This committee, as its name implies, is the first step towards a party for the working man. For the obvious reason, I could not quite share his enthusiasm. I find the details of this evening's debate difficult to grasp. Some Trade Unions seem to be more sympathetic to the Liberal Party, which includes many Fabians. There is no clear outcome, as far as I can gather, arising from tonight's discussion.

The guest speaker looks around for any further questions from the floor. Mrs Cooper grabs my arm and raises it. 'My young friend, here, would like to know which might be the better path to achieve votes for the working woman.'

Despite the other women's 'Hear! Hear!' a sound, not unlike a groan, meets Mrs Cooper's words. My cheeks are flaming yet I feel that inner chill, as if the temperature in the room had dropped.

'I quite understand your point, madam,' the speaker addresses Mrs Cooper. 'All I can suggest is that sometimes in the cause of progress it is necessary to take one step at a time.'

There are muttered agreements, the speaker is thanked and, after a few local announcements, the meeting is concluded. We all stand, glad of the relief and are about to go when the young man who slipped in beside me introduces himself, 'Fred Rawlins'. After I have given him my name, he shakes hands with the group, then turns his attention back to me. 'And what do you do, Rose? I can call you Rose, not Miss Alleyn?' I assent and tell him briefly of my life in Widdock. 'Very good,' he says, several times. I ask him about himself.

'My first meeting, too. I work for a big market gardener's in Chesford, raising fruit and cut flowers under glass. I came here on the train. Just think, I could have gone up the line instead.' He names a place of which I've vaguely heard. 'They've got a Fabian Society, too. I'm glad I didn't.' He checks his watch and says that he must go to catch his train. 'I hope to see you, Rose, at next month's meeting.'

By and large, I have to echo what Fred Rawlins said about the sense of friendliness here. As we make our way towards the door, all those we pass acknowledge us cordially and many people call a warm goodnight.

In the morning, Mr Pritchard is full of inspiration from the meeting. 'This is the start of it,' he says. He asks me what I made of the discussion. I start to tell him that, although I had to concentrate hard I found the evening to be yet another interesting part of my new life. 'And I met a very agreeable young man who works in Chesford. Do you remember when you rode your bicycle down to see the Eleanor Cross? Well, he works in all those acres of glasshouses . . .' I find myself petering to a halt. Mr Pritchard has a slightly fixed expression. Perhaps, he has stopped listening. It comes to me that I might be boring him. After all, glasshouses and the cultivation of exotic fruit and vegetables are hardly his concern. I go through to the shop and start to tidy shelves.

The morning passes and my employer, thank goodness, becomes once more his normal self. He divulges, when we close the shop at one o'clock, that of all annoying things his first attendance at the Parish Council meeting clashes with Mr Philpott's lecture.

'Even if they were to whip through the agenda, which I doubt they will, and I were to hoof it from the council offices to the

Assembly Rooms, I would only catch the tail end, so I think I must be philosophical and make my peace with the situation. Good job Philpott's subject is the novelists. At least I won't be missing something completely new to me.'

This might explain why he appeared so preoccupied.

On Thursday morning, he is as inspired as I have ever seen him, 'though it might all come to nothing, of course,' he says, by way of tempering his enthusiasm. The Parish Council has requested him to investigate models of housing for the poor and then to write a report about them.

'I shall have plenty to discuss with Philpott over dinner tonight, not least last week's excellent lecture on philanthropic housing. I'm glad I didn't miss that one.'

At one o'clock, I am just about to turn the sign to CLOSED when I see my brothers coming towards the shop. I step outside into spring sunshine. I can guess their purpose and have been to the station twice to talk to them, but found neither to be available. After we have said hello, Joe comes directly to the point: Mothering Sunday. We have all received letters from Hilda, asking if we're coming home to visit Mother's grave. My heart drops at the words. I have had a letter, too, from Phyllis. 'We've been given special dispensation so if you can't, I'll be there for you. I'd dearly love to see you, Rose. We all would, but we understand. It's a long way and a difficult journey to organise for such a short time.'

'We were thinking of going early in the morning by bicycle,' says Joe, 'to get there for Matins and back before the first train runs on Sunday afternoon.'

'But then we thought, Rose is bound to want to go if she can,' says Hubert.

'Well, yes, I –'

'Which complicates matters,' says Joe.

'I do realise –'

'I've just had a thought,' Hubert says to Joe, 'supposing I hired a tandem.'

149

'Does she know how to cycle?'

'She wouldn't have to. She'd just sit behind and pump her legs.'

'You'd have to allow for the fact that she would slow us up.'

'Well, let me know what you decide about me,' I say, 'I'm going for walk.'

'Right you are, Rose,' says Hubert, unaware of my sarcasm.

'Yes, we must be getting back,' says Joe, equally unaffected. 'We'll tell you in good time what we've arranged.'

I manage to say thank you and goodbye without malice. They mean no harm. In fact, they're trying to be helpful.

If ever I were tempted to disbelieve in the Divine Existence, this would be the moment when I might lose my faith. It is a week to the day after our last encounter. We meet in the street outside the shop, big, soft snowflakes swirling between us and settling on my brothers' dark capes, already coated like plum puddings dredged with powdered sugar. For a moment, it seems none of us can speak.

With the hand not holding my umbrella, I reach out and touch their sleeves. 'Come in by the fire.' But they won't. They haven't time. So, we stand in the archway through to the backyard, and the snowflakes drift, twirling past our eyes.

'It's no good,' says Hubert. 'We can't risk being stranded in deep snow at Markly.'

'Especially if the lines were still open and trains able to operate here,' says Joe. 'We'd lose our jobs.'

'We've written to Hilda,' says Hubert.

I nod. It is exactly what I expected to hear, though the effect of the words is like a stone settling in my heart.

Joe is struggling to articulate something. 'It's not as if we need a special day . . .' He can hardly finish. Hubert turns abruptly, head down. I nod but cannot speak. The snow blurs before my eyes. We stand with our own thoughts until we have recovered, then say a subdued goodbye.

Across the road, Kate is selling nosegays of violets. I buy one and shall put it in a small vase on my bedside cabinet. I would have left it on Mother's grave tomorrow, together with the posy of primroses I also buy. I give this straight to Mrs Fuller. It is a rare moment when the two of us have the kitchen to ourselves, which is just as well. Suddenly, we are both in tears. I have learnt that the kindly gentleman in the portrait was her dear husband, some years older than herself. I step into Mrs Fuller's arms and hold her tight.

It is Mothering Sunday. In the range oven, I have left a piece of brisket, potatoes and a rice pudding with a sweep of dusky nutmeg, all the more reason to hasten home from church.

As we turn the corner of New Road, I spot Mr Pritchard in his navy greatcoat and red muffler, dark hair escaping from his cap. He is walking with vigour, on his way to luncheon at Mr Philpott's, which now seems to be his custom. He gives us a wave, which Lettie and I return for all of us. Even at this distance, I can tell his face is full of the anticipation of a good meal and stimulating discourse. For a moment, I wish that I were with him.

We pass the large modern church whose services are not to Mrs Fuller's taste, chiefly on account of their great length. The congregation is just emerging and there, to my surprise, is my brother, Joe. He doesn't see me. He is chatting to a stocky man who has his back to me, a middle-aged woman holding the man's arm and, facing me, someone whom I assume to be their daughter. My heart knocks. Under the wide hat are large blue eyes in a face framed by auburn kiss-curls. At a glance, she could be mistaken for Hilda or, when she was younger, Mother.

Dear Rose,

We were so sorry that the weather prevented you from coming home. I thought you'd like to know how it all went this afternoon. Excuse the scribble. I'm hoping to finish this before I'm wanted again upstairs.

151

Jack rode to Markly on that old horse he likes here at Sawdons and brought the cart back. So, Ralph, Dot and I sat on the seat and he was our postilion. It was quite cosy under the rug and made us all feel a little better about what we were going to face, though I won't deny it was an ordeal. When we reached the churchyard, we found there were blue and white violets as well as primroses growing in the bank next to Mother's grave, and daffodils had come up by the headstone. Just what Mother would have loved. We stood in a row and Dot said, 'God bless Mother's soul' and we all said, 'Amen'. I said it, thinking of you, too, Rose. It was icy-cold, so we didn't linger. We got in the cart and headed home.

I went in first. Father was sitting by the fire. He looked all in. They'd been to church this morning and gone to the grave then. He cheered up when the others trooped through the door and Hilda started cutting her simnel cake. Jack was very sorry you weren't there. He says he hopes you're coming home for Easter because he'll be there. I'll see you in the afternoon on Easter Day, I hope.

With love,
Phyllis

I stay sitting, with the letter in my hand. I can see the little, shivering group at the pretty graveside and, afterwards, in the warmth of the cottage. How I wish I had been there. I shut my eyes and take a steadying breath, in which there is the delicate scent of the violets by my bed. Although it is past the time when I should be setting out for work, I open the other letter which came for me this morning.

Dear Rose,

We were bitterly disappointed not to see you and the boys. I had made a simnel cake. I will make another one at Easter. On that subject, Jack's been told he can go to another house after Easter and learn about motor cars, so he'll be home. Father will collect you in the morning on Maundy Thursday and take you back in the morning on Easter Monday.

152

I will not write more now, as Phyllis said that she would be writing to you when she got back yesterday. It was a very sad occasion, but we all felt better for seeing each other, I think.

Your loving sister,
Hilda
xxx

Though this letter, too, gives me a pang, I cannot help but smile at Hilda's unhesitating assumption that I can be spared from the shop.

By the time I am buttoning my coat and putting on my hat and gloves, I am no longer smiling. I very much want to see my family, of course I do, but how can I ask Mr Pritchard for all that holiday?

'How would you like a holiday, Rose? Oh dear, there's no need to look so startled.'

It is as if he has been reading the thoughts rampaging in my head. I take off my outdoors clothes and leave the shopping, following Mr Pritchard through to the shop. He looks very genial this morning.

'Couldn't have gone better, last night's meeting – apart from Bledington trying to draw Mr Allenbury out about his intentions over some parcels of land. He shouldn't bother. It just creates an unpleasant atmosphere.'

Of course, it was the Chamber of Trade. How could I have forgotten? 'But, they were pleased about your role at the parish council, then?'

'Oh,' he makes a dismissive gesture, 'they were pleased that I've been given something that will keep me quiet, they think. No, most of the meeting was spent discussing whether we should have uniformity in our opening hours over Easter.'

I can feel my heartbeat. 'What did they decide?' My voice sounds thin.

'It was down to the discretion of the individual shopkeeper.'

I cannot speak.

'Obviously, shops like grocers and bakers may open for a few hours on Easter Saturday but, broadly speaking, there was a general consensus to remain closed from Good Friday till the following Tuesday. Rose, are you all right, you look rather faint?'

Then, I tell him about Hilda's letter.

We are in the kitchen. I am frying our Sunday morning bacon, whilst Lettie breaks eggs into a bowl. Meg lays the table, Win is making tea. Jenny, to staunch the cajoling *yirrup-yirrup* of Morris and Ruskin rubbing round her legs, is in the scullery pouring milk into their bowls. Mrs Fuller isn't down yet. There is, unusually, no sign of Priscilla either.

Then, we hear pounding feet. The door bursts open.

'No church this morning!'

We all stop.

'It burnt down in the night!'

In the instant of being dumbstruck, I am filled with intense sorrow for the beautiful old building – just as my brain catches up –

'April Fool!' Priscilla crows at all of us.

It is as if, with that emphatic declaration of Priscilla's, we turned from blackthorn winter towards spring. Now, the days count themselves till Easter. Events become 'the last before', as in tonight's meeting of the Fabian Society. Our poetry discussion this afternoon (Mr Pritchard reading 'Spring the Sweet Spring' by Thomas Nashe, whilst I contribute William Wordsworth's 'Daffodils') affects me with a disproportionate poignancy, as if it were to be our very last. I feel unsettled as I walk home, on my own now as it is light.

'Everyone will be using this soon.'

'Don't tell us it's cheaper than Collett's. The brushes hardly were,' says Lettie.

'Collett's don't even sell this yet – but they will, mark my words,' says Priscilla, evenly.

'May I?' Mrs Fuller takes the tin and studies it. '"Wonder tooth-cleaning powder", H'm.' She grips the lid and turns it.

We all stare at the white grains inside.

'It's very good. I can show you —'

'And I can tell you that I should like to take it in to work and have it tested,' says Winnie.

'I was about to say the same,' says Meg. 'They put all kinds of things in these so-called powders — chalk, brick-dust, charcoal.'

'There's nothing like that in there!' Priscilla protests but this time Science, endorsed by Mrs Fuller and the rest of us, is not disposed to take her side.

The altercation leaves me feeling out of sorts. We are in the body of the room tonight and I fear I must seem inattentive to the speaker on the contentious topic: 'Empire: this meeting moves that we should put our own house in order before embarking on further expansionist policies'. I apologise for my distractedness to Mr Rawlins, who has joined us once again. He doesn't seem to mind.

'It's a bit heated, isn't it?' He wipes an imaginary line of sweat from his brow.

I agree and, unsure I wish to venture an opinion, am glad that Mr Pritchard has come to sit on his other side. He engages Fred in lively conversation allowing me to see what Mrs Neale makes of it.

'I'll look out for you tonight, of course,' says Mr Pritchard.

The thought that there will be no more Wednesday lectures after Easter gives me such a pang and combines with a strange feeling which has been creeping up on me all afternoon so that now, just before I leave the shop, I have a sudden stupid impulse to cry. This is ridiculous. I want to see my family. The long break is perfect for me and for my employer, too. He is going up to London with Mr Philpott, who is acquainted with Octavia Hill. 'Cooper's coming and bringing photographic equipment. He has a dark room.' They are also going to visit 'that chap, Howard, who's planning garden cities. He lives somewhere west of Widdock.' Mr Pritchard is as excited as a boy with a new bicycle. I busy myself putting on my coat, adjusting my hat and gloves, so that he cannot see my silly, brimming eyes until I make sure they've subsided. I realise my life here in this bookshop, in Apple Tree House and in Widdock, at large, has become my world. In light of this, I suppose my state of mind is not so inexcusable.

The scientific sisters enter the kitchen one behind the other, Meg with the tin of tooth-powder, Winnie holding a piece of paper with symbols written on it. Dimly, I recognise having seen something like them in a book on Grandpa Clarke's bookshelf. We are all there to hear Winnie's pronouncement:

'$NaHCO_3$ – Sodium Bicarbonate.'

Lettie claps a hand over her mouth.

'*And*,' Winnie looks at Meg.

'$NaCl$,' says Meg. 'Our old friend Sodium Chloride. Salt.'

'As if we need buy either of those!' Lettie chortles, summing up the mood of this particular meeting.

This time, Mr Pritchard has 'hoofed it' from the Parish Council meeting, having tendered his apologies and promised his report on housing for the next session. 'I'm jolly well not missing Philpott's final lecture.' Seated next to me, his is the loudest applause in what is truly an outpouring of admiration. This evening we have learnt how Mr and Mrs Webb are working to extend the franchise, including women's suffrage. (There have been vociferous comments from a certain strait-laced section of the audience, not all men, a position I fail to comprehend.) Names such as Annie Besant and Josephine Butler have become people to us in the unfolding drama of our times. Other enthusiastic members of the audience joined in the debate, the mood overwhelmingly optimistic and appreciative of Mr Philpott's breadth of vision as, in conclusion, he looked back over what we have discussed from John Ruskin and Charles Darwin to Karl Marx, William Morris and those who have crossed the threshold of this twentieth century, as different from each other as the poet, William Butler Yeats and the Labour representative, Keir Hardie. A new spirit of creativity and honest endeavour, deriving from the best of those who went before points the way, we dare to hope, into the current age.

Mr Pritchard leaps up to thank our speaker, petitioning him to run another lecture course. There are shouts of 'Hear! Hear!', and more men press forward to pump his hand. He thanks us all and says he will be honoured to do so 'in the autumn'. Mr Pritchard has told me that Mr Philpott takes his family to spend the summer in Italy. Before then, he must tour with his publisher, giving readings from his latest book, the subject of this course. We have ordered extra copies to take advantage of his popularity before the memory of him fades during the months he is away.

The meeting is beginning to break up. Mr Pritchard catches his friend's eye. They both nod in recognition of the fact that my employer will take dinner at the Philpott household tomorrow evening, Maundy Thursday. We step outside into the starry night, the string quartet walking ahead of us, chatting.

'I always feel exhilarated and expanded after these evenings,' Mr Pritchard says.

'You know so much already.'

'Ah, but the mental stimulation in itself is – intoxicating. Even if what is said is sometimes an affirmation of what I already know, or think I know, the way it is presented is always refreshing. And the critical examination of the topic is, as you know, first class.'

I feel the urge to speak, but am suddenly shy.

'Don't you agree?'

The thing I burn to say fills my mind. I open my mouth. 'It's like our Monday afternoon poetry reading and discussion. That's how I feel then.' My cheeks are flaming despite the cool night.

'Yes, yes. How right you are, Rose. Intellectual companionship. What a joy! We are very lucky, aren't we?'

'We certainly are, Mr Pritchard.'

'Leonard. We're not in the shop now.'

We have stopped at the bottom of New Road. Mrs Fuller and Miss Robertson are saying their farewells.

Suddenly, neither of us seems to know the right words for our parting. I'm being wrenched inside. That silly wobbly feeling threatens again. I take a deep breath and, for a moment, close my eyes. When I open them, I notice Mr Pritchard, Leonard, is staring fixedly at the ground. He steps towards me. 'I shall think of you with all your family, Rose. I wish you well.'

I step towards him. 'And I shall think of you – Leonard.'

Our gloved hands touch.

'Goodbye.'

'Goodbye.'

We both turn away.

Chapter Eleven

'Come and tell me when your father gets here, Rose. If I'm not in the house, I'll be in the studio.'

Mrs Fuller is wearing her artist's smock, the green of young leaves, of her eyes. Embroidered on its yoke is a pretty honeysuckle pattern in a darker shade with yellow flowers. She has drawn her hair back simply from her face with two tortoiseshell combs. It almost reaches her waist in strands of silvery reddish-gold. She aims to spend the next five days, 'while you are all away and nothing much else is happening', working to improve artistic skills which, during the winter months of cold and poor light have 'gone to pot.' This she alleges despite apparently fearless attendance on the first Thursday of the month at meetings of the Widdock Art Society, where members may take their work for appraisal by a distinguished guest artist.

She has been much amused to receive an invitation on behalf of her old professor, Mr Poynter, to a grand exhibition, at which he is represented, opening over Easter in Paris. 'I'm an afterthought,' says Mrs Fuller. 'If he'd really wished me to attend, he'd have written weeks ago.' And in answer to Lettie's excited question, 'Even if I could afford to make the trip, the thought that he'll be there is an excellent incentive not to go.' She tears the card neatly in four and drops it in the fire. Curiously, though, the episode seems to have shaken her from her so-called winter torpor.

This morning, she looks determined and energetic as she steps outside to go down to her studio, closing the back door behind her.

Mrs Munns, emerging from the scullery with brush and dustpan, nods at her receding footsteps. 'She'll have been hoping for a letter from Italy.' She shakes her head.

I know, because Mrs Fuller has told me, she has a married daughter and a little grandson living in Rome. I know, too, that for the half dozen or so letters she has written since my arrival, there has been one reply and that so general it told her nothing or, putting it another way, too much. 'I don't like the sound of all this blandness. She's hiding something, Rose.' Mrs Fuller is far too shrewd to be fobbed off with platitudes such as, 'I expect she's very busy'. I could only pat her hand.

'Keeping herself occupied so she doesn't dwell on it.'

Mrs Munns is right, in part. I nod, but excuse myself to go and pack my few essentials. Shortly afterwards, I hear the muffled tramp of her footsteps on the stairs and the random hollow knock of wood on wood as she descends, brushing.

By the time I come down, I can see her through the front door's stained glass and hear her attacking the knocker. I fill the pastry case I have just baked blind and return it to the oven. It will make an egg and bacon flan to last two days for Mrs Fuller and Priscilla who will be staying since, she says, she has 'no home to go to, but don't fret about me. I've got plenty to keep me busy'.

As I carry the flan through to the larder, I hear my father following Mrs Munns through the back door, scuffing his boots on the mat while she offers him tea which, with thanks, he refuses. 'I don't want to leave the mare too long.'

It seems strange to see him here, looking somehow smaller than my recollection of him, in this high-ceilinged room. Neither of us seems to know how to address each other. I tell him I must fetch Mrs Fuller. Mrs Munns presses him to take tea.

I make my way down the path through the formal garden whose borders are now awake with daffodils and scarlet tulips. I pass a screen of fruit trees, not yet blossoming, into the vegetable garden, which Mrs Fuller and Mr Munns have planted up and staked out with neat rows of criss-cross bean poles just as Father will have done at home. A weathered brick wall, from a time before the street of houses, runs along the far end of the garden, its length punctuated by a door, wide enough for agricultural traffic but now kept locked. Indicative of the land's previous usage are a range of barn-like buildings which run to meet the boundary wall. Since these face north, Mrs Fuller has renovated one of them to make a painter's studio. I knock with some hesitation. This will be the first time I have entered her place of work. 'Come in, Rose,' Mrs Fuller trills.

She walks towards me, smiling and wiping her hands on a rag. She has a smudge of turquoise paint on her cheek. Behind her, though I don't like to look too much, I see whitewashed walls and on them canvases glowing with colour.

As if she has read my reticence Mrs Fuller says, 'When you come back I will show you my work, but I expect you must go now, mustn't you?'

'Well, my father is always anxious,' I say.

'Of course. Don't you be, on my behalf while you are away. I shall be all right. Priscilla and I can keep each other company. Then on Sunday, after church, I'm invited to Imogen Cooper's for luncheon.'

'That will make a break.'

'Yes, she's a dear friend. Though sometimes I think it's worse to come back after a social outing than to spend the whole time alone. I tell you this, Rose, and you'll understand it from your own experience, one learns to adjust to solitude.'

'Very nice, your Mrs Fuller,' Father says, as we move off, 'even if she doesn't entirely look after herself.'

I agree that she is, indeed, very nice. I catch a last glimpse of the house behind its eponymous apple tree, whose branches are clothed in a fuzz of lemony green.

'I bet the old girl keeps you all in in order,' says Father, as we pass down New Road. 'Does she do the cooking as well?'

I realise that there is a lot Father doesn't know, but I'm finding it difficult to maintain a conversation. We turn into the High Street and, for a moment, point to where the road rises towards the river with the men leaning on the bridge. Beyond this lie the shops of Holywell End.

Then we turn East onto the Markly road and we're passing the riverside cottages, the public house with its little garden, the new mill. We have left behind us the burnt toffee smell of roasting malt. Here, in open country, the air smells sweet. It is as if Widdock no longer exists.

After a while I stop speaking, trying not to feel nettled by the old irritation. Father's interest in my life does not extend beyond the facts that I am safe, well and supporting myself. Knowing that he will not welcome questions about his, I keep quiet falling into a pleasant daze to the thud of Sable's hooves, the creak of the cart and the embrace of the quiet countryside.

I barely notice as we pass through the village of Hadle Street, and afterwards I am half asleep, Father a wall beside me. It comes to me with shame that he has good reason not to wish to hear the details of my existence. He is exercised enough coping with his own.

And now we're passing the outlying houses, the stray cottages on the edge of my home town which is really, I now see, one long street. How quickly Widdock Road becomes the High Street, quiet this Maundy Thursday in the middle of the day. We pass the church, with The Green Man opposite, a scent of woodsmoke suggesting that the bar is open. Father touches his cap to Ned Thurgood who, looking up from locking his forge, returns the pleasantry with a brief smile which barely reaches me before he has turned again to his keys, and we are passing Father's workshop next door, then Will Sturgess's yard. Sable's head turns momentarily to her winter quarters, but Father encourages her progress with a gentle slap of the reins and a 'Go *arn*'. We come to the houses and cottages at our side of town, then Doctor Jepp's house in its modest grounds. Now we're at the field between the Jepps and us. Sable enters our lane, breaking into a little trot as she anticipates her nosebag and our field which I can see above the hedge starred with blackthorn and misted in new green. At the end of the lane, set a little way into the field, is home. I am having to breathe deeply. Hilda appears at the door, smiling and wearing Mother's apron. It is almost too much.

No one quite meets anyone's eye. Father takes Sable quickly round to the back. Hilda tells me how well I look and shows me to the room which I will share with her. The fact that it is my old room is borne in on both of us as we stand there under the eaves in the scent of clean bedlinen and the savour of Hilda's barley broth, drifting up the stairs.

'Come down when you're ready,' she says, and turns quickly.

I stand for a moment, disconcerted. How small the cottage seems, low-ceilinged and dark. The thought makes me feel almost like a traitor. So much that has mattered in my life happened here. I think again of that terrible morning only three months ago. Before I can quell them, the tears slide down my cheeks.

It would be wrong to say that we are on best behaviour with each other. That description would imply a sense of deference. Rather, our awkwardness stems from adjustment to being a family again and, with it, concern for feelings which are, I think, close to the surface in all three of us including, in his own way, Father. As soon as Hilda and I clear away the dishes, he returns to his workshop, 'a few things to tidy up'. Hilda produces her mixing bowl to make the dough for tomorrow's hot cross buns. 'No, you may not help me, you're the guest. Sit and talk to me.'

It feels strange not to be the cook, to be referred to as a guest, but I'm happy to oblige. As I've said before, Hilda's dough is lighter than mine. I'm glad my friends at Apple Tree House are never likely to make the comparison.

I begin to tell Hilda of Mrs Fuller and Lettie and the others, my days at the bookshop with Mr Pritchard ('I'm glad he really is as nice as I always thought him,' says Hilda) and my evenings going to meetings, Mr Philpott's lectures and the Fabian Society –

'Stop! Stop!' cries Hilda. 'You're filling my head.'

For the second time today, I check myself. I should have simply sketched instead of spouting in such a self-important way. Now, there is just the sound of Hilda's capable hand turning the mixture in the bowl from which exudes the fragrance of cinnamon and nutmeg. How could I have been so slow? 'Hilda, I'm sorry.' My heart is banging fit to burst out of my chest. 'I didn't mean to be thoughtless.'

'It's all right, Rose, I know you didn't.' She gives me a small, tight smile which then relaxes and broadens. 'There's no need to look so pained.' She starts to clean her fingers with a damp cloth. 'Though I won't deny it has been hard at times.'

I hear the extent of it in her restraint. Hilda has borne the brunt of Father's grief as well as her own. Before my swimming eyes, hers are as full of loving sympathy as Mother's and as blue. 'There, there,' she says, sounding like Mother as she pats my sleeve.

'I'm sorry,' I say again in a whisper. 'I wish . . .' But what? I don't wish I could have stayed here at home, God forgive me. The thought of such a possibility, even though it never existed, touches me with its own subtle shade of dismay laced with guilt, which seems to settle like a cloak, adding to my grief.

'I wish I could help somehow,' I say, feeling the inadequacy of the words.

'Well, you're here now,' Hilda sighs, covering the bowl with a muslin cloth, 'and you *can* help. You can put this in the pantry, please.'

When we've cleared up, Hilda fishes in the dresser drawer for her spectacles blowing on them first and cleaning them on the hem of her apron. She places them on her nose furtively, casting a glance towards the window before settling to her task. Whilst she catches up the loose threads on the intricate lace which borders our venerable best tablecloth, to be used on Sunday, I take the wooden mushroom from the sewing basket and, rolling down one stocking and then the other, darn their well-worn heels. 'What would we do, Rose, if someone came to call?' She giggles.

'I don't know why you worry so much about sometimes wearing spectacles,' I say. 'You know Mr Pritchard wears them, too, when he reads.' Mention of his name brings the image of him vividly to me. I wonder what he is doing at this moment.

Hilda gives me a pitying smile. 'It's different for men, Rose, as well you know.'

This time she sounds, in turn of phrase if not voice, just like Father.

In the regular rhythm of our needles and in the moments when our heads lift, pulling up the thread, we re-establish sisterly ease. I listen as Hilda tells me, quietly and in few words, how she has tried to comfort Father by keeping a spotless home with good food always on the table.

'You couldn't have done more. I'm sure it all helps,' I say, meaning it. 'Father seems ...' I search for the right word, '... reconciled.'

'Do you think so?'

I nod, vigorously. 'I do.'

'Then I have not been mistaken. Thank you, Rose.' Hilda gives me the first truly warm smile of our reunion.

'Oh!' Hilda's exclamation makes me look up from laying the table. She is outside inspecting the thyme bush beside the bench to see if there is enough new growth to spare a sprig for the rabbit stew whose delicious odours have been distracting me increasingly. 'There's a man on a white horse coming down Oak Meadow.' This is on the other side of us from the Jepps, away from town.

Passers-by are few at our cottage, especially as evening closes in. I put down the handful of cutlery and go to join my sister. Somewhere in a tree silhouetted by evening sunshine, a blackbird gives forth its eloquent roosting song.

The horse and rider have now reached the gate at the top of our field. There is something about the easy way the man walks the horse up, bends and unlatches the gate and, backing the horse, swings the gate just wide enough so that it will close again stoutly of its own accord when they are through the neatly judged gap.

My heart leaps. 'It's Jack.'

'So it is! He wasn't supposed to come till Saturday,' says Hilda, almost reproachfully. 'Funny, though. Something told me to save the stew for tonight.'

But I'm already hurrying down the path waving, trying not to run as Jack waves back.

I catch up with him as he is coming through our field. 'Rose,' he says, beaming.

I find I cannot speak, my smile is so huge.

Sable raises her head as if she, like the rest of the family, cannot believe what she sees. Her ears flick back for a moment but then she simply stands, observing, as we reach the garden gate.

'What's all this about?' says Father, who comes round from the woodshed as Jack dismounts.

'I'll tell you later,' he says, shortening stirrups, talking to the horse at the same time as he speaks to us. 'I want to make sure these two get on together first.'

'Food's on the table,' says Hilda, hurrying down the path. 'Don't take too long.'

Father clasps the bulk of the saddle against him as Jack slips the harness and pats the horse gently on the rump. 'Off you go, boy.'

We all stand and watch as the gelding reclaims his independence moving with assured, even strides up the field. Sable gives a little whicker and comes to meet him.

'Oh, look, they're kissing,' says Hilda.

'They're blowing down each other's nostrils,' says Jack. 'They have met before. See? They remember they're friends.'

With both horses placidly grazing we, too, can go to eat.

'So, what's happened? Nothing bad, I hope.'

We are barely seated and served before Father's anxiety surfaces.

'I haven't lost my job, if that's what you're fearing,' says Jack, exchanging a wry smile with me, seated opposite him.

'Nothing to joke about,' says Father.

Jack apologises and goes on, 'As I knew you were collecting Rose today, I decided to tell them I was required sooner at Harkerswell – the place where I'm going to learn about motor cars.'

'Good Lord!' says Father.

Hilda has clapped a hand over her mouth, her eyes wide with trepidation.

'There's no need to look like that. The Squire'll never know. The whole thing's based on Master Greville chatting to the son of the house while they were both in their cups at his London club. You know how Greville always wants to be up-to-date?'

'Up to no good, more like,' says Hilda, with venom.

Jack goes on, 'Well, according to Greville, this fellow says to him, "Send your man over. Ours can teach him everything. Then, you can present your father with a —"' Jack stalls, 'some French word. He meant shutting the stable door after the horse has bolted.'

'And you won't be missed, this weekend, at Sawdons?' Father is incredulous.

'None of 'em's going anywhere,' says Jack. 'There's no London Season, what with the war and Harry's got the boy to help him while I'm away. He's not complaining, so . . .' He makes a dismissive gesture. Clearly, the senior groom is considered too old to be taught the mysteries of motor transportation.

'Well, I have to say, I don't like the deceitful way you went about it, Jack,' says Father. 'We've always been honest in this family.'

This time Jack does not apologise, but looks out of the window as if he has sufficiently justified his actions. There is a slightly awkward silence. Father does not upbraid him further, except to shake his head.

'I thought Greville had been told to curb his spendthrift ways,' says Hilda, spitting the name out.

Jack snorts by way of answer.

For a while, all that can be heard is the music of busy cutlery.

'This stew's delicious, Hilda,' I say.

The men agree.

'And they let you borrow the horse?' says Father. 'Or did you take him?'

'I bought him.'

'*What*?' The spoon, with which Father has been supping gravy, clatters to his dish.

'The two misses never ride him now, and they're off to Switzerland next year. He's an old boy, but sweet-natured. I offered Greville what the knacker would have given for him, but he wouldn't take it. I said I wanted to buy him fair and square. "Give me a penny, then," he says. So, I did and we shook hands on it. I don't deny Greville's a swine where womankind's concerned,' he acknowledges Hilda, 'but he's always played fair with me.'

Our quietness, as Hilda and I clear the plates for pudding, suggests that we are all reflecting on Jack's career at Sawdons.

. . . We are trotting, just fast enough to be exciting. I am wearing a pair of Jack's out-grown breeches. I am not frightened as I bounce along, my arms round his waist. I can feel his confidence. It is a June morning, sunny after rain, and this path beside the river has a pleasing open aspect across meadowland. I know that I must make the most of Jack because if, like my four oldest brothers, he finds no work here he will have to leave. I shall miss these Saturday jaunts, purely for the pleasure of each other's company.

'What the-?' Jack slows Sable to a steady walk. Ahead of us is a commotion of frantic barking. On the other bank, a young gentleman dressed for country walking pretends to throw, then does, a stick for his terrier into the fast-running river. The dog, plunging in, saves the large stick but cannot find purchase, try as he might, on the slippery bank. He is loathed to give up the stick but it is the very thing which is impeding movement. Sable turns her head. 'Walk on,' says Jack.

'Let it go, you fool,' the man shouts. He does not bend to offer any help.

The struggling dog relinquishes the stick and manages to pull himself up the bank, but he is disconcerted now. Barking anew, he capers from the man and dashes across a small, low footbridge to where we stand, stationary. He starts to snap round Sable's legs, leaping and growling. She steps sideways to avoid him.

'It's all right, old girl,' says Jack, trying to soothe her. 'Walk on,' but the dog is all around her as she skitters.

We had always laughed at Will Sturgess's insistence that Sable was half blood-horse. 'I'd like to know which half,' Father would say. Suddenly, as I feel bone and sinew turn to quicksilver beneath me, the thought that Will might have been right barely has time to register as the mare gathers herself. I am ice.

'All right, whoa, all right,' Jack is saying. I can feel his solid presence holding down all that pent-up energy, but only just. I try not to be petrified, to feed my nerves to Sable. We teeter.

Jack exudes calm. I sense Sable feeling it, the fear leaving her. In a voice which carries, but is still calm, Jack says, 'Would you please call off your dog, sir?'

Perhaps knowing he should have acted sooner, the man accepts Jack's authoritative tone. 'Rufus!' The dog pauses. 'Rufus – come here!'

The terrier trots obediently across the footbridge and accepts his leash.

'Thank you, sir,' calls Jack. 'Walk on,' he says to Sable.

We move forward in a sedate way, as if nothing had interrupted our measured progress . . .

A week later, word came from Phyllis that Jack should seek the post of stable boy at Sawdons. How I felt for him, his spirits plummeting as the young master of the house strode into the tack room, 'Oh, it's you,' then, to his father entering the room, 'I want this lad. He knows how to handle horses.' The anecdote has become a family legend.

'So, what do you plan to do with your horse,' asks Father, 'pretend to be Lord Muck?'

'I thought he could stay here,' says Jack, with a certain bravado. 'It would mean you weren't always reliant on Sable.'

'H'm,' says Father.

Hilda wants to be reminded of the horse's name.

'Iolo, he's a Welsh cob,' says Jack.

'Oh, yes, I remember,' says Hilda. 'Yollo, that's nice.'

'Have you any more surprises for us?' Father asks.

★

169

I am behind Jack on Sable, the dog leaping and snarling. This time, Jack cannot control her and she rears. I fall and hit the ground, wide awake in the darkness, heart pounding. As I subside, I become aware of a sound which sets my nerves on edge again. For a moment, I think it is Father. Hilda has gently warned me that, for nights on end in those first dark months and sometimes still, she has heard his quiet tears. But the muffled sound does not issue from the adjacent room. I strain to hear but now, with a sense almost of horror, I am certain. It emanates from downstairs.

Anxiety washes over me. It comes to me that although I was overjoyed to see Jack, more than a day earlier than expected because he couldn't wait to see me, there was about his stories of daring, the leave of absence and purchase of the horse, almost a recklessness which I haven't remarked in him before.

As yeast rises, so am I roused to my senses by the aroma of nutmeg, cinnamon, candied peel and baking dough. 'A treat and a sadness,' she says, as I taste the starchier texture of the rice-paper cross and hear my younger self saying, 'It should be called Bad Friday.' Then, I wake properly knowing that Mother will not be downstairs. It is Hilda I can hear, talking to Jack. Jack. Such a desperate, shocking sound, I wonder that I managed to sleep after it. What can it have meant? Was it simply due to the renewed confrontation with loss which I, too, have had to face since being back at home?

I wash and dress quickly, going downstairs to a warm, cheery kitchen full of the scents of home and of this special day.

'These buns are delicious,' says Jack. 'You'd better hurry up, Rose, before I eat yours.'

He looks so contented and well. Could I have imagined that episode in the night or, more likely, have dreamt it?

After breakfast, Jack says that he will tend to Iolo and Sable. I am about to offer to join him, but Hilda requests my help in carrying water from the pump at Dr Jepp's which he kindly lets us use. We hear the doctor before we turn the corner at the back of his house.

He is in the act of mowing his lawn, but he breaks off as soon as he sees us.

'Rose! How well you look! Metropolitan life must suit you.' He takes my buckets and fills them, plying me with questions.

Hesitantly, I begin to tell him of my friends at Apple Tree House, my interesting work which really doesn't feel like work in the enjoyable company of Mr Pritchard and, because he encourages me with further questioning, about the evening lectures I attend. By now all four buckets are full. Hilda bends to take hers, offers thanks and leaves.

'No, let her,' says Dr Jepp, quietly, holding my gaze for an intense moment, so that I straighten up again from the intention to take mine. 'This is just the chance I hoped that you would have, Rose. Stay a moment, there's a book . . .' He darts indoors. 'Don't be put off by the title. Read it like a story. No, keep it, keep it. I think you'll find it fascinating.'

With great thanks, I pick up my buckets and say goodbye, the small volume tucked securely in my skirt pocket. I am immensely flattered that the doctor thinks me equal to the subject. It is: 'The Formation of Vegetable Mould Through The Action of Worms with Observations on Their Habits', the final work of Charles Darwin.

'That'll teach the doctor to cut his grass on a Good Friday,' says Hilda of the rain shower just before she called us to eat at half past twelve, but she offers no criticism when Father commandeers Jack to help him afterwards in his beloved vegetable patch, which Jack seems to enjoy. She is indefatigable, rolling twenty-two small marzipan balls, eleven apiece to be apostles on two simnel cakes, one for us and one for Aunt Mary, Uncle Adam and Grandmother. I hard-boil four eggs and, when they have cooled enough in water for me to handle them, I attempt rudimentary decoration with the pastry brush using egg white as a binding agent and cochineal as paint. I'm glad that Mrs Fuller will not see the end result though Phyllis, the most artistic of us, is bound to comment when she sets eyes on them on Sunday.

At dinner, or tea as we call it here, conversation dwindles in the enjoyment of fish pie and spring greens from the garden followed by milk jelly. I think about mentioning Dr Jepp's kindness, but the moment passes. Somehow even Jack, I sense, might interpret it as bragging. When Hilda and I return from clearing up after the meal, Father and Jack are seated by the fire. 'Come and sit next to me, Rose,' says Jack. 'Let's be just like we used to be before I left home.' We all spend the evening reminiscing. It is as if Mother were here amongst us.

This time, there is no mistaking it. I sit bolt upright in bed. What should I do? I imagine pulling my dressing gown around me in the darkness, letting my bare feet find the silent places they know so well on the floorboards, the stairs. Would Jack want me to see him in his distress, though? Would he confide in me? And even if he did wish to do so, how could we talk about his troubles forced to converse in whispers? I will my heavy heart to calmness. I must save my energy for tomorrow. I have to find a time and private place.

I make a point of coming downstairs early, but the bunk bed is already neatly made. I walk out into the garden in the sombre light of a grey day and look, instinctively, towards the field, but it's empty and I remember Father saying that Will Sturgess had a family use today for Sable. Jack must have gone out on Iolo. By the time I step indoors again, Hilda is down and brewing tea. She wants us to eat promptly at midday because we are all to take afternoon tea over at the mill. We spend the morning on domestic tasks. Jack returns in time for the meal.

Interregnum. I know that Latin word with its sense of balance. Today is one such time between. It is a void, like the primordial Chaos. Perhaps I am being fanciful but I always feel, instead of a sense of waiting, a lowering of the spirits as if there might not be an Easter. I hope that it is only this cast of mind which makes me see shadows where there are none. We are all rather quiet over our macaroni cheese. As we walk along the towpath to the mill, each of us must be apprehensive about how we shall find Grandmother and, in light of her condition, how we shall be received by Aunt Mary.

But when we reach Mill Cottage, Grandmother is asleep, head flung back against the antimacassar, mouth sagging open. Father, perhaps distressed at being confronted by his mother in such an indecorous pose, edges back towards the door turning the brim of his hat in his hands. 'I think I'll just . . .' he begins.

'You'll find him in his greenhouse,' says Aunt Mary.

Father looks relieved and sidles out to join Uncle Adam.

'Yes, you go too, Jack,' says my aunt. 'I can see you don't want to be cooped up in here.'

Her tone of voice startles him so that whatever had been his intention, if any, when his gaze lingered on Father's retreating figure, he almost jumps, a look of guilt replacing that of blankness as he obeys. I manage to catch his eye in sympathy before he steps outside.

And now, except with the addition of Hilda, it is just as it was that day in January after Mother's death and before my life in Widdock. Here is the hot, airless little room full of furniture, a bleak sky pressing against the ungenerous windowpanes. I give a response which matches my aunt's enquiry, neither too extensive nor so mean that it might elicit a request for further details. I need not have worried. Having thanked Hilda for the simnel cake, 'but we'll never eat that much, just the three of us, you'd better take half back as you've got all the family coming tomorrow,' she falls into town gossip with my sister, which does not cease even when Grandmother wakes and Aunt starts to make tea.

'Grandmother, it's me, Rose.' In the moment in which the words are uttered, I see what may be a fleeting recognition, gone as quickly as a crack of sunlight in a grey sky. I sit down again, my own thoughts wandering. Was this the day that the three men, Messrs. Pritchard, Philpott and Cooper, planned to go to London to look at models of housing for the poor? Suddenly, I feel a great pang to be with them or sitting in the kitchen at Apple Tree House drinking tea with Mrs Fuller and the others. It is my turn to feel guilty, as if I'm being disloyal to my family. Sensing, perhaps, a need in me to make amends, Aunt Mary sends me to go and fetch the menfolk for their tea and cake.

I step outside into the cool air, feeling the former confinement slipping from my shoulders even as I grasp my shawl around them. A chill breeze lifts the loose wisps of my hair but I enjoy it. I walk round to the back of the cottage, where Uncle has his vegetable beds. I follow the low voices of Father and Uncle beyond the wood-shed and the privy. I find them outside the greenhouse gazing into Uncle's cold frames at his seedlings and discussing the perils of late frosts. I announce that tea is ready. 'Where's Jack?'

Both men have been so engaged with their topic that they barely take in what I tell them, let alone the question I ask.

'Jack?' says Father. 'Oh, he went home.'

'He said he wasn't feeling well,' Uncle adds. 'He did look a bit rough.'

I feel a great surge of emotion: fear, even anger. I try to keep my voice from wobbling. 'Do say I'm sorry to Aunt Mary, please. I'm going home to make sure he's all right.'

I dart off while the men are still recovering their senses. Once I reach the towpath, I break into a run, but have to slow to a fast walk so as not to attract undue attention from the couple of families I pass. Out of sight I run again, but once more have to slow because I find I'm sobbing. What if he is really ill? That would be reason enough for anguished tears. *Dear God, no . . . please, please, no . . .*

I stumble up through the field, the horses lifting their heads for a moment at my uneven progress. I pause by the cottage window, trying to regain my self-control. He is slumped in Father's chair, legs stretched out before him gazing into the fire. I take a deep breath and enter, closing the door softly behind me. He briefly glances my way.

'Thank God it's you, Rose.'

I sit down opposite him. 'Jack,' I swallow, 'please tell me, your illness –'

174

He gives a bark of a laugh. 'I'm not ill. But *you* . . .' Now he is looking at me, 'You've been crying.'

'Of course I have! I thought . . .' But I can't speak. I fish for my handkerchief.

'I'm not sick. Only sick at heart.'

I wipe my eyes and nose. 'I suppose I should be relieved, but –'

'The fact is I'm not interested in ruddy motor cars.'

I have never heard him speak with such vehemence, let alone swear.

'I'm sorry to be so coarse, but you can imagine how I feel. Your life's with books. Mine is with horses. This whole business of going to Harkerswell – it's set me thinking. If they do buy one of these motor cars at Sawdons, they'll have me being their chauffeur and I'll never work with horses again.'

'Well . . . you could go somewhere else, I suppose . . .' Even to me, my voice sounds unconvincing.

'No, no,' he shakes his head. 'What's happening at Sawdons isn't unusual, it's the way the wind is blowing. I'll be out of work unless I can adapt to change. I tell you, Rose, I don't know whether I can face it.'

There is something about the way he speaks which frightens me. I try, desperately, to find some note of cheer. 'You never know, you might find, once you get to Harkerswell and start to learn things, you *are* interested after all.'

He gives the barest of dismissive shrugs. We fall into silence but my mind is in turmoil. Clutching at straws I say, 'If more people do go in for motor cars and you can look after them, perhaps you could do that and get paid for it *and* you could run a stable, too. You could start by hiring out Iolo.'

'Ever the optimist, that's you, Rose,' says Jack. He smiles, but it's a rueful one. 'That's what I miss. You see, I was really looking forward to you coming to work at Sawdons. If you'd been there, you could have cheered me up and I might not have got so low.'

For a moment, I am as confused as Father and Uncle when interrupted. My employment at Sawdons was to have taken place

175

before . . . before Mother died. It feels far away, like something which may or may not have happened during childhood. I am distraught inside. To be part and parcel of Jack's melancholy is appalling. While I am trying, once again, to find words of comfort, I am aware that he has risen and is feeding the fire.

'As a matter of fact,' he says, replacing the hod beside the range, 'there's a job going at Sawdons which would just suit you.'

I feel as if I have turned to stone unable to breathe or speak, but my brother continues. 'One of the Squire's more intellectual friends pointed out to him that he has some rare book in his library which other men might pay good money to see. The Squire, of course, has never bothered to look at any of them, let alone read them, but now he wants to sort them all out in case there are any other hidden treasures. He wants someone dependable with a fair hand to make a list. It will be a long job and he's willing to pay good money.'

'He'll want a man,' I manage to say.

'Not necessarily,' says Jack. 'Anyway, you think about it, Rose,' he adds, hurriedly, as we hear the voices of the others returning.

And I know, from the way he's trying not to sound as if it matters too much to him, that he has already put my name forward.

None of the others notices my quietness. Once Jack has convinced Hilda that he doesn't need dandelion and burdock or, at the other extreme, kaolin and morphine, she agrees to let him retire to bed after we finish the leftover macaroni. This does not inconvenience us. We are all tired from the afternoon's social exertion, so are glad to go up, too. I tell Hilda I'm not equal to thinking up a bedtime story. While she relays the gossip which I missed and then falls asleep, I am deep in contemplation.

Am I my brother's keeper? Much as I tell myself they don't apply to me, those words of Cain's toll in my head. Jack's state of mind has faced me with a terrible dilemma. Can I live with my conscience if I ignore my dearest brother's plea? There is no doubt that cataloguing the library at Sawdons would be an interesting job. That, at least, would be some compensation. Compensation for what? For the second time today, Mr Pritchard appears in my mind, this time standing in the bookshop reading poetry to me. I feel the beat of anger at the unfairness of my situation. But this is selfishness when set against my brother's desperate need. I know what I *should* do. There is a kind of inevitability in it, as if Fate is telling me I aimed too high in trying to escape my destiny. The thought of giving up my life in Widdock makes me sad enough to cry myself to sleep.

Chapter Twelve

Movement below me . . . Furniture . . . Meg and Win in the kitchen? But no, I'm back at home. Yesterday comes to me with a thud. That must be Jack I can hear, up early. First light is showing grey around the edges of the curtains, the dawn chorus finding its voice behind a leading thrush. Last night, I was so exhausted I must have slept right through oblivious to Jack's tears, if any. I am too numb to feel remorse. Dread has settled upon me, but I know I must speak to him. There's that sound again: the drawer under the bunk bed quietly closing. What can Jack have been searching for in the layers of less good linen and garments so patched that even we have relegated them to use as rags? I put my curiosity aside and pull on my dressing gown. I open the bedroom door and close it behind me without a sound.

The soft glow of lamplight welcomes me and the smell of toasted bread. As I come down the stairs, I see the butter dish and honeypot on the table. Jack turns, smiling, with two cups of tea.

'Hello,' he whispers. 'I thought it sounded like you. I hoped it was.'

My smile is as tight as the bands round my heart. I must not show resentment otherwise my decision is in vain.

While I try to compose myself, Jack is speaking. 'Have something to eat, do,' he says, softly, placing a plate before me. He walks to the window and pulls back the curtain. 'It's going to be a lovely day.' Already, the sky is tinged with a growing blue.

I look at the toast cooling on my plate. I cannot eat.

'Look what I found, still there at the bottom of the drawer.' He sounds almost excited.

'Shh . . .' I put a finger to my lips, but recognise what he's picked up from the seat beside him and waves before me. 'Goodness!' I exclaim in a whisper. It's his old breeches which I used to wear, and he's found the shirt, socks and jerkin, all crushed from their long incarceration.

'Come on, Rose, it's a lovely morning for a ride. You can have Iolo. Let's go and get them.' With that he rises. As he opens the door to leave the cottage, morning sunlight streams in together with birdsong.

I sit for a moment not knowing what to feel or do. I had been all ready to make a speech, but he's right. This is a perfect Easter morning which should not be wasted. I manage to eat a piece of toast while I am getting dressed in Jack's old clothes. I finish my tea, quench the lamp and go to join him in the sweet freshness of the field with the dew still thick on the grass.

'Don't worry, he'll come to you,' and Iolo does, allowing me to slip the halter over his head and lead him down the field to the yard. As we walk, I feel his nose against my back, almost lifting me. I look round into his liquid dark eyes with their blue fleck, fathoms deep.

'He won't knock you over. That's his way of patting you.'

And so it seems, a feeling of affability emanating from the horse. Evidence of his good nature continues whilst we are picking out, a job I've never liked but Iolo raises each hoof as I go round him so that I can hold it and remove the small amount of dry, compacted mud caught in the v shape of the frog. I slip the bridle over his head, his great tongue allowing me to accommodate the bit. I do up the throat lash but when Jack places the saddle on his back, I don't have the strength to tighten the girth sufficiently and am all thumbs with the stirrup leathers. Sable is already harnessed, so I ask for help. While my brother works, I take in his demeanour. There is something about him more than the immediate anticipation of a good ride, which seems, dare I think, optimistic? I decide to say nothing regarding the future until we've had our ride.

179

I grab the reins and a handful of Iolo's mane, feeling the rich, sticky texture of its good condition between my fingers. Jack makes a step for me with his hands and I propel myself upwards onto Iolo's back, settling into the saddle. I am feeling slightly wary but enjoying the special scent of horse and the warmth of him, as Jack goes round making adjustments to the girth. I surprise myself by being unafraid to slip each leg from the stirrup iron and back out of the way so that Jack can tighten the leather still further to my lesser height. Now, Jack's in the saddle and we're ambling forward, looking down on Father's rows of leeks and kale.

We take the path up our field, dotted with cowslips, through the gate into Oak Meadow. It is as if all the birds in the world are singing. Jack is ahead of me, but he slows to let me come up and walk beside him. 'You know, I can't explain it but I feel . . . as if something has lifted.'

'You do look better,' I say, guardedly. 'I'm so glad.'

Jack says nothing more for a while and nor do I. There is just the clop of the horses' hooves on the dirt path, the subtle creak of their harness. In the distance, a cockerel crows. I feel a weight slip from me, too. *Let's just see what happens.* Was this my own thought or Mother's voice?

'That's a nice soft stretch,' says Jack, nodding towards a strip of grass running beside a ploughed field sown with clover.

I know what he's thinking. 'Yes, why not?' I say. Indeed, why not?

'I'll lead. Iolo will go like a bolt to start with but he'll soon drop to a trot, so don't worry.'

'I'll try not to.' Already I can feel the horse's muscles melting under me. I trust him.

Jack half-turns. 'Ready?'

'Yes.' I shorten my reins, sit tight and we leap forward. And now we're flying, Iolo and I, as if we would cross three counties, seven seas, as if we would easily catch the fleet mare ahead of us, her dark coat burnished by the sunlight which brightens Jack's hair to gold, his teeth to a flash of white as he smiles over his shoulder, checking to see I'm all right. I'm already smiling. All around us now is glorious open meadow, starred with celandines. In the blue sky above, larks criss-cross and hover, pouring forth their rippling notes above the drumming of hooves. When, at last, Iolo begins to slow from his rollicking canter and Sable follows suit, I feel regret. I wonder if I have just glimpsed a corner of heaven.

Topside of beef and potatoes, roasting while we were in church and little Yorkshire puddings, all served with purple sprouting broccoli fresh from the garden, and rich gravy. It is a tribute to Hilda's culinary skills that everyone's consequent sense of well-being has smoothed over the sharp words spoken during the meal, when Hubert asked what time the others were expected.

'I shall go and fetch them,' Jack says. 'Dot and Phyllis wouldn't have time to come otherwise.'

Father gives him a penetrating look. 'You can't. You're supposed to be at Harkerswell, aren't you?'

'I've arranged to meet them down the lane a bit from the Sawdons gates — the Chilsbury Farm turn-off, you might not know it.'

'I course I know it,' Father says, with anger in his voice, 'but what if someone from Sawdons sees you?'

Jack looks evasive. 'Well, they won't, will they? Who's going to be wandering —'

'You don't know that,' Father interrupts. 'You see,' he points his knife at Jack, 'this is where deception leads you. The next thing will be outright lying.'

'I agree,' says Joe.

'I don't understand your reasoning. You could have come yesterday all above board,' says Hubert.

My cheeks are flaming. Jack's now staring fixedly at his plate. I shoot Hilda a beseeching glance which she interprets and, thank goodness, says nothing about my role in this.

'I'm sorry, Father,' Jack says in a small voice.

'So am I, Jack,' says Father, 'so am I.'

There is a horrible pause.

Father sighs. 'You get the mare harnessed, Jack, and *I* will go to the Chilsbury turn-off and meet them. I'm doing it to keep your reputation. This is the one and only time, though, is that clear?'

'Yes, Father,' says Jack. 'Thank you, Father.'

'Let that be an end of the matter, then,' says Father before either Joe or Hubert can open their mouths, and deliberately, 'very nice crumble, Hilda.'

'Thank you, Father,' says Hilda who, with me, has cleared the plates and served the pudding. 'Your rhubarb's extra tasty this year, isn't it?'

She looks around at us. We all nod and murmur, with which enthusiastic praise Father seems mollified and Jack to have come out of his humiliation.

All is ready for our guests with Mother's best tea set, which I especially love because its graceful pattern of summer flowers features a soft, deep-pink rose. Hilda skims butter across the surface of a loaf held in the crook of her arm as Mother would, then cuts each slice off so finely that it has the texture of a baby's christening shawl. I arrange her handiwork on the rectangular bread-and-butter plate. On another are her remarkable scones, their tops as shiny brown as new boots. There is homemade blackberry jam. In pride of place is the grand simnel cake.

Joe and Hubert are upstairs resting on our beds. Their bicycling exertion having already taken its toll, which required our prodding during the sermon, Hilda's home cooking has finished them. Jack, too, is dozing, but outside. Lightly, I slide onto the bench beside him. I study his face for any signs of a return to melancholia but he looks, as far as I can tell, at peace with himself. The sun has moved round to the other side of the cottage but, with no breeze, it is comfortably warm here still. I shut my eyes, feel my muscles relaxing . . . The bench gives slightly . . . Hilda. I settle between my brother and my sister.

They're here. I wake with complete ease as if bidden and ready, having slept my fill. I can hear the cart coming up the lane, so I run out of the garden and am ready to hold Sable's head as Father helps Dot down and then Phyllis while Ralph, who never wears Sunday best but always his shabby, comfortable gardener's clothes, climbs out of the inside of the cart.

As on the evening when Jack came, I am grinning from ear to ear at the sight of my dearest sister wearing a sprigged blouse and a straw hat from which her unruly fair hair is trying to escape in just the way that I have always loved and she has always found exasperating. Her strong face is shaded by the brim, but there's a glitter to her eyes as blue as the forget-me-nots she has used to trim it. She is carrying her jacket and a small bag, but she clutches at me and I hug her back. For a moment, I think I'm going to cry. I hear Phyllis take a loud, sniffing breath, then Hilda is marshalling us into the cottage to have our tea before it's too late and everyone has to go again.

It turns out that Phyllis has, in her bag, a chocolate egg. 'They made themselves ill, the misses, before they even went down to breakfast. I was in Miss Caroline's room, opening the window because she felt sick and wanted fresh air. "You may have this and keep it,"' Phyllis adopts a spoilt, flouncing voice, '"I don't want to see another chocolate egg as long as I live!"'

Everyone laughs whether or not they have ever worked at Sawdons. Ralph takes it on himself to break the egg into nine small pieces, no easy task.

'We won't need these, then.' I remove the plate bearing my decorative disasters, which Hilda has tried to ameliorate by embedding them in straw, as if in a nest.

'Oh dear, did the hen have an accident?' says Phyllis of my garish red streaks and dashes. We're off into giggles which do not subside when we have to share Mother's rocker, the two of us being the slightest in the room. There are not enough chairs for everyone. It is clear that, whilst I am still full from the Sunday roast and pudding, the party from Sawdons are ravenous. They had their dinner at midday, before serving the family upstairs with theirs. We four happily hold back on the bread and butter, which disappears straightaway together with my hard-boiled eggs, thank goodness. We are at the scone and cake stage when Joe clears his throat.

'I have an announcement to make.' We all give him our attention. 'I am engaged to be married to Miss Catherine Tyler of Belle Vue House, Widdock.'

Jack and Ralph offer immediate, sincere congratulations. Hubert, of course, already knows the news and so, it is clear, does Father, but both echo what has been said, as do we sisters.

'How did you meet her? What's she like?' asks Hilda.

'I became acquainted with the family through church,' says Joe. 'Her father is a well-respected businessman and Town Councillor. Catherine is the most beautiful young lady in Widdock, but completely natural and modest.'

I can't resist looking from the corner of my eye. Nor can Phyllis. I feel and hear her shaky breath as she, like me, tries not to giggle. The chair shifts slightly on its rockers.

'Goodness,' says Hilda. 'I hope she's nice with it.'

'Indeed,' says Joe. 'She is altogether charming and capable.'

This somehow makes it worse.

'Crumb . . . stuck in my throat,' croaks Phyllis, which may be true.

Hilda leaps up, glad to fetch water since I can't, Phyllis and I being pinioned in the chair by its arms and our hips.

Fortunately, Joe has launched into an account of his promotion, which will take place when the station on the other side of Widdock expands, opening a line to London. This gives him the means to support a wife and household. We all congratulate him once again.

'I'm meeting Mr Tyler tomorrow after I've dropped you,' says Father. 'His idea. Decent of him, I thought.'

'May I make a suggestion, Father,' says Joe. 'If he proposes eating, ask for the dish of the day. That'll save any . . . embarrassment.'

'We're meeting in the King's Head not The Railway Hotel,' says Father. 'They'll *tell* me what they've got.'

'I'm going to do bread and cheese for the three of you,' Hilda pipes up, 'so you can truthfully say you've eaten earlier.'

'I'll truthfully say what I feel like saying,' says Father, 'though I thank you for the offer, Hilda, and I might be glad of it if I get peckish on the journey. I'm not stupid, you know, Joe. I can make out "pie",' he describes the sweep of the p, the dotted i, the curl of the e. 'There's always a pork pie to be had. I can make out "pork", too, and "fish".' He does both, fairly accurately.

'I doubt there'll be any fish,' says Hubert. 'They won't have put to sea this weekend.'

'I think Father has the measure of the situation,' says Phyllis.

'Thank you, Phyllis,' says Father, his disgruntled look subsiding.

Joe takes out his watch and consults it. 'Well . . .'

'As a matter of fact, I have an announcement,' says Dot. 'I was waiting till we'd all finished eating, but Joe – well, never mind.'

'What is it, then, because we must –' Joe starts.

'I'm getting married, too, and I have the date,' says Dot.

'Really?'

'They've let you?'

'Oh congratulations!'

We three sisters all speak at once. Joe looks slightly put out, but recovers himself to offer his best wishes with the other men.

'They've told us we may have Saturday afternoon, the fourth of August,' says Dot. 'Upstairs are at home and not entertaining because they're going to Scotland for the twelfth. We'll get married in the Chapel and they've said we may have the Wedding Breakfast downstairs. Immediate family and the staff, of course, but as George only has his sister, Clara, you are all invited with pleasure.'

'Bank Holiday weekend, hmmn . . . difficult,' says Hubert.

In my mind, I'm echoing Hubert's reservation. To be available on a Saturday afternoon at Sawdons would mean leaving Mr Pritchard alone on our busiest day. I feel I cannot ask the favour, though I say nothing now to spoil Dot's arrangements. Suddenly, I have a strange feeling like an ache. How enjoyable it would have been to have Mr Pritchard with us on the day. After all, it was his place of employment for some years. Perhaps he might not want to be reminded.

I realise Joe and Hubert are saying their goodbyes. We wave them

185

off, then we four sisters take the dishes to the scullery. No sooner are we out of earshot of the men, than Hilda turns to Dot.

'Well . . . They've always been dead set against marriage among the servants. What made them change their minds?'

'They think the Head Gardener should be married, especially a man of George's age. It's not like being a servant. It's a position that commands respect,' says Dot, with pride.

'Yes, I realise that, but what are you going to do if, you know,' she drops her voice, 'something happens?'

'Clara keeps house for him and she will stay, of course. She's nowhere else to go. So, if anything does come along, she's said she'll help.'

'And you don't mind sharing the house with her?'

'I shouldn't think so, it's bigger than this one! And anyway, the arrangement means I can marry George. Besides, she's a very nice woman. It's not her fault she hasn't found a husband. I know what it's like to think you never will.' Dot involuntarily touches the cheek which her dark birthmark stains.

Phyllis and I leave Dot and Hilda discussing weddings and walk outside again, where Father is taking Ralph round the garden for the benefit of his professional advice. Jack is listening, too. It is still warm, so we sit on the bench again and, in answer to her eager questioning, I tell Phyllis all about Widdock imitating the schoolmasterly tones of Mr Davidson, the combative manner of Mr Vance and a host of other customers whose idiosyncrasies I find I can remember. I tell her about our poetry reading sessions and discussions.

'You lucky thing. Tell Leonard I miss his intelligent conversation, won't you?' says Phyllis.

Leonard. Of course, she knew him by his first name. I say I will.

'He was the only person I felt was fighting on the same side as me. Still, never mind. I'm glad for him and for you. I mean it.'

'Would it have made a difference if I'd come to Sawdons?' I have to say it.

'Listen, Rose,' Phyllis turns to me, 'I said at the beginning: you did the right thing. And I'm used to that place, I'll survive. As a matter of fact, I'm planning a diversion for myself, but,' she lowers her voice, 'it involves Father.'

'How?' We both look at him, a few feet away now in front of his favourite rose bush, discussing pruning methods with Ralph. Jack has gone for Iolo.

'I've been doing a little woodwork using Ralph's tools, Grandfather's tools that were.'

'Oh, Phyl, that's wonderful!'

'Shh . . .Don't get too excited. I have hardly any time, of course, but Sunday afternoons like this, a couple of hours when Upstairs leave us all alone, I'm allowed to work in the gardeners' bothy, where Ralph goes to do his carpentry for the garden and has a lathe. I've only managed it once, so far. I did a bit of mitring for him on an ornamental plant frame, just to get my hand back in. Heaven knows, I need the practice, but I want to make my own small things. The problem is the wood. I can't steal from the estate even though they wouldn't miss it. I was going to pluck up courage and ask Father if he'd let me have some, from time to time. I'd pay for it, but Jack's upset him and Joe makes him cross, I could ruin my chances. What do you think, Rose?'

There is a history here. When we were not playing our games of make-believe Phyllis and I, aged about eight years old and six, would sometimes go down to Father's workshop. Sitting quietly in a corner, she would watch Father as he worked. I would sit beside her for companionship, reading a storybook. Sometimes Ralph, the most able with his hands of all my brothers, would be there using the small set of tools made in Great-Grandfather's time, passed to each successive son to introduce the growing boy to his craft. When Ralph wasn't there, Phyllis would pick up the chisel and the mallet and work at a piece of wood. How the image has stayed with me of the little bird she fashioned. I remember Father's pride in her, mingled with regret for what did not come to pass.

His entire working life has been spent in a time of great hardship for country folk. Fear for his own livelihood formed part of the fabric of our childhood. When his four eldest sons left Markly, he could hardly blame them. But I think he always hoped that Ralph would, after all, stay and be the one who would ensure the name of Alleyn stood beside that of Will Sturgess and his son. In a way, Phyllis's aptitude and interest only intensified his lingering disappointment when it was clear this would not happen. When she asked to join him as apprentice, he refused outright. 'Carpentry is not a job for womenfolk.'

Phyllis has long ago accepted that decision, but the tension between them has become a subtle part of how they behave with one another.

All of this is there in her dilemma about asking Father for some wood.

'When will you next be this way?' I ask.

'Who knows?' For the moment, she looks downcast.

'I think I'd approach him, then.'

She nods and straightens up, raising her voice. 'Father? May I speak to you about something?'

'In a moment, Phyllis.' Father turns to Ralph. 'Go and see if Jack is ready to bring the cart round, will you? We should be getting on.'

When Ralph is out of earshot, Father says, 'I caught the gist of what you were saying, Phyllis.'

I reach for Phyllis's hand and squeeze it.

'You youngsters seem to have a very different attitude to your employment from what we had, I must say, but perhaps that's how things are going to be now we're in the twentieth century.' He pauses. Neither of us dares to speak. 'However, Phyllis, if it will make you happy –'

Phyllis's head jerks up.

'I will look out some wood for you. I'll tell Jack to collect it when he comes back from his trip. You don't have to pay me, Phyllis. I'm glad you did the honest thing and asked me. I'll also give you Great-Grandfather's tools. Then, you won't be bothering Ralph for his. Besides, you should have your own, if you're going to do it properly.'

We're all smiling now, even though the next thing we have to do is say goodbye.

Another fine day. I pack my two summer dresses and a cotton blouse to go with the one already hanging in the wardrobe at Apple Tree House. Father is anxious to start straightaway so we eat an early breakfast, the three of us sitting on the bench in the sunshine, while Hilda plies us with more tea and toast.

I scan Jack's face, but it gives nothing away as to his internal state. He has that slight air of bravado with which he came, but that might be simple nervousness about what lies ahead rather than a re-emergent sickness of heart, as he aptly called it. I truly hope so.

Father has placed sacking on the cart seat. He is anxious not to spoil his best clothes with the gritty dust from the horses' coats and their moulting hair, 'especially his,' he nods at Iolo on whom Jack is mounted, like an outrider.

Hilda and I clasp hands, warmly. Father helps me up onto the seat and springs up himself. Then, we're off, Hilda becoming a smaller and smaller figure, waving till the budding trees in the lane mask her from view. I remember Gertrude's words to Hamlet, though in an entirely different context: 'You have cleft my heart in twain'. Half my heart is here at our cottage but, yes, the other half is seeking its resting place at Apple Tree House and looking forward, if a heart can do so, to meeting all my friends again and my employer. I say his name to myself as Phyllis spoke it: Leonard. I can't wait to see him again tomorrow and find out how he has spent the five days of our separation.

Just before we get to Widdock, I take the reins from Father while he eats his bread and cheese. In no time, we're saying goodbye to him and, as it's such a truly lovely day, we take the path down on to the water meadows. While Iolo crops, Jack and I eat our picnic lunch as other families are doing under the big white clouds and strong blue sky. Then, it's time for him to go, too. We come up on the path into Holywell End, Jack leading Iolo. I grip his free hand. 'I'll be thinking of you. Write, if you can. Let me know how you are.'

'I'll be all right,' he says, with a toss of the head which doesn't quite convince me.

He swings up into the saddle and urges Iolo forward across the bridge with the ubiquitous men enjoying the sunshine. I follow, as he turns into the High Street. I wave as he waves, after which he has to concentrate on the way forward in the town's traffic. I walk on up New Road, imagining him leaving Widdock on the road north towards Cambridge. Somewhere, there lies the manor house called Harkerswell.

When I enter the hall at Apple Tree House, with its faint scent of beeswax polish and faded lavender, and I see afresh the William Morris wallpaper and Mrs Fuller's tender portrait of her husband, I know that this, too, is home. I feel this warmth again as I close my eyes, head upon pillow, surrounded by all my dear friends.

I sense the others rising even earlier, remember their summer time-table has begun. I drift back to sleep. When I do wake and get up, Lettie still oblivious, I see that it's another lovely day. I decide to wear my ivory cotton blouse with the sailor collar.

Lettie, too, when she comes down to the kitchen, is wearing a white lawn blouse with a lace trim. She has been chosen to be one of the May Queen's two attendants. The Queen is from one of the oldest families in town. For diplomatic reasons, I imagine, this is neither Ibbot nor Hobbs, the two from whom Bella, the eloping cook, and her true love came.

We shed coats for jackets, put on straw hats and lace gloves.

'Ne'er cast a clout till May be out,' reproves Mrs Munns, as we guessed she would. We smile and step from the house into an unseasonably warm April day.

As I approach the shop, I notice butterflies in my stomach. This has been such a long break, it's like starting work all over again.

Mr Pritchard has changed the window display. I feel a pang that I was not there to enjoy helping him. He was right to do so, though. In tune with the improving weather, he has placed the ever-popular Reverend Gilbert White's *The Natural History and Antiquities of Selborne* in the centre, flanked by some local authors' works on the fauna and flora of this county. He has also, kindly, fanned out copies of the little leaflet after which the old gentleman who wrote it, many years ago, comes in every week to enquire if any have been sold.

I see Mr Pritchard in the shop. He opens the door. 'Rose! It's good to have you back. What's that you're reading?'

Today, I have no shopping save for the two meat pies which I have presumed to buy from the baker's for Mr Pritchard and me to have for luncheon. This is because, as we all discussed last night at dinner, Lettie and I will now be the last ones to arrive home in the evening. Mrs Fuller, therefore, has said that she will buy what's needed for the meal. Meg and Winnie, helped by Jenny and Priscilla, if she can be believed, will start to prepare it. If they are all hungry, which is likely, they can eat first, leaving some for Lettie and me. 'It can be a high tea,' says Mrs Fuller. 'That's all Bella ever did the whole year round, Rose. We've been spoilt by you.' They others all agree. They are provided with a midday dinner at their factory canteens, but they're always starving in the winter by the time that they get home. We decide on ham, greens and potatoes. Therefore, I have no bag but the paper one with pies and, in my other hand, Mr Darwin's observations on the habits of worms.

'Your thirst for knowledge is admirable,' says Mr Pritchard.

I feel I have to own that it was Dr Jepp who pointed me in this direction.

'That doesn't matter,' says Mr Pritchard. 'We all need teachers. And how appropriate to this week's theme.' He strides over to the shelves, puts on his spectacles and reaches for another copy of *The Natural History and Antiquities of Selborne*, which he consults enthusiastically. 'There, there!' He points to a paragraph from which he reads an extract aloud: ' "Worms seem to be the great promoters of vegetation, which would proceed but lamely without them." You see, White anticipates Darwin and probably informed his study of the subject. We should have a copy of the Darwin in the window, too.' I go to fetch one. 'Thank you. What would I do without you?'

I blush to the roots of my hair. To cover my embarrassment, I go through to the sitting room with the pies and to remove my outdoor clothes.

When I return, Mr Pritchard is wielding the feather duster round the shelves. 'I'm afraid I rather let things slip.'

I take it from him, while he gets ready to open shop.

'I'll tell you later,' he says, in answer to my question about the weekend. Three men have stopped outside our window. 'I changed the display yesterday morning. Then I thought I'd open for a couple of hours and see what happened. It was worth it, as you might guess.' The men step inside. 'Good morning, gentlemen. What a lovely day for a stroll in the countryside!'

'You can keep your sales talk, Pritchard,' says Mr Vance. It being school holidays, he is accompanied by the other two.

'A thoroughly worthwhile proposition, though,' says Mr Davidson in his booming, schoolmasterly voice.

'As if he ever goes for a walk in the country,' says Mr Nash, with twinkling good humour.

Whilst Mr Pritchard defends himself with equal humour, I think of my impersonations for Phyllis. I wonder what she's doing at this moment and how she is. And Jack.

We are busy all morning. When it comes to one o'clock, Mr Pritchard announces that it's far too fine a day to stay indoors, and goes out for a walk. I eat my pie, then borrow one of the old gentleman's ancient leaflets from the pile remaining under the counter. I spend an absorbing half an hour outdoors and see, as if for the first time, a willow warbler on an alder stump along the towpath. On the water meadows, I recognise marsh marigolds and yellow flags. The shiny turquoise and orange of a kingfisher is gone in a flash.

When I tell him later, 'Ah,' says Mr Pritchard, looking knowing.

Of course, his familiarity with the local fauna and flora is likely to be greater than mine. Even so, I feel slightly dispirited by his mere acknowledgement of my keen observations. Just for a moment, it is as if he has stepped back from his usual openness, almost as if he is appraising me.

I go through to the shop to open up, wondering whether I'm to blame. All morning, although kept active and engaged with customers, I have found my gaze straying to my employer. Having spent these past days in the company of blond Jack whose eyes are the colour of sun-warmed stone, to be once more in the presence of Mr Pritchard could not be a more startling contrast, with his black hair and eyes of the deepest cornflower blue. I become aware that the subject of my musings is giving me a quizzical look. I move quickly to the shelves to tidy them.

'I surmise we both have led a very full weekend,' he says.

'Well, yes,' I pause. Is this an invitation to discourse in detail? What is of great significance to me, the fundamentals of my family life will, almost certainly, sound tedious and irrelevant when related. More to the point, a large part of what took place was personal and private even from Mr Pritchard though, curiously, I find I should have loved to share it and ask for his advice. 'You've yet to tell me how you spent your time,' I say. 'Perhaps you could do that in place of my reading poetry, as I've had no chance –'

'Rose, Rose,' he cuts across me, gently, 'this is a Tuesday, not a Monday.'

I clap my hand to my mouth. 'What a fool! I knew it was, of course, and yet it feels so like a Monday. I'm sorry, Mr Pritchard.' I feel intense disappointment.

He laughs. 'There's no need to apologise. It's an odd week and you're not quite yourself, I expect. On reflection, I think I'll wait till Cooper's photographs are available before I launch into my account. In fact, I could read the first draft of my report to you while you look at them. I wrote it straightaway when I got back. It'll make a lot more sense if you can see the buildings under discussion. I'm hoping family commitments won't prevent him from working in his dark room this weekend. Anyway, I'll let you know.'

'Please do. I'd really like that.'

'Would you? Good, good,' he says.

But there's that look again.

Chapter Thirteen

'I have some very exciting news,' I say, turning from hanging up my coat and hat, Mr Pritchard having just greeted me with the customary enquiry when we first meet in the morning.

'Oh, what's that?'

He pauses with his hand on the doorknob, before going through to the shop, and turns back to face me looking – what exactly? Suspicious would be too strong a word. Wary, perhaps, a look which, though not identical, is in accord with others occasionally directed my way over the past four days since my return to work.

'Come on, I'm curious.' He looks tense.

I try to keep my composure. 'It's about Mrs Fuller.'

'Really?'

Is it my imagination or does he appear more relaxed?

'You may know she'd entered a competition to paint the mural in the Training College hall.'

'I didn't.'

'No, nor did we. She must have kept it completely to herself, then.'

'In case of disappointment? Go on.' He's beginning to smile.

'Well, I think you've guessed it. She's had a letter from the College Governors. She's won!'

Mr Pritchard claps his hands. 'Oh! Well done to her! Do give her my congratulations.' He really does look delighted.

'Good Lord, Jack, you're making a habit of surprising me.'

Thank goodness the opening flurry of customers is over. Mr

Pritchard is dealing with the last. Here is Jack shy, in these surroundings which must to him seem intimidating. But he is smiling from ear to ear. I find I am smiling back.

'I had to call by and tell you,' he says, in a respectfully lowered voice, 'I actually enjoyed myself at Harkerswell. He's a decent chap, Styles, and a good teacher. I understood everything. So, it was much more interesting than I ever thought it could be.'

'That's very good,' I say, aware that Mr Pritchard and his customer have concluded their transaction.

'But I just wanted you to know – your idea – the motor repair workshop and the stables, we're going to do it.'

'Well, well,' I say.

'Not straight away, of course, we'll have to save, but we're going to go in for it together. Styles reckons these motor cars always need attention, so we'll never be out of work. If they *don't* catch on as much as seems likely, we'll just be full-time job-masters with a couple of horses for hire.'

'So, you feel better – about everything, I mean?' I realise I'm holding my breath.

Mr Pritchard's customer bids him good day and leaves the shop.

'Yes, yes, you can stop fretting about me, dearest Rose.'

I nearly faint with relief.

'Do you need any assistance, Miss Alleyn?'

I turn to face my employer, who is frowning.

'Mr Pritchard, you remember Jack, don't you? My brother,' I add, when he still looks blank.

Mr Pritchard hits his forehead with his fist, smiling in an embarrassed way. 'I do *now*. How stupid of me,' he adds in an undertone, which seems excessive self-admonishment.

'I can't believe it was only Monday, Rose, when we had our picnic by the river,' Jack is saying. 'So much seems to have happened since then.'

'I think I saw the two of you,' says Mr Pritchard, slowly. 'I thought I recognised Rose, but I didn't . . . Well, it doesn't matter now. Will you stay and take tea, Jack? Rose could have an early break.'

But Jack declines saying he must, in fairness, get back to Sawdons. We all step outside, where Iolo is waiting, and both wave my brother off.

'Fancy my not remembering Jack,' says Mr Pritchard, with a self-deprecating smile. 'Not that I came across him much at That Place. Even so.'

It occurs to me that whilst I had given no thought to the fact that Jack and I were eating our bread and cheese together unchaperoned, having arrived in Widdock with Father who is not a complete stranger here, could it be that Mr Pritchard glimpsed us later, after Father left, and mistook Jack for some other young man? It might explain his quizzical manner over the past four days. Just what sort of a girl does he think I am? I feel a little disappointed. I always thought he didn't care about convention but when it comes to it, as with my shopping for him to save his blushes, he's just the same as other men. *But that's not true, is it? He isn't like most other men.* I suppose I should be touched that he cares so much about my reputation. He certainly seemed relieved when he remembered Jack.

The rest of the day, he seems in a particularly good humour. I put this down to the weather, which appears to be set fair, and to the corresponding sales of books concerned with nature and activities outdoors. He also has a visit, just before we close, from Mr Cooper, inviting him to Sunday luncheon together with Mr and Mrs Philpott. The London photographs are ready for inspection.

' "Good evening, Ladies and Gentleman". Does that sound too much as if I'm addressing a hall full of people rather than a group not much bigger than this?' asks Mr Pritchard.

We are seated round the table in the Coopers' lovely dining room, which is just the right size to be intimate without being poky, the walls clad in a warm crimson stripe appropriate to the age of the house, built during the Regency.

'Are there any? Ladies, I mean,' asks Mrs Fuller.

'There are two,' says Mr Pritchard.

'*You* know,' says Mrs Cooper, 'Whatsername . . . Scott-Nichols,

Celia Scott-Nichols and dear old Sally Hewlish, always falls asleep during our concerts, bless her.'

'She falls asleep during council meetings,' says Mr Pritchard. 'I can't blame her, sometimes.'

'You could say, "Good evening, fellow councillors,"' offers Mr Cooper.

'But he isn't, is he?' says his wife. 'He's co-opted. And he can't say, "Good evening, fellow members, it's not a club."'

'What are you going on to say, Pritchard?' asks Mr Philpott who, perhaps unsurprisingly, has come to the meeting without his reputedly pretty but non-intellectual wife.

'"I consider it a great privilege to have been asked by you to compile this report." Just to remind them that they did, in case they start getting defensive,' says Mr Pritchard.

'What about "Good evening, Ladies and Gentlemen of the Parish Council,"?' suggests Mr Cooper.

'Seconded,' says Mr Philpott, quickly, in a slightly exasperated voice.

We all nod and raise our hands. There are murmurs of 'carried'.

Mr Pritchard starts again with the approved introduction. 'I shall talk about three different models of housing, two of which have been put into practice. I refer to Bourneville, Birmingham, developed by George Cadbury for his factory workers; and The Boundary Street Estate, Tower Hamlets, built by the London County Council to house the urban poor. The third model is that of Ebenezer Howard, as proposed in his treatise of 1898: "Tomorrow; a Peaceful Path to Social Reform", namely, the Garden City. I shall discuss the first two together with photographs by courtesy of Mr Charles Cooper –'

'Better not mention me,' says Mr Cooper. 'They might think I've got some kind of vested interest.' He runs an architectural practice with his son who shares the house, and whose small children we occasionally hear thudding about overhead or crossing the landing, their chattering shushed by a nursemaid as they go about their bedtime routine.

'Go on, Pritchard,' says Mr Philpott, '". . . the first two together with photographs . . ."'

'And, with the kind permission of Mr Howard, a plan of how the last might be executed. I shall briefly consider the advantages and disadvantages of each. I shall go on to report the essence of conversations I have had with representative families, suffering deprivation, about their needs and aspirations. I shall attempt to put forward suggestions based on all the above and taking into account the possible availability of land. I appreciate, however, that council members will be better equipped than I am to address this last and, no doubt, many other aspects of my topic.'

All parties in the room are nodding, myself included. Mr Pritchard cuts an impressive figure even before he reaches the substance of his report.

As he goes on speaking, he passes round Mr Cooper's photographs of Bourneville, which Leonard has not visited himself. Both men, I have already gathered, regard the village as an exemplary model. I see attractive cottages with generous gardens, set in wide and wooded streets. An interior shows a kitchen with a sunken bath, which can be covered over when not in use. Young women workers, with their bicycles, stand smiling outside a large cycle shed made of what seems to be quite beautiful brickwork. Even the shops around the green have pleasant windows and look like cottages with half-timbering. All has an open, airy feeling.

The buildings of the Boundary Street Estate are altogether sterner in appearance. They rise five storeys in order to accommodate as many as possible of the East End's considerable population. Even so, they benefit from generous casements divided into squares not unlike the pattern of those in this very house. This fenestration, as Mr Pritchard calls it, is designed to let in light and air. Detail, such as the chequered tiling over a wide entrance porch, is pleasing to the eye. There is a large central garden with a bandstand and many trees.

Mr Howard's plans, I learn, draw inspiration from the work of John Ruskin and William Morris. I am getting the impression that, with all these schemes, there is an emphasis on good design and truth to material, as in the Arts and Crafts tradition, and also on healthy outdoor exercise such as that to be derived from cycling and digging vegetables on one's own allotment. This last is what the Burnses, Wrights and Kembles, our neighbours in the yard behind the shop would, it turns out, like to do if ever they were given the opportunity of being re-housed with a garden. Mr Pritchard makes an estimation of the numbers of families squeezed into the insanitary courts and yards of Widdock and also makes suggestions, based on his own observations, about sites which might be suitable for housing. His conclusion is that even on the smallest scale principles of good design should be observed, just as they are at Bourneville. This should apply both to the layout of the site and the detailed plans for dwellings. The Parish Council might care to consider whether larger schemes should be envisaged to cater, not just for the town's poor, but for its growing population of those who take the train to and from work in London. As the twentieth century progresses, this is hardly likely to decrease. In light of this, he says that he has noticed, amongst reformers such as Henrietta Barnett, a desire to mix the classes, this being beneficial to a more balanced and humane society. He thanks us, as if we were the Parish Council, and asks the Chair's permission to throw the meeting open to discussion.

The applause would be more than simply hearty, but Mrs Cooper gestures to us to keep it within bounds in case the children have now dropped off to sleep.

'The Parish Council probably knows all this already,' says Mr Pritchard, modestly.

'Assume nothing,' says Mr Philpott. 'And they won't have had it put as cogently.'

'I don't expect they'll wear the London model, Boundary Street,' says Mr Cooper. 'Those blocks are a bit too . . . austere.'

'But don't you think the buildings look a little like our maltings?' says Leonard.

'Whatever the buildings look like, it's clear that some sort of area for growing plants must be provided,' I dare to say and everyone agrees, Mr Pritchard smiling encouragement at my contribution.

199

'I suppose it depends if anyone would mind living in a structure that looked like a place of work,' says Mrs Fuller.

'Anywhere is better than where they are, Florence,' says Mrs Cooper. 'One hopes that good, practical design would encourage a sense of pride in the place.'

'Octavia Hill told me she employed lady inspectors in her housing schemes,' says Mr Pritchard.

'I've heard this,' says Mr Cooper. ' "Patience, gentleness and hope", the feminine perspective.'

'Yes, and attention to detail,' says Mr Pritchard. 'They also render help to tenants in finding work.'

'What was she like? Octavia Hill,' asks Mrs Fuller. 'She sounds very sympathetic.'

'Admirable but stern,' says Mr Pritchard.

And so the talk goes on as, beyond the graceful windows, the blue sky gradually darkens.

I love this time of year, with its lengthening evening light. As I walk home, I think about the week just passed, so different from the previous one in which, until that Saturday of Jack's visit, Mr Pritchard had seemed uncharacteristically out of sorts. Perhaps it was just overwork and worry, centred on production of his report. This week, with its continuing fine weather, has been altogether different. I dwell upon our Monday poetry reading, a celebration of the great William Shakespeare in honour of his birthday that very day, April the twenty-third, or so it's thought. As I walk up New Road, I think again of Mr Pritchard delivering Jaques's speech from *As You Like It*: 'All the world's a stage/ And all the men and women merely players', which I knew from Mother's *Complete Works*, but had forgotten in its detail. 'Don't look so crestfallen, Rose,' said Mr Pritchard. 'Yes, the speech gives a bleak picture of human life, but as soon as it finishes young Orlando enters and puts Jaques's cynicism into perspective by his devotion to his old servant Adam.' I had read first, choosing Portia's well-known speech taken from *The Merchant of Venice*: 'The quality of mercy is not strained; /It droppeth as the gentle rain from Heaven'. 'Excellent,' said Mr Pritchard. As I explained, it is a favourite of mine and particularly of Phyllis, who loved to read it for the appreciation of Mother and me.

Then, on Wednesday, there was Mr Pritchard's impressive rehearsal of his report. Of course, none of us could predict how it will be received next Wednesday at the Parish Council meeting, but we all agreed that Mr Pritchard had made a fine job of his task. Yes, his mood this week, thank goodness, has been transformed, or rather returned to his usual energetic good humour. Business has been brisk today, Saturday, all of which helps the general atmosphere.

Quickly accustomed to their summer timetable, the four factory girls are hungry early and have already eaten their smoked mackerel and bread and butter. This is a pity, since I have bought a watercress, from Kate across the road, to complement the oily fish with its fiery zest.

'All the more for us,' says Lettie, who is in just before me.

We are alone except for Morris and Ruskin, hopeful of the fish skins. A note from Mrs Fuller says she will be working in her studio till the light fails, would we leave some food for her? The house has the quiet of emptiness, the others also, probably, taking advantage of the fine evening before night draws in.

Lettie asks how my day has been, and I tell her all about its place in this week, contrasting it with the last but, unusually for one who loves so much to talk of what A might have said to B but didn't and C's interpretation of the exchange or lack of it, she seems barely to be listening.

'Something's wrong, isn't it?' I say, gently. 'Do you want to tell me?'

Lettie looks instinctively at the door, even though we have heard no noise. 'Not here. Let's have some of your custard tart and then go out.'

Assuming that the others are likely to be walking a circuit of the town, by the river and in the park, we take the towpath the other way, east, towards the flour mill.

'If we were to keep on following the river, we would eventually come to my home town,' I say, but Lettie isn't open to such light-hearted observations.

She looks over her shoulder. 'I keep expecting her to pop up,' she says. 'Not that I'm afraid of her, if she does,' she snarls, so fiercely that a mallard drake starts up from the water and flies off, squawking.

One of the pleasures of most factory girls, during their rare hours of freedom, is to tour the shops on a Saturday afternoon. They are part of our clientele, sometimes in groups surprised that we don't stock more light novels, often lone individuals, hungry for self-improvement. One of the High Street shops which they most frequent though is, of course, Gifford's, for the means to brighten up their wardrobe.

There is an inevitability about Lettie's tale, which she grinds out between clenched teeth. The wonder is it hasn't happened sooner. In short, Priscilla was instrumental in encouraging a group of colleagues to derive great sport from making Lettie empty out drawer after drawer of trimmings and bindings, to be unwound from their cards and tried against a brim which supposedly needed decoration, or a hem which had apparently come down.

'She loved the fact I had to be polite all the time, as if I didn't know what they were up to.'

'I suppose she's jealous that you're going to have your photograph taken,' I say, referring to the tableau which will be on display in Gifford's main window on the first of May. 'It's a way of getting her own back for the fact of your being chosen because you're popular and pretty.'

'I'm only one of the attendants, not the blasted Queen! Sorry, sorry, Rose.' She pats my arm.

'It's all right.' I am shocked less by the swear word than by my friend's distress. 'Well, it's not all right, I mean about how you feel.' We have walked as far as the lock-keeper's cottage. I sit down on the bench outside and Lettie joins me. The way we have come looks like cloth of gold, river reflecting sky. 'What are we going to do?'

'Nothing, nothing,' says Lettie, quickly. 'I wouldn't give her the satisfaction of knowing she's annoyed me. Act as if nothing has happened. I'll get over it. Just talking to you has helped already.'

'Good,' I say, though I'm still troubled. I'm sure Lettie is right in her approach, but I feel as if I should be doing something. What, though?

'Funny thing,' Lettie says as we begin the walk back, 'now I think of it.' She has calmed down and seems to have regained her poise, thank goodness. 'I happen to know that Madam wasn't with the others when they were in the High Street and she did her best to avoid them. They all came bundling out of Long's. She saw them and pretended to be looking at Harvey's window.'

I picture a lively group of young women, having treated themselves to quarter pounds of rhubarb and custard or jelly babies, perhaps on their way to eat them in the park, Priscilla on the opposite pavement walking towards them, but turning suddenly away as if fascinated by the foundry's never-changing fan of malting shovels.

'I was in our window,' Lettie is saying. 'I'd just set up the board, telling people to look at it again on the first of May to see the photographs. It was odd, viewing it all like a mime except when one of them spotted her and they called her name. I could hear "Prissie". You could tell she didn't like that. Then they crossed the road, still calling. I left the window, but the movement must have caught her eye because by the time I got back to my counter, they were entering the shop.'

'So, she'd been humiliated in front of you?'

'If that's how she cares to take it.' Lettie tosses her head.

We are walking up New Road now, the houses on our side of the street dark against a westerly sky. The street lamps spring to life, their pools of light casting all outside them to instant night.

'Remember, Rose,' says Lettie, as we turn towards the looming bulk of Apple Tree House, 'say nothing.'

Despite my sense of things being on a knife edge, this turns out to be an order with which it is easy to comply. As we approach the kitchen door, we hear a familiar sound. 'Snap!' Priscilla's favourite card game and, as we turn the handle, 'Ah, here they are!' cries Winnie.

'We were beginning to get worried,' Jenny adds.

'Where have you been?' asks Meg.

'Never mind where we've been, budge up and deal us in,' says Lettie, with a beaming smile which blesses everyone and comes to rest, if only for a moment before we take our chairs, on Priscilla.

If ever Lettie should tire of dressing windows and advising customers about the latest fashions, she should become an actress. Her performance this evening, as carefree friend of us all, could not have been eclipsed by Sarah Bernhardt herself.

It is almost too warm to sit in comfort, even in the shade cast by the evergreen branches of a venerable silk-tassel tree whose silvery catkins, like extravagant drop-earrings, were a heartening sight in the dark days of winter and early spring. Lettie, deckchair fully extended, is sleeping off her Sunday roast, mouth slightly open and lightly snoring. Jenny has already gone upstairs to lie on her bed, curtains nearly closed but window wide to catch what little breeze stirs. I do not envy Meg and Winnie, resolutely setting out to teach at The Friends' First Day School.

I step in from the garden and take off my boots. The scullery tiles are cool to my burning soles. I plan to go up to my room, free myself from itchy woollen stockings, and return to the garden barefoot, just as I would at home.

I round the bend at the top of the staircase onto the landing, facing Priscilla's room. Her door stands open, no doubt to catch any passing airs. She is seated at her open window looking out, but turns at my approaching footstep. It is hard to say whether the look she gives me is a smile. I feel that the whole scene is some kind of invitation, not necessarily of Pricilla's making, to do what, I am unsure. I make myself enter the room.

'We're in the garden,' I say, unnecessarily because she knows this, at the same time wondering if I should not raise the topic of her behaviour towards Lettie yesterday even though the latter requested that I should let it rest.

'It's cooler up here,' says Priscilla, which is true in this east-facing room.

I allow my gaze to follow hers. 'There's Mrs Munns,' I say, searching for guidance, as the small figure of our cleaner comes into view, then disappears behind the greening branches of the apple tree.

As she reappears the other side and starts to mount the homeward hill, Priscilla yells into the Sunday stillness, starting low and rising to a strident second syllable: 'Edie!'

Mrs Munns falters, looking all around her but never once thinking to widen her scope beyond the immediate street, let alone upwards to a first-floor window set back from the road.

Priscilla is laughing, a high, sneering note. Although it has to be admitted that Mrs Munns did, God forgive me, look a little comic, in the exaggerated movements of her complete incomprehension, she also looked confused and upset having lost, if only for a matter of moments, her stoic dignity. I do not like myself for feeling any kind of amusement at her expense. I am reminded of the time, which seems long ago now, when I'd barely met Priscilla and she poked fun at the stern appearance of the Sunday School teacher whom we passed in the street. Later that same afternoon, she carolled Mr Pritchard's name outside the shop.

'Priscilla, why do you –' As I speak we both hear, from the adjacent room, a creak of bedsprings, a footstep and a door emphatically opened.

My face can only be an echo of Priscilla's blank shock. Neither of us knew that Mrs Fuller was still at home, let alone resting in her room. She had said she would be calling on the Coopers. Now, here she is drawn up to her full, formidable height.

'May I have a word with you, Priscilla, please?' Her eyes are glittering green chips. 'Rose, would you be kind enough . . . ?'

She does not need to complete the sentence. Mind fixed on nothing but escape, I am already hurrying past her and back downstairs as she steps inside Priscilla's room and shuts the door. I am still clutching my boots, I realise.

*

I decide to honour the continuing fine weather with a blue muslin dress, whose texture is just right for a spring day which could prove warm even indoors. Father, when he first saw me in it, said, 'Ah, Hilda's old frock.' She had outgrown it. 'She used to look lovely in that, what with her blue eyes.'

Any concerns I might have had about whether Mr Pritchard would consider it less suitable for work than my usual navy skirt and white or cream blouse are unfounded. Either he does not notice the difference or he chooses not to comment, probably the former. I have the feeling that, although he is observant of the world around us and understands much about what goes on inside people's heads, he pays little regard to their physical appearance which, I suppose, is to his credit. The marvel is he always looks so stylish himself, especially since his wardrobe is as limited as mine.

Today, he is in good spirits and bounding with energy, having completed revisions to his report based on suggestions arising from our meeting on Wednesday. 'I just hope I can convince them,' he says, referring to next week's meeting of the Parish Council.

'Well, if anybody can, you are the one.'

'Thank you,' he says, 'for your unfailing support.'

And now I'm blushing. What was I thinking, allowing my gaze to linger? Thinking about Hilda's eyes must have made me susceptible to the deepest blue of Mr Pritchard's as they looked into mine. I have never been so keen to greet a customer.

We follow the example of the other shopkeepers and prop our door wide open with the little steps I use to reach the highest shelves. It is an even quieter Monday afternoon than usual. Those who do not have to work, we imagine, are finding reasons to stroll by the river or in the park or needing no reason at all, sit and enjoy the peaceful respite of their gardens.

I can think of nowhere I would rather be, though, than seated ready to listen in the miraculous cave of our shop, whose old walls are a cool, welcome embrace and whose windows and doorway allow a taste of summer warmth. We have fallen into the habit of alternating who reads first. Today, it is Mr Pritchard's turn. My preference is the other way round, as it was last week, so that I can get my rendition out of the way and relax afterwards, the more fully to appreciate Mr Pritchard's always absorbing contribution. I would never admit to this failure of self-confidence.

We have an identical book each, Volume Eight of a large anthology, *The Poets and the Poetry of the Century*, edited by Alfred Henry Miles, which I have come to know thanks to my employer. I have seen today's poet's name in this book, without reading any of the seven or eight things by him. I have noticed that his poems were published posthumously, so we are unlikely to come across much more of his work. It is Mr Pritchard's custom to read with no introduction, so that we can respond simply to the poem rather than being influenced by someone else's interpretation. It is perfectly still. No sound distracts us as Mr Pritchard begins, as usual, by announcing the title and the author.

'"Spring,"' he says, 'by Gerard Manley Hopkins.' Then he begins:

> 'Nothing is so beautiful as Spring –
> When weeds, in wheels, shoot long and lovely and lush;
> Thrush's eggs look little low heavens, and thrush
> Through the echoing timber does so rinse and wring
> The ear, it strikes like lightnings to hear him sing;
> The glassy peartree leaves and blooms, they brush
> The descending blue; that blue is all in a rush
> With richness; the racing lambs too have fair their fling.
>
> What is all this juice and all this joy?
> A strain of the earth's sweet being in the beginning
> In Eden garden. – Have, get, before it cloy,
> Before it cloud, Christ, lord, and sour with sinning,
> Innocent mind and Mayday in girl and boy,
> Most, O maid's child, thy choice and worthy the winning.'

I look up in a state of astonishment, both puzzled and delighted. I have never heard or read anything quite like this. With the first line I thought I knew where I was – 'Nothing is so beautiful as Spring.' I was expecting a celebration of opening flowers, and singing birds, and warmer days, in language I was used to. But that is not what I heard. I see Mr Pritchard smiling at me, reading my expression, knowing that I am both confused and enthralled. I think he must have known the poem would have this effect. Perhaps it had it on him when he first came across it.

'I'd like you to read it again,' I say.

'You read it, Rose,' he says, and I know not to demur and say that I won't do it as well as him. But I am daunted. It is a long time since I felt so unsure how to go about reading a poem aloud. I can't see the regular patterns of rhythm or grammar I am used to. I take a deep breath and make a beginning. That first line at least welcomes me in. Then I find the words lead me into how to say them, not being afraid of the apparently overdone repetition of sounds, what Mr Pritchard calls the alliteration and assonance, the repeated w and l consonants and the e and o sounds, and so on through the poem. I quickly catch on, not trying to minimise these repetitions but almost exaggerating them, so that the e sound in weeds and wheels lingers on my own ear as I say it. Pronouncing the l and u sounds in the same line is a lip-smacking delight, like eating a tasty snack.

'It all becomes much clearer when you read it aloud,' I say. 'You can feel the sheer pleasure in every phrase and line. But what a very strange way to write! I thought good poets were supposed to be subtle in the way they made music out of the sounds of words, but this is not subtle at all. And it seems quite awkward in places. I might have expected the poem to say that the eggs are sky-blue, and I could have coped with it saying that they look like the sky or the heaven. But leaving out the word "like" seems to make the whole sentence awkward. It's as if the poet is so keen to tell you something that his excitement is infectious and the awkwardness seems the most eloquent thing you ever heard.'

Mr Pritchard is looking at me intently and nodding, and he has a strange expression on his face. 'Well said, Rose,' he says at last. 'That's it exactly. I hoped you would rise to the challenge of this new kind of writing, and you have done, wonderfully. But I never expected you would be able to talk about it so well.'

I can feel a self-consciousness beginning to betray me into a blush. This is a special moment we are sharing. To ease my confusion, I speak again, this time talking not about the style of the poem but the pictures and sounds it brings to mind.

'I have never thought of the thrush's song as being like a lightning flash,' I say, 'but it has that sudden sharpness and speed. And it does echo in the woods, just as the poet says, talking about "echoing timber." But, then, it's all good. "The glassy peartree leaves", I know just what he means. When the sun is shining on them, they do look glassy.'

'Yes, the whole of that first stanza is sublime,' says Mr Pritchard. 'The introduction of religion into the sestet is a bit of a surprise, don't you think? Though I expect you find it a natural progression to move from the joy of nature to the love of God.' He shoots me a wry look.

'I do think the first stanza is so lovely it stands on its own,' I say. This is true, though at the same time I'm remembering how, on Easter morning, when I rode out with Jack the whole experience made me feel exalted, as if heaven had not only manifested itself in my surroundings but had, for a moment, entered me. Surely Eden, in the inhabitants' first innocence, must have felt like that? I do not mention any of these notions, but I do say, 'The description made me think of spring at home, my old home, I mean.' The moment I've said it, I feel a little wobbly, but Mr Pritchard is going on speaking.

'Of course,' he is saying, 'the whole idea of Mayday has nothing to do with innocence in the Christian sense, or any other come to that. The tradition of dancing round the Maypole is actually pagan in its origin.'

I am taken aback to think that something which I had accepted at face value as an emblem of spring, and always loved for its prettiness, should have ulterior connotations. I try to look neither embarrassed nor ignorant, but I am not sure I succeed.

Mr Pritchard comes to my rescue with a change of subject. 'I'm very much looking forward to hearing your poem, Rose, so shall we do that?'

I have a poem appropriate to tomorrow's date, so I try to subdue my usual self-distrust about my choices. I open Mother's anthology and read 'A Chanted Calendar' by Sydney Thompson Dobell. It is, admittedly, a rather odd poem, which juxtaposes description of spring flowers with images of war.

> 'First came the primrose,
> On the bank high,
> Like a maiden looking forth
> From the window of a tower
> When the battle rolls below,
> So look'd she,
> And saw the storms go by.'

The third stanza mentions the date:

> 'Then came the daisies,
> On the first of May,
> Like a banner'd show's advance
> While the crowd runs by the way,
> With ten thousand flowers about them
> they came trooping through the fields.'

After more military and floral images, the poem concludes on a theme of rejoicing.

'When I looked the poem up, much of it seemed new to me. Then, I realised that when Mother read it to us she cut out the lines about war, but she must have done it cleverly, because I don't recall it seeming disjointed.'

Mr Pritchard draws up his stool. I can feel his intense presence concentrating on the page. 'Yes, I can see how it could be done. No wonder your mother wasn't keen for you to hear all of it. How old were you?'

'About eight, I think, and Phyllis would have been about ten or eleven. Mother read it to the two of us.'

'The cowslip is a delightful image to round the poem off, though. "She spread her little mat of green". That's so evocative, isn't it?'

'I thought you might think the whole thing was a bit . . .' I leave my sentence unfinished.

'Sentimental? You needn't disparage your choice. It has some striking moments. And your mother obviously knew what she was doing.' He hesitates. 'I wish I could have met her.'

'So do I.' Suddenly, everything's rushing up and my eyes are brimming.

'I'm sorry, I shouldn't even have said it. Forgive me.'

I am scrabbling for my handkerchief but, of course, this is not my usual outfit. Where's the pocket in this dress?

I hear Mr Pritchard's stool scrape and now he's standing right beside me. 'Here, have mine. It's clean.'

'Thank you. I'm sorry,' I hiccup.

'Shhh.'

I feel his hand closing round my reaching fingers. I seem to be slightly dizzy. I put the fine linen gratefully to my eyes and nose, smell its freshness, entirely different from any laundered cloth I own. It has the scent of lemon, but something spicy, too, which I have come to recognise from these reading sessions when we sit side by side. All this I notice, even while I wonder if I am about to faint.

'Are you going to be all right?'

I take a deep breath and look into his kind, worried eyes. 'I am perfectly recovered, Mr Pritchard.' Though, truth to tell, I don't feel quite myself. 'Thank you for your understanding. I shall wash and return the hand –'

'Never mind the handkerchief,' he says.

My insides lurch. Whatever is happening to me?

A moment passes without either of us seeming able to relinquish each other's gaze.

'I do . . .' Mr Pritchard begins, but seems to think better of what he was about to say. He returns to sit on his stool. 'I do hope you are well enough to conclude our discussion.'

I assure him I am.

He clears his throat. 'Interesting chap, Sydney Dobell. He became a passionate supporter of Mazzini in the fight for a united Italy.'

'I thought . . . Garibaldi was the leader.'

'He was, but they were both important in the struggle. It shows you where Dobell got his imagery from, doesn't it? He also supported women's rights, by the way.'

I hear Mother's voice, 'He believed that women were the equal of men.' And now, I find that I am telling Mr Pritchard about the very incident, concerning Phyllis and me, which I have been pushing to the back of my mind for fear of being amused whilst reading out the penultimate line about the cowslip with 'A golden fillet round her brow'. I tell Mr Pritchard how Mother, who had started to tell us about the poet, looked across at the two of us, failing to keep straight faces, and said in a tired voice, 'Not that kind of fillet.' She must have caught the moment, while she was reading, when Phyllis and I mouthed to each other what must have struck us simultaneously as a joke, the word haddock.

Mr Pritchard gives a great laugh, thank goodness, so I haven't disgraced myself. 'Ha! Yes, a piece of smoked haddock plastered across the dancer's forehead. I can just imagine you and Phyllis as giggling young girls. It's a rather charming picture.'

I'm smiling, too, but the feeling which has overtaken me in the telling is not, after all, a reprise of our hilarity but regret. 'We disappointed Mother.'

'I'm sure she understood.'

'Yes, she did. She always saw the best in us. In everyone, actually.' I take several deep breaths.

'Come on,' says Mr Pritchard, gently, 'it's almost time to close.'

He walks up Holywell End with me. 'It's too lovely an evening

212

to stay indoors. I think I'll have a good walk round Widdock and check my facts, so that I'm ready for anything the Parish Council may fling at me.'

After we part company at Bridgefoot, I linger a moment and watch him following the river west in the evening sunlight.

As I walk on home along a street which has become so familiar, I reflect that this afternoon, with its powerful emotions, could hardly fail to bring it all back to me. A quarter of the year has passed since that terrible day of Mother's death, yet what I'm left with, what I feel above all, is a sense not only of her sweetness but of her strength. I feel something else, too, as elusive as the hint of fragrance from some spring blossom which, as I pass, I can't quite place. How my life has changed. My thoughts return to the figure who helped me – no, inspired me to make that change. I see him as he was just now, a silhouette against water flecked with golden light.

Acknowledgements

I should like to thank my husband, John Freeman, who was my first reader, and my daughter, Eleanor Dawson, who was my second, for their detailed feedback and unfailing encouragement. Thanks, also to my son, Trevor Dawson, and to all my extended family and my friends, for their ever-sustaining support and belief.

I am grateful for useful conversations and correspondence with Valerie Don, Gavin Goodwin, Anne Maskell and Valerie Riley.

Finally, a big thank you to the kind and always helpful staff of Hertford Museum.

Acknowledgments